THE MURDER OF ROGER ACKROYD

By AGATHA CHRISTIE

CONTENTS

- CHAPTER I 2
- CHAPTER II 5
- CHAPTER III 10
- CHAPTER IV 16
- CHAPTER V 25
- CHAPTER VI 32
- CHAPTER VII 37
- CHAPTER VIII 45
- CHAPTER IX 51
- CHAPTER X 57
- CHAPTER XI 65
- CHAPTER XII 70
- CHAPTER XIII 75
- CHAPTER XIV 79
- CHAPTER XV 85
- CHAPTER XVI 91
- CHAPTER XVII 96
- CHAPTER XVIII 103
- CHAPTER XIX 107
- CHAPTER XX 112
- CHAPTER XXI 118
- CHAPTER XXII 122
- CHAPTER XXIII 126
- CHAPTER XXIV 133
- CHAPTER XXV 135
- CHAPTER XXVI 139
- CHAPTER XXVII 141

Author: Agatha Christie
The cover design: Eleonora Kirpichnikova, copyright 2024

CHAPTER I
DR. SHEPPARD AT THE BREAKFAST TABLE

MRS. FERRARS died on the night of the 16th–17th September—a Thursday. I was sent for at eight o'clock on the morning of Friday the 17th. There was nothing to be done. She had been dead some hours.

It was just a few minutes after nine when I reached home once more. I opened the front door with my latch-key, and purposely delayed a few moments in the hall, hanging up my hat and the light overcoat that I had deemed a wise precaution against the chill of an early autumn morning. To tell the truth, I was considerably upset and worried. I am not going to pretend that at that moment I foresaw the events of the next few weeks. I emphatically did not do so. But my instinct told me that there were stirring times ahead.

From the dining-room on my left there came the rattle of tea-cups and the short, dry cough of my sister Caroline.

"Is that you, James?" she called.

An unnecessary question, since who else could it be? To tell the truth, it was precisely my sister Caroline who was the cause of my few minutes' delay. The motto of the mongoose family, so Mr. Kipling tells us, is: "Go and find out." If Caroline ever adopts a crest, I should certainly suggest a mongoose rampant. One might omit the first part of the motto. Caroline can do any amount of finding out by sitting placidly at home. I don't know how she manages it, but there it is. I suspect that the servants and the tradesmen constitute her Intelligence Corps. When she goes out, it is not to gather in information, but to spread it. At that, too, she is amazingly expert.

It was really this last named trait of hers which was causing me these pangs of indecision. Whatever I told Caroline now concerning the demise of Mrs. Ferrars would be common knowledge all over the village within the space of an hour and a half. As a professional man, I naturally aim at discretion. Therefore I have got into the habit of continually withholding all information possible from my sister. She usually finds out just the same, but I have the moral satisfaction of knowing that I am in no way to blame.

Mrs. Ferrars' husband died just over a year ago, and Caroline has constantly asserted, without the least foundation for the assertion, that his wife poisoned him.

She scorns my invariable rejoinder that Mr. Ferrars died of acute gastritis, helped on by habitual over-indulgence in alcoholic beverages. The symptoms of gastritis and arsenical poisoning are not, I agree, unlike, but Caroline bases her accusation on quite different lines.

"You've only got to look at her," I have heard her say.

Mrs. Ferrars, though not in her first youth, was a very attractive woman, and her clothes, though simple, always seemed to fit her very well, but all the same, lots of women buy their clothes in Paris and have not, on that account, necessarily poisoned their husbands.

As I stood hesitating in the hall, with all this passing through my mind, Caroline's voice came again, with a sharper note in it.

"What on earth are you doing out there, James? Why don't you come and get your breakfast?"

"Just coming, my dear," I said hastily. "I've been hanging up my overcoat."

"You could have hung up half a dozen overcoats in this time."

She was quite right. I could have.

I walked into the dining-room, gave Caroline the accustomed peck on the cheek, and sat down to eggs and bacon. The bacon was rather cold.

"You've had an early call," remarked Caroline.

"Yes," I said. "King's Paddock. Mrs. Ferrars."

"I know," said my sister.

"How did you know?"

"Annie told me."

Annie is the house parlormaid. A nice girl, but an inveterate talker.

There was a pause. I continued to eat eggs and bacon. My sister's nose, which is long and thin, quivered a little at the tip, as it always does when she is interested or excited over anything.

"Well?" she demanded.

"A bad business. Nothing to be done. Must have died in her sleep."

"I know," said my sister again.

This time I was annoyed.

"You can't know," I snapped. "I didn't know myself until I got there, and I haven't mentioned it to a soul yet. If that girl Annie knows, she must be a clairvoyant."

"It wasn't Annie who told me. It was the milkman. He had it from the Ferrars' cook."

As I say, there is no need for Caroline to go out to get information. She sits at home, and it comes to her.

My sister continued:

"What did she die of? Heart failure?"

"Didn't the milkman tell you that?" I inquired sarcastically.

Sarcasm is wasted on Caroline. She takes it seriously and answers accordingly.

"He didn't know," she explained.

After all, Caroline was bound to hear sooner or later. She might as well hear from me.

"She died of an overdose of veronal. She's been taking it lately for sleeplessness. Must have taken too much."

"Nonsense," said Caroline immediately. "She took it on purpose. Don't tell me!"

It is odd how, when you have a secret belief of your own which you do not wish to acknowledge, the voicing of it by some one else will rouse you to a fury of denial. I burst immediately into indignant speech.

"There you go again," I said. "Rushing along without rhyme or reason. Why on earth should Mrs. Ferrars wish to commit suicide? A widow, fairly young still, very well off, good health, and nothing to do but enjoy life. It's absurd."

"Not at all. Even you must have noticed how different she has been looking lately. It's been coming on for the last six months. She's looked positively hag-ridden. And you have just admitted that she hasn't been able to sleep."

"What is your diagnosis?" I demanded coldly. "An unfortunate love affair, I suppose?"

My sister shook her head.

"*Remorse*," she said, with great gusto.

"Remorse?"

"Yes. You never would believe me when I told you she poisoned her husband. I'm more than ever convinced of it now."

"I don't think you're very logical," I objected. "Surely if a woman committed a crime like murder, she'd be sufficiently cold-blooded to enjoy the fruits of it without any weak-minded sentimentality such as repentance."

Caroline shook her head.

"There probably are women like that—but Mrs. Ferrars wasn't one of them. She was a mass of nerves. An overmastering impulse drove her on to get rid of her husband because she was the sort of person who simply can't endure suffering of any kind, and there's no doubt that the wife of a man like Ashley Ferrars must have had to suffer a good deal——"

I nodded.

"And ever since she's been haunted by what she did. I can't help feeling sorry for her."

I don't think Caroline ever felt sorry for Mrs. Ferrars whilst she was alive. Now that she has gone where (presumably) Paris frocks can no longer be worn, Caroline is prepared to indulge in the softer emotions of pity and comprehension.

I told her firmly that her whole idea was nonsense. I was all the more firm because I secretly agreed with some part, at least, of what she had said. But it is all wrong that Caroline should arrive at the truth simply by a kind of inspired guesswork. I wasn't going to encourage that sort of thing. She will go round the village airing her views, and every one will think that she is doing so on medical data supplied by me. Life is very trying.

"Nonsense," said Caroline, in reply to my strictures. "You'll see. Ten to one she's left a letter confessing everything."

"She didn't leave a letter of any kind," I said sharply, and not seeing where the admission was going to land me.

"Oh!" said Caroline. "So you *did* inquire about that, did you? I believe, James, that in your heart of hearts, you think very much as I do. You're a precious old humbug."

"One always has to take the possibility of suicide into consideration," I said repressively.

"Will there be an inquest?"

"There may be. It all depends. If I am able to declare myself absolutely satisfied that the overdose was taken accidentally, an inquest might be dispensed with."

"And are you absolutely satisfied?" asked my sister shrewdly.

I did not answer, but got up from table.

CHAPTER II
WHO'S WHO IN KING'S ABBOT

BEFORE I proceed further with what I said to Caroline and what Caroline said to me, it might be as well to give some idea of what I should describe as our local geography. Our village, King's Abbot, is, I imagine, very much like any other village. Our big town is Cranchester, nine miles away. We have a large railway station, a small post office, and two rival "General Stores." Able-bodied men are apt to leave the place early in life, but we are rich in unmarried ladies and retired military officers. Our hobbies and recreations can be summed up in the one word, "gossip."

There are only two houses of any importance in King's Abbot. One is King's Paddock, left to Mrs. Ferrars by her late husband. The other, Fernly Park, is owned by Roger Ackroyd. Ackroyd has always interested me by being a man more impossibly like a country squire than any country squire could really be. He reminds one of the red-faced sportsmen who always appeared early in the first act of an old-fashioned musical comedy, the setting being the village green. They usually sang a song about going up to London. Nowadays we have revues, and the country squire has died out of musical fashion.

Of course, Ackroyd is not really a country squire. He is an immensely successful manufacturer of (I think) wagon wheels. He is a man of nearly fifty years of age, rubicund of face and genial of manner. He is hand and glove with the vicar, subscribes liberally to parish funds (though rumor has it that he is extremely mean in personal expenditure), encourages cricket matches, Lads' Clubs, and Disabled Soldiers' Institutes. He is, in fact, the life and soul of our peaceful village of King's Abbot.

Now when Roger Ackroyd was a lad of twenty-one, he fell in love with, and married, a beautiful woman some five or six years his senior. Her name was Paton, and she was a widow with one child. The history of the marriage was short and painful. To put it bluntly, Mrs. Ackroyd was a dipsomaniac. She succeeded in drinking herself into her grave four years after her marriage.

In the years that followed, Ackroyd showed no disposition to make a second matrimonial adventure. His wife's child by her first marriage was only seven years old when his mother died. He is now twenty-five. Ackroyd has always regarded him as his own son, and has brought him up accordingly, but he has been a wild lad and a continual source of worry and trouble to his stepfather. Nevertheless we are all very fond of Ralph Paton in King's Abbot. He is such a good-looking youngster for one thing.

As I said before, we are ready enough to gossip in our village. Everybody noticed from the first that Ackroyd and Mrs. Ferrars got on very well together. After her husband's death, the intimacy became more marked. They were always seen about together, and it was freely conjectured that at the end of her period of mourning, Mrs. Ferrars would become Mrs. Roger Ackroyd. It was felt, indeed, that there was a certain fitness in the thing. Roger Ackroyd's wife had admittedly died of drink. Ashley Ferrars had been a drunkard for many years before his death. It was only fitting that these two victims of alcoholic excess should make up to each other for all that they had previously endured at the hands of their former spouses.

The Ferrars only came to live here just over a year ago, but a halo of gossip has surrounded Ackroyd for many years past. All the time that Ralph Paton was growing up to manhood, a series of lady housekeepers presided over Ackroyd's establishment, and each in turn was regarded with lively suspicion by Caroline and her cronies. It is not too much to say that for at least fifteen years the whole village has confidently expected Ackroyd to marry one of his housekeepers. The last of them, a redoubtable lady called Miss Russell, has reigned undisputed for five years, twice as long as any of her predecessors. It is felt that but for the advent of Mrs. Ferrars, Ackroyd could hardly have escaped. That—and one other factor—the unexpected arrival of a widowed sister-in-law with her daughter from Canada. Mrs. Cecil Ackroyd, widow of Ackroyd's ne'er-do-well younger brother, has taken up her residence at Fernly Park, and has succeeded, according to Caroline, in putting Miss Russell in her proper place.

I don't know exactly what a "proper place" constitutes—it sounds chilly and unpleasant—but I know that Miss Russell goes about with pinched lips, and what I can only describe as an acid smile, and that she professes the utmost sympathy for "poor Mrs. Ackroyd—dependent on the charity of her husband's brother. The bread of charity is so bitter, is it not? *I* should be quite miserable if I did not work for my living."

I don't know what Mrs. Cecil Ackroyd thought of the Ferrars affair when it came on the tapis. It was clearly to her advantage that Ackroyd should remain unmarried. She was always very charming—not to say gushing—to Mrs. Ferrars when they met. Caroline says that proves less than nothing.

Such have been our preoccupations in King's Abbot for the last few years. We have discussed Ackroyd and his affairs from every standpoint. Mrs. Ferrars has fitted into her place in the scheme.

Now there has been a rearrangement of the kaleidoscope. From a mild discussion of probable wedding presents, we have been jerked into the midst of tragedy.

Revolving these and sundry other matters in my mind, I went mechanically on my round. I had no cases of special interest to attend, which was, perhaps, as well, for my thoughts returned again and again to the mystery of Mrs. Ferrars's death. Had she taken her own life? Surely, if she had done so, she would have left some word behind to say what she contemplated doing? Women, in my experience, if they once reach the determination to commit suicide, usually wish to reveal the state of mind that led to the fatal action. They covet the limelight.

When had I last seen her? Not for over a week. Her manner then had been normal enough considering—well—considering everything.

Then I suddenly remembered that I had seen her, though not to speak to, only yesterday. She had been walking with Ralph Paton, and I had been surprised because I had had no idea that he was likely to be in King's Abbot. I thought, indeed, that he had quarreled finally with his stepfather. Nothing had been seen of him down here for nearly six months. They had been walking along, side by side, their heads close together, and she had been talking very earnestly.

I think I can safely say that it was at this moment that a foreboding of the future first swept over me. Nothing tangible as yet—but a vague premonition of the way things were setting. That earnest *tête-à-tête* between Ralph Paton and Mrs. Ferrars the day before struck me disagreeably.

I was still thinking of it when I came face to face with Roger Ackroyd.

"Sheppard!" he exclaimed. "Just the man I wanted to get hold of. This is a terrible business."

"You've heard then?"

He nodded. He had felt the blow keenly, I could see. His big red cheeks seemed to have fallen in, and he looked a positive wreck of his usual jolly, healthy self.

"It's worse than you know," he said quietly. "Look here, Sheppard, I've got to talk to you. Can you come back with me now?"

"Hardly. I've got three patients to see still, and I must be back by twelve to see my surgery patients."

"Then this afternoon—no, better still, dine to-night. At 7.30? Will that suit you?"

"Yes—I can manage that all right. What's wrong? Is it Ralph?"

I hardly knew why I said that—except, perhaps, that it had so often been Ralph.

Ackroyd stared blankly at me as though he hardly understood. I began to realize that there must be something very wrong indeed somewhere. I had never seen Ackroyd so upset before.

"Ralph?" he said vaguely. "Oh! no, it's not Ralph. Ralph's in London——Damn! Here's old Miss Ganett coming. I don't want to have to talk to her about this ghastly business. See you to-night, Sheppard. Seven-thirty."

I nodded, and he hurried away, leaving me wondering. Ralph in London? But he had certainly been in King's Abbot the preceding afternoon. He must have gone back to town last night or early this morning, and yet Ackroyd's manner had conveyed quite a different impression. He had spoken as though Ralph had not been near the place for months.

I had no time to puzzle the matter out further. Miss Ganett was upon me, thirsting for information. Miss Ganett has all the characteristics of my sister Caroline, but she lacks that unerring aim in jumping to conclusions which lends a touch of greatness to Caroline's maneuvers. Miss Ganett was breathless and interrogatory.

Wasn't it sad about poor dear Mrs. Ferrars? A lot of people were saying she had been a confirmed drug-taker for years. So wicked the way people went about saying things. And yet, the worst of it was, there was usually a grain of truth somewhere in these wild statements. No smoke without fire! They were saying too that Mr. Ackroyd had found out about it, and had broken off the engagement—because there *was* an engagement. She, Miss Ganett, had proof positive of that. Of course *I* must know all about it—doctors always did—but they never tell?

And all this with a sharp beady eye on me to see how I reacted to these suggestions. Fortunately long association with Caroline has led me to preserve an impassive countenance, and to be ready with small non-committal remarks.

On this occasion I congratulated Miss Ganett on not joining in ill-natured gossip. Rather a neat counterattack, I thought. It left her in difficulties, and before she could pull herself together, I had passed on.

I went home thoughtful, to find several patients waiting for me in the surgery.

I had dismissed the last of them, as I thought, and was just contemplating a few minutes in the garden before lunch when I perceived one more patient waiting for me. She rose and came towards me as I stood somewhat surprised.

I don't know why I should have been, except that there is a suggestion of cast iron about Miss Russell, a something that is above the ills of the flesh.

Ackroyd's housekeeper is a tall woman, handsome but forbidding in appearance. She has a stern eye, and lips that shut tightly, and I feel that if I were an under housemaid or a kitchenmaid I should run for my life whenever I heard her coming.

"Good morning, Dr. Sheppard," said Miss Russell. "I should be much obliged if you would take a look at my knee."

I took a look, but, truth to tell, I was very little wiser when I had done so. Miss Russell's account of vague pains was so unconvincing that with a woman of less integrity of character I should have suspected a trumped-up tale. It did cross my mind for one moment that Miss Russell might have deliberately invented this affection of the knee in order to pump me on the subject of Mrs. Ferrars's death, but I soon saw that there, at least, I had misjudged her. She made a brief reference to the tragedy, nothing more. Yet she certainly seemed disposed to linger and chat.

"Well, thank you very much for this bottle of liniment, doctor," she said at last. "Not that I believe it will do the least good."

I didn't think it would either, but I protested in duty bound. After all, it couldn't do any harm, and one must stick up for the tools of one's trade.

"I don't believe in all these drugs," said Miss Russell, her eyes sweeping over my array of bottles disparagingly. "Drugs do a lot of harm. Look at the cocaine habit."

"Well, as far as that goes——"

"It's very prevalent in high society."

I'm sure Miss Russell knows far more about high society than I do. I didn't attempt to argue with her.

"Just tell me this, doctor," said Miss Russell. "Suppose you are really a slave of the drug habit. Is there any cure?"

One cannot answer a question like that offhand. I gave her a short lecture on the subject, and she listened with close attention. I still suspected her of seeking information about Mrs. Ferrars.

"Now, veronal, for instance——" I proceeded.

But, strangely enough, she didn't seem interested in veronal. Instead she changed the subject, and asked me if it was true that there were certain poisons so rare as to baffle detection.

"Ah!" I said. "You've been reading detective stories."

She admitted that she had.

"The essence of a detective story," I said, "is to have a rare poison—if possible something from South America, that nobody has ever heard of—something that one obscure tribe of savages use to poison their arrows with. Death is instantaneous, and Western science is powerless to detect it. That is the kind of thing you mean?"

"Yes. Is there really such a thing?"

I shook my head regretfully.

"I'm afraid there isn't. There's *curare*, of course."

I told her a good deal about curare, but she seemed to have lost interest once more. She asked me if I had any in my poison cupboard, and when I replied in the negative I fancy I fell in her estimation.

She said she must be getting back, and I saw her out at the surgery door just as the luncheon gong went.

I should never have suspected Miss Russell of a fondness for detective stories. It pleases me very much to think of her stepping out of the housekeeper's room to rebuke a delinquent housemaid, and then returning to a comfortable perusal of *The Mystery of the Seventh Death*, or something of the kind.

CHAPTER III
THE MAN WHO GREW VEGETABLE MARROWS

I TOLD Caroline at lunch time that I should be dining at Fernly. She expressed no objection—on the contrary——

"Excellent," she said. "You'll hear all about it. By the way, what is the trouble with Ralph?"

"With Ralph?" I said, surprised; "there's isn't any."

"Then why is he staying at the Three Boars instead of at Fernly Park?"

I did not for a minute question Caroline's statement that Ralph Paton was staying at the local inn. That Caroline said so was enough for me.

"Ackroyd told me he was in London," I said. In the surprise of the moment I departed from my valuable rule of never parting with information.

"Oh!" said Caroline. I could see her nose twitching as she worked on this.

"He arrived at the Three Boars yesterday morning," she said. "And he's still there. Last night he was out with a girl."

That did not surprise me in the least. Ralph, I should say, is out with a girl most nights of his life. But I did rather wonder that he chose to indulge in the pastime in King's Abbot instead of in the gay metropolis.

"One of the barmaids?" I asked.

"No. That's just it. He went out to meet her. I don't know who she is."

(Bitter for Caroline to have to admit such a thing.)

"But I can guess," continued my indefatigable sister.

I waited patiently.

"His cousin."

"Flora Ackroyd?" I exclaimed in surprise.

Flora Ackroyd is, of course, no relation whatever really to Ralph Paton, but Ralph has been looked upon for so long as practically Ackroyd's own son, that cousinship is taken for granted.

"Flora Ackroyd," said my sister.

"But why not go to Fernly if he wanted to see her?"

"Secretly engaged," said Caroline, with immense enjoyment. "Old Ackroyd won't hear of it, and they have to meet this way."

I saw a good many flaws in Caroline's theory, but I forbore to point them out to her. An innocent remark about our new neighbor created a diversion.

The house next door, The Larches, has recently been taken by a stranger. To Caroline's extreme annoyance, she has not been able to find out anything about him, except that he is a foreigner. The Intelligence Corps has proved a broken reed. Presumably the man has milk and vegetables and joints of meat and occasional whitings just like everybody else, but none of the people who make it their business to supply these things seem to have acquired any information. His name, apparently, is Mr. Porrott—a name which conveys an odd feeling of unreality. The one thing we do know about him is that he is interested in the growing of vegetable marrows.

But that is certainly not the sort of information that Caroline is after. She wants to know where he comes from, what he does, whether he is married, what his wife was, or is, like, whether he has children, what his mother's maiden name was—and so on. Somebody very like Caroline must have invented the questions on passports, I think.

"My dear Caroline," I said. "There's no doubt at all about what the man's profession has been. He's a retired hairdresser. Look at that mustache of his."

Caroline dissented. She said that if the man was a hairdresser, he would have wavy hair—not straight. All hairdressers did.

I cited several hairdressers personally known to me who had straight hair, but Caroline refused to be convinced.

"I can't make him out at all," she said in an aggrieved voice. "I borrowed some garden tools the other day, and he was most polite, but I couldn't get anything out of him. I asked him point blank at last whether he was a Frenchman, and he said he wasn't—and somehow I didn't like to ask him any more."

I began to be more interested in our mysterious neighbor. A man who is capable of shutting up Caroline and sending her, like the Queen of Sheba, empty away must be something of a personality.

"I believe," said Caroline, "that he's got one of those new vacuum cleaners——"

I saw a meditated loan and the opportunity of further questioning gleaming from her eye. I seized the chance to escape into the garden. I am rather fond of gardening. I was busily exterminating dandelion roots when a shout of warning sounded from close by and a heavy body whizzed by my ear and fell at my feet with a repellant squelch. It was a vegetable marrow!

I looked up angrily. Over the wall, to my left, there appeared a face. An egg-shaped head, partially covered with suspiciously black hair, two immense mustaches, and a pair of watchful eyes. It was our mysterious neighbor, Mr. Porrott.

He broke at once into fluent apologies.

"I demand of you a thousand pardons, monsieur. I am without defense. For some months now I cultivate the marrows. This morning suddenly I enrage myself with these marrows. I send them to promenade themselves—alas! not only mentally but physically. I seize the biggest. I hurl him over the wall. Monsieur, I am ashamed. I prostrate myself."

Before such profuse apologies, my anger was forced to melt. After all, the wretched vegetable hadn't hit me. But I sincerely hoped that throwing large vegetables over walls was not our new friend's hobby. Such a habit could hardly endear him to us as a neighbor.

The strange little man seemed to read my thoughts.

"Ah! no," he exclaimed. "Do not disquiet yourself. It is not with me a habit. But can you figure to yourself, monsieur, that a man may work towards a certain object, may labor and toil to attain a certain kind of leisure and occupation, and then find that, after all, he yearns for the old busy days, and the old occupations that he thought himself so glad to leave?"

"Yes," I said slowly. "I fancy that that is a common enough occurrence. I myself am perhaps an instance. A year ago I came into a legacy—enough to enable me to realize a dream. I have always wanted to travel, to see the world. Well, that was a year ago, as I said, and—I am still here."

My little neighbor nodded.

"The chains of habit. We work to attain an object, and the object gained, we find that what we miss is the daily toil. And mark you, monsieur, my work was interesting work. The most interesting work there is in the world."

"Yes?" I said encouragingly. For the moment the spirit of Caroline was strong within me.

"The study of human nature, monsieur!"

"Just so," I said kindly.

Clearly a retired hairdresser. Who knows the secrets of human nature better than a hairdresser?

"Also, I had a friend—a friend who for many years never left my side. Occasionally of an imbecility to make one afraid, nevertheless he was very dear to me. Figure to yourself that I miss even his stupidity. His *naïveté*, his honest outlook, the pleasure of delighting and surprising him by my superior gifts—all these I miss more than I can tell you."

"He died?" I asked sympathetically.

"Not so. He lives and flourishes—but on the other side of the world. He is now in the Argentine."

"In the Argentine," I said enviously.

I have always wanted to go to South America. I sighed, and then looked up to find Mr. Porrott eyeing me sympathetically. He seemed an understanding little man.

"You will go there, yes?" he asked.

I shook my head with a sigh.

"I could have gone," I said, "a year ago. But I was foolish—and worse than foolish—greedy. I risked the substance for the shadow."

"I comprehend," said Mr. Porrott. "You speculated?"

I nodded mournfully, but in spite of myself I felt secretly entertained. This ridiculous little man was so portentously solemn.

"Not the Porcupine Oilfields?" he asked suddenly.

I stared.

"I thought of them, as a matter of fact, but in the end I plumped for a gold mine in Western Australia."

My neighbor was regarding me with a strange expression which I could not fathom.

"It is Fate," he said at last.

"What is Fate?" I asked irritably.

"That I should live next to a man who seriously considers Porcupine Oilfields, and also West Australian Gold Mines. Tell me, have you also a penchant for auburn hair?"

I stared at him open-mouthed, and he burst out laughing.

"No, no, it is not the insanity that I suffer from. Make your mind easy. It was a foolish question that I put to you there, for, see you, my friend of whom I spoke was a young man, a man who thought all women good, and most of them beautiful. But you are a man of middle age, a doctor, a man who knows the folly and the vanity of most things in this life of ours. Well, well, we are neighbors. I beg of you to accept and present to your excellent sister my best marrow."

He stooped, and with a flourish produced an immense specimen of the tribe, which I duly accepted in the spirit in which it was offered.

"Indeed," said the little man cheerfully, "this has not been a wasted morning. I have made the acquaintance of a man who in some ways resembles my far-off friend. By the way, I should like to ask you a question. You doubtless know every one in this tiny village. Who is the young man with the very dark hair and eyes, and the handsome face. He walks with his head flung back, and an easy smile on his lips?"

The description left me in no doubt.

"That must be Captain Ralph Paton," I said slowly.

"I have not seen him about here before?"

"No, he has not been here for some time. But he is the son—adopted son, rather—of Mr. Ackroyd of Fernly Park."

My neighbor made a slight gesture of impatience.

"Of course, I should have guessed. Mr. Ackroyd spoke of him many times."

"You know Mr. Ackroyd?" I said, slightly surprised.

"Mr. Ackroyd knew me in London—when I was at work there. I have asked him to say nothing of my profession down here."

"I see," I said, rather amused by this patent snobbery, as I thought it.

But the little man went on with an almost grandiloquent smirk.

"One prefers to remain incognito. I am not anxious for notoriety. I have not even troubled to correct the local version of my name."

"Indeed," I said, not knowing quite what to say.

"Captain Ralph Paton," mused Mr. Porrott. "And so he is engaged to Mr. Ackroyd's niece, the charming Miss Flora."

"Who told you so?" I asked, very much surprised.

"Mr. Ackroyd. About a week ago. He is very pleased about it—has long desired that such a thing should come to pass, or so I understood from him. I even believe that he brought some pressure to bear upon the young man. That is never wise. A young man should marry to please himself—not to please a stepfather from whom he has expectations."

My ideas were completely upset. I could not see Ackroyd taking a hairdresser into his confidence, and discussing the marriage of his niece and stepson with him. Ackroyd extends a genial patronage to the lower orders, but he has a very great sense of his own dignity. I began to think that Porrott couldn't be a hairdresser after all.

To hide my confusion, I said the first thing that came into my head.

"What made you notice Ralph Paton? His good looks?"

"No, not that alone—though he is unusually good-looking for an Englishman—what your lady novelists would call a Greek God. No, there was something about that young man that I did not understand."

He said the last sentence in a musing tone of voice which made an indefinable impression upon me. It was as though he was summing up the boy by the light of some inner knowledge that I did not share. It was that impression that was left with me, for at that moment my sister's voice called me from the house.

I went in. Caroline had her hat on, and had evidently just come in from the village. She began without preamble.

"I met Mr. Ackroyd."

"Yes?" I said.

"I stopped him, of course, but he seemed in a great hurry, and anxious to get away."

I have no doubt but that that was the case. He would feel towards Caroline much as he had felt towards Miss Ganett earlier in the day—perhaps more so. Caroline is less easy to shake off.

"I asked him at once about Ralph. He was absolutely astonished. Had no idea the boy was down here. He actually said he thought I must have made a mistake. I! A mistake!"

"Ridiculous," I said. "He ought to have known you better."

"Then he went on to tell me that Ralph and Flora are engaged."

"I know that too," I interrupted, with modest pride.

"Who told you?"

"Our new neighbor."

Caroline visibly wavered for a second or two, much as a roulette ball might coyly hover between two numbers. Then she declined the tempting red herring.

"I told Mr. Ackroyd that Ralph was staying at the Three Boars."

"Caroline," I said, "do you never reflect that you might do a lot of harm with this habit of yours of repeating everything indiscriminately?"

"Nonsense," said my sister. "People ought to know things. I consider it my duty to tell them. Mr. Ackroyd was very grateful to me."

"Well?" I said, for there was clearly more to come.

"I think he went straight off to the Three Boars, but if so he didn't find Ralph there."

"No?"

"No. Because as I was coming back through the wood——"

"Coming back through the wood?" I interrupted.

Caroline had the grace to blush.

"It was such a lovely day," she exclaimed. "I thought I would make a little round. The woods with their autumnal tints are so perfect at this time of year."

Caroline does not care a hang for woods at any time of year. Normally she regards them as places where you get your feet damp, and where all kinds of unpleasant things may drop on your head. No, it was good sound mongoose instinct which took her to our local wood. It is the only place adjacent to the village of King's Abbot where you can talk with a young woman unseen by the whole of the village. It adjoins the Park of Fernly.

"Well," I said, "go on."

"As I say, I was just coming back through the wood when I heard voices."

Caroline paused.

"Yes?"

"One was Ralph Paton's—I knew it at once. The other was a girl's. Of course I didn't mean to listen——"

"Of course not," I interjected, with patent sarcasm—which was, however, wasted on Caroline.

"But I simply couldn't help overhearing. The girl said something—I didn't quite catch what it was, and Ralph answered. He sounded very angry. 'My dear girl,' he said. 'Don't you realize that it is quite on the cards the old man will cut me off with a shilling? He's been pretty fed up with me for the last few years. A little more would do it. And we need the dibs, my dear. I shall be a very rich man when the old fellow pops off. He's mean as they make 'em, but he's rolling in money really. I don't want him to go altering his will. You leave it to me, and don't worry.' Those were his exact words. I remember them perfectly. Unfortunately, just then I stepped on a dry twig or something, and they lowered their voices and moved away. I couldn't, of course, go rushing after them, so wasn't able to see who the girl was."

"That must have been most vexing," I said. "I suppose, though, you hurried on to the Three Boars, felt faint, and went into the bar for a glass of brandy, and so were able to see if both the barmaids were on duty?"

"It wasn't a barmaid," said Caroline unhesitatingly. "In fact, I'm almost sure that it was Flora Ackroyd, only——"

"Only it doesn't seem to make sense," I agreed.

"But if it wasn't Flora, who could it have been?"

Rapidly my sister ran over a list of maidens living in the neighborhood, with profuse reasons for and against.

When she paused for breath, I murmured something about a patient, and slipped out.

I proposed to make my way to the Three Boars. It seemed likely that Ralph Paton would have returned there by now.

I knew Ralph very well—better, perhaps, than any one else in King's Abbot, for I had known his mother before him, and therefore I understood much in him that puzzled others. He was, to a certain extent, the victim of heredity. He had not inherited his mother's fatal propensity for drink, but nevertheless he had in him a strain of weakness. As my new friend of this morning had declared, he was extraordinarily handsome. Just on six feet, perfectly proportioned, with the easy grace of an athlete, he was dark, like his mother, with a handsome, sunburnt face always ready to break into a smile. Ralph Paton was of those born to charm easily and without effort. He was self-indulgent and extravagant, with no veneration for anything on earth, but he was lovable nevertheless, and his friends were all devoted to him.

Could I do anything with the boy? I thought I could.

On inquiry at the Three Boars I found that Captain Paton had just come in. I went up to his room and entered unannounced.

For a moment, remembering what I had heard and seen, I was doubtful of my reception, but I need have had no misgivings.

"Why, it's Sheppard! Glad to see you."

He came forward to meet me, hand outstretched, a sunny smile lighting up his face.

"The one person I am glad to see in this infernal place."

I raised my eyebrows.

"What's the place been doing?"

He gave a vexed laugh.

"It's a long story. Things haven't been going well with me, doctor. But have a drink, won't you?"

"Thanks," I said, "I will."

He pressed the bell, then, coming back, threw himself into a chair.

"Not to mince matters," he said gloomily, "I'm in the devil of a mess. In fact, I haven't the least idea what to do next."

"What's the matter?" I asked sympathetically.

"It's my confounded stepfather."

"What has he done?"

"It isn't what he's done yet, but what he's likely to do."

The bell was answered, and Ralph ordered the drinks. When the man had gone again, he sat hunched in the arm-chair, frowning to himself.

"Is it really—serious?" I asked.

He nodded.

"I'm fairly up against it this time," he said soberly.

The unusual ring of gravity in his voice told me that he spoke the truth. It took a good deal to make Ralph grave.

"In fact," he continued, "I can't see my way ahead.... I'm damned if I can."

"If I could help——" I suggested diffidently.

But he shook his head very decidedly.

"Good of you, doctor. But I can't let you in on this. I've got to play a lone hand."

He was silent a minute and then repeated in a slightly different tone of voice:—

"Yes—I've got to play a lone hand...."

CHAPTER IV
DINNER AT FERNLY

IT was just a few minutes before half-past seven when I rang the front door bell of Fernly Park. The door was opened with admirable promptitude by Parker, the butler.

The night was such a fine one that I had preferred to come on foot. I stepped into the big square hall and Parker relieved me of my overcoat. Just then Ackroyd's secretary, a pleasant young fellow by the name of Raymond, passed through the hall on his way to Ackroyd's study, his hands full of papers.

"Good-evening, doctor. Coming to dine? Or is this a professional call?"

The last was in allusion to my black bag, which I had laid down on the oak chest.

I explained that I expected a summons to a confinement case at any moment, and so had come out prepared for an emergency call. Raymond nodded, and went on his way, calling over his shoulder:—

"Go into the drawing-room. You know the way. The ladies will be down in a minute. I must just take these papers to Mr. Ackroyd, and I'll tell him you're here."

On Raymond's appearance Parker had withdrawn, so I was alone in the hall. I settled my tie, glanced in a large mirror which hung there, and crossed to the door directly facing me, which was, as I knew, the door of the drawing-room.

I noticed, just as I was turning the handle, a sound from within—the shutting down of a window, I took it to be. I noted it, I may say, quite mechanically, without attaching any importance to it at the time.

I opened the door and walked in. As I did so, I almost collided with Miss Russell, who was just coming out. We both apologized.

For the first time I found myself appraising the housekeeper and thinking what a handsome woman she must once have been—indeed, as far as that goes, still was. Her dark hair was unstreaked with gray, and when she had a color, as she had at this minute, the stern quality of her looks was not so apparent.

Quite subconsciously I wondered whether she had been out, for she was breathing hard, as though she had been running.

"I'm afraid I'm a few minutes early," I said.

"Oh! I don't think so. It's gone half-past seven, Dr. Sheppard." She paused a minute before saying, "I—didn't know you were expected to dinner to-night. Mr. Ackroyd didn't mention it."

I received a vague impression that my dining there displeased her in some way, but I couldn't imagine why.

"How's the knee?" I inquired.

"Much the same, thank you, doctor. I must be going now. Mrs. Ackroyd will be down in a moment. I—I only came in here to see if the flowers were all right."

She passed quickly out of the room. I strolled to the window, wondering at her evident desire to justify her presence in the room. As I did so, I saw what, of course, I might have known all the time had I troubled to give my mind to it, namely, that the windows were long French ones opening on the terrace. The sound I had heard, therefore, could not have been that of a window being shut down.

Quite idly, and more to distract my mind from painful thoughts than for any other reason, I amused myself by trying to guess what could have caused the sound in question.

Coals on the fire? No, that was not the kind of noise at all. A drawer of the bureau pushed in? No, not that.

Then my eye was caught by what, I believe, is called a silver table, the lid of which lifts, and through the glass of which you can see the contents. I crossed over to it, studying the things. There were one or two pieces of old silver, a baby shoe belonging to King Charles the First, some Chinese jade figures, and quite a number of African implements and curios. Wanting to examine one of the jade figures more closely, I lifted the lid. It slipped through my fingers and fell.

At once I recognized the sound I had heard. It was this same table lid being shut down gently and carefully. I repeated the action once or twice for my own satisfaction. Then I lifted the lid to scrutinize the contents more closely.

I was still bending over the open silver table when Flora Ackroyd came into the room.

Quite a lot of people do not like Flora Ackroyd, but nobody can help admiring her. And to her friends she can be very charming. The first thing that strikes you about her is her extraordinary fairness. She has the real Scandinavian pale gold hair. Her eyes are blue—blue as the waters of a Norwegian fiord, and her skin is cream and roses. She has square, boyish shoulders and slight hips. And to a jaded medical man it is very refreshing to come across such perfect health.

A simple straight-forward English girl—I may be old-fashioned, but I think the genuine article takes a lot of beating.

Flora joined me by the silver table, and expressed heretical doubts as to King Charles I ever having worn the baby shoe.

"And anyway," continued Miss Flora, "all this making a fuss about things because some one wore or used them seems to me all nonsense. They're not wearing or using them now. The pen that George Eliot wrote *The Mill on the Floss* with—that sort of thing—well, it's only just a pen after all. If you're really keen on George Eliot, why not get *The Mill on the Floss* in a cheap edition and read it."

"I suppose you never read such old out-of-date stuff, Miss Flora?"

"You're wrong, Dr. Sheppard. I love *The Mill on the Floss*."

I was rather pleased to hear it. The things young women read nowadays and profess to enjoy positively frighten me.

"You haven't congratulated me yet, Dr. Sheppard," said Flora. "Haven't you heard?"

She held out her left hand. On the third finger of it was an exquisitely set single pearl.

"I'm going to marry Ralph, you know," she went on. "Uncle is very pleased. It keeps me in the family, you see."

I took both her hands in mine.

"My dear," I said, "I hope you'll be very happy."

"We've been engaged for about a month," continued Flora in her cool voice, "but it was only announced yesterday. Uncle is going to do up Cross-stones, and give it to us to live in, and we're going to pretend to farm. Really, we shall hunt all the winter, town for the season, and then go yachting. I love the sea. And, of course, I shall take a great interest in the parish affairs, and attend all the Mothers' Meetings."

Just then Mrs. Ackroyd rustled in, full of apologies for being late.

I am sorry to say I detest Mrs. Ackroyd. She is all chains and teeth and bones. A most unpleasant woman. She has small pale flinty blue eyes, and however gushing her words may be, those eyes of hers always remain coldly speculative.

I went across to her, leaving Flora by the window. She gave me a handful of assorted knuckles and rings to squeeze, and began talking volubly.

Had I heard about Flora's engagement? So suitable in every way. The dear young things had fallen in love at first sight. Such a perfect pair, he so dark and she so fair.

"I can't tell you, my dear Dr. Sheppard, the relief to a mother's heart."

Mrs. Ackroyd sighed—a tribute to her mother's heart, whilst her eyes remained shrewdly observant of me.

"I was wondering. You are such an old friend of dear Roger's. We know how much he trusts to your judgment. So difficult for me—in my position, as poor Cecil's widow. But there are so many tiresome things—settlements, you know—all that. I fully believe that Roger intends to make settlements upon dear Flora, but, as you know, he is just a *leetle* peculiar about money. Very usual, I've heard, amongst men who are captains of industry. I wondered, you know, if you could just *sound* him on the subject? Flora is so fond of you. We feel you are quite an old friend, although we have only really known you just over two years."

Mrs. Ackroyd's eloquence was cut short as the drawing-room door opened once more. I was pleased at the interruption. I hate interfering in other people's affairs, and I had not the least intention of tackling Ackroyd on the subject of Flora's settlements. In another moment I should have been forced to tell Mrs. Ackroyd as much.

"You know Major Blunt, don't you, doctor?"

"Yes, indeed," I said.

A lot of people know Hector Blunt—at least by repute. He has shot more wild animals in unlikely places than any man living, I suppose. When you mention him, people say: "Blunt—you don't mean the big game man, do you?"

His friendship with Ackroyd has always puzzled me a little. The two men are so totally dissimilar. Hector Blunt is perhaps five years Ackroyd's junior. They made friends early in life, and though their ways have diverged, the friendship still holds. About once in two years Blunt spends a fortnight at Fernly, and an immense animal's head, with an amazing number of horns which fixes you with a glazed stare as soon as you come inside the front door, is a permanent reminder of the friendship.

Blunt had entered the room now with his own peculiar, deliberate, yet soft-footed tread. He is a man of medium height, sturdily and rather stockily built. His face is almost mahogany-colored, and is peculiarly expressionless. He has gray eyes that give the impression of always watching something that is happening very far away. He talks little, and what he does say is said jerkily, as though the words were forced out of him unwillingly.

He said now: "How are you, Sheppard?" in his usual abrupt fashion, and then stood squarely in front of the fireplace looking over our heads as though he saw something very interesting happening in Timbuctoo.

"Major Blunt," said Flora, "I wish you'd tell me about these African things. I'm sure you know what they all are."

I have heard Hector Blunt described as a woman hater, but I noticed that he joined Flora at the silver table with what might be described as alacrity. They bent over it together.

I was afraid Mrs. Ackroyd would begin talking about settlements again, so I made a few hurried remarks about the new sweet pea. I knew there was a new sweet pea because the *Daily Mail* had told me so that morning. Mrs. Ackroyd knows nothing about horticulture, but she is the kind of woman who likes to appear well-informed about the topics of the day, and she, too, reads the *Daily Mail*. We were able to converse quite intelligently until Ackroyd and his secretary joined us, and immediately afterwards Parker announced dinner.

My place at table was between Mrs. Ackroyd and Flora. Blunt was on Mrs. Ackroyd's other side, and Geoffrey Raymond next to him.

Dinner was not a cheerful affair. Ackroyd was visibly preoccupied. He looked wretched, and ate next to nothing. Mrs. Ackroyd, Raymond, and I kept the conversation going. Flora seemed affected by her uncle's depression, and Blunt relapsed into his usual taciturnity.

Immediately after dinner Ackroyd slipped his arm through mine and led me off to his study.

"Once we've had coffee, we shan't be disturbed again," he explained. "I told Raymond to see to it that we shouldn't be interrupted."

I studied him quietly without appearing to do so. He was clearly under the influence of some strong excitement. For a minute or two he paced up and down the room, then, as Parker entered with the coffee tray, he sank into an arm-chair in front of the fire.

The study was a comfortable apartment. Book-shelves lined one wall of it. The chairs were big and covered in dark blue leather. A large desk stood by the window and was covered with papers neatly docketed and filed. On a round table were various magazines and sporting papers.

"I've had a return of that pain after food lately," remarked Ackroyd casually, as he helped himself to coffee. "You must give me some more of those tablets of yours."

It struck me that he was anxious to convey the impression that our conference was a medical one. I played up accordingly.

"I thought as much. I brought some up with me."

"Good man. Hand them over now."

"They're in my bag in the hall. I'll get them."

Ackroyd arrested me.

"Don't you trouble. Parker will get them. Bring in the doctor's bag, will you, Parker?"

"Very good, sir."

Parker withdrew. As I was about to speak, Ackroyd threw up his hand.

"Not yet. Wait. Don't you see I'm in such a state of nerves that I can hardly contain myself?"

I saw that plainly enough. And I was very uneasy. All sorts of forebodings assailed me.

Ackroyd spoke again almost immediately.

"Make certain that window's closed, will you?" he asked.

Somewhat surprised, I got up and went to it. It was not a French window, but one of the ordinary sash type. The heavy blue velvet curtains were drawn in front of it, but the window itself was open at the top.

Parker reëntered the room with my bag while I was still at the window.

"That's all right," I said, emerging again into the room.

"You've put the latch across?"

"Yes, yes. What's the matter with you, Ackroyd?"

The door had just closed behind Parker, or I would not have put the question.

Ackroyd waited just a minute before replying.

"I'm in hell," he said slowly, after a minute. "No, don't bother with those damned tablets. I only said that for Parker. Servants are so curious. Come here and sit down. The door's closed too, isn't it?"

"Yes. Nobody can overhear; don't be uneasy."

"Sheppard, nobody knows what I've gone through in the last twenty-four hours. If a man's house ever fell in ruins about him, mine has about me. This business of Ralph's is the last straw. But we won't talk about that now. It's the other—the other——! I don't know what to do about it. And I've got to make up my mind soon."

"What's the trouble?"

Ackroyd remained silent for a minute or two. He seemed curiously averse to begin. When he did speak, the question he asked came as a complete surprise. It was the last thing I expected.

"Sheppard, you attended Ashley Ferrars in his last illness, didn't you?"

"Yes, I did."

He seemed to find even greater difficulty in framing his next question.

"Did you never suspect—did it ever enter your head—that—well, that he might have been poisoned?"

I was silent for a minute or two. Then I made up my mind what to say. Roger Ackroyd was not Caroline.

"I'll tell you the truth," I said. "At the time I had no suspicion whatever, but since—well, it was mere idle talk on my sister's part that first put the idea into my head. Since then I haven't been able to get it out again. But, mind you, I've no foundation whatever for that suspicion."

"He *was* poisoned," said Ackroyd.

He spoke in a dull heavy voice.

"Who by?" I asked sharply.

"His wife."

"How do you know that?"

"She told me so herself."

"When?"

"Yesterday! My God! yesterday! It seems ten years ago."

I waited a minute, and then he went on.

"You understand, Sheppard, I'm telling you this in confidence. It's to go no further. I want your advice—I can't carry the whole weight by myself. As I said just now, I don't know what to do."

"Can you tell me the whole story?" I said. "I'm still in the dark. How did Mrs. Ferrars come to make this confession to you?"

"It's like this. Three months ago I asked Mrs. Ferrars to marry me. She refused. I asked her again and she consented, but she refused to allow me to make the engagement public until her year of mourning was up. Yesterday I called upon her, pointed out that a year and three weeks had now elapsed since her husband's death, and that there could be no further objection to making the engagement public property. I had noticed that she had been very strange in her manner for some days. Now, suddenly, without the least warning, she broke down completely. She—she told me everything. Her hatred of her brute of a husband, her growing love for me, and the—the dreadful means she had taken. Poison! My God! It was murder in cold blood."

I saw the repulsion, the horror, in Ackroyd's face. So Mrs. Ferrars must have seen it. Ackroyd is not the type of the great lover who can forgive all for love's sake. He is fundamentally a good citizen. All that was sound and wholesome and law-abiding in him must have turned from her utterly in that moment of revelation.

"Yes," he went on, in a low, monotonous voice, "she confessed everything. It seems that there is one person who has known all along—who has been blackmailing her for huge sums. It was the strain of that that drove her nearly mad."

"Who was the man?"

Suddenly before my eyes there arose the picture of Ralph Paton and Mrs. Ferrars side by side. Their heads so close together. I felt a momentary throb of anxiety. Supposing—oh! but surely that was impossible. I remembered the frankness of Ralph's greeting that very afternoon. Absurd!

"She wouldn't tell me his name," said Ackroyd slowly. "As a matter of fact, she didn't actually say that it was a man. But of course——"

"Of course," I agreed. "It must have been a man. And you've no suspicion at all?"

For answer Ackroyd groaned and dropped his head into his hands.

"It can't be," he said. "I'm mad even to think of such a thing. No, I won't even admit to you the wild suspicion that crossed my mind. I'll tell you this much, though. Something she said made me think that the person in question might be actually among my household—but that can't be so. I must have misunderstood her."

"What did you say to her?" I asked.

"What could I say? She saw, of course, the awful shock it had been to me. And then there was the question, what was my duty in the matter? She had made me, you see, an accessory after the fact. She saw all that, I think, quicker than I did. I was stunned, you know. She asked me for twenty-four hours—made me promise to do nothing till the end of that time. And she steadfastly refused to give me the name of the scoundrel who had been blackmailing her. I suppose she was afraid that I might go straight off and hammer him, and then the fat would have been in the fire as far as she was concerned. She told me that I should hear from her before twenty-four hours had passed. My God! I swear to you, Sheppard, that it never entered my head what she meant to do. Suicide! And I drove her to it."

"No, no," I said. "Don't take an exaggerated view of things. The responsibility for her death doesn't lie at your door."

"The question is, what am I to do now? The poor lady is dead. Why rake up past trouble?"

"I rather agree with you," I said.

"But there's another point. How am I to get hold of that scoundrel who drove her to death as surely as if he'd killed her. He knew of the first crime, and he fastened on to it like some obscene vulture. She's paid the penalty. Is he to go scot-free?"

"I see," I said slowly. "You want to hunt him down? It will mean a lot of publicity, you know."

"Yes, I've thought of that. I've zigzagged to and fro in my mind."

"I agree with you that the villain ought to be punished, but the cost has got to be reckoned."

Ackroyd rose and walked up and down. Presently he sank into the chair again.

"Look here, Sheppard, suppose we leave it like this. If no word comes from her, we'll let the dead things lie."

"What do you mean by word coming from her?" I asked curiously.

"I have the strongest impression that somewhere or somehow she must have left a message for me—before she went. I can't argue about it, but there it is."

I shook my head.

"She left no letter or word of any kind. I asked."

"Sheppard, I'm convinced that she did. And more, I've a feeling that by deliberately choosing death, she wanted the whole thing to come out, if only to be revenged on the man who drove her to desperation. I believe that if I could have seen her then, she would have told me his name and bid me go for him for all I was worth."

He looked at me.

"You don't believe in impressions?"

"Oh, yes, I do, in a sense. If, as you put it, word should come from her———"

I broke off. The door opened noiselessly and Parker entered with a salver on which were some letters.

"The evening post, sir," he said, handing the salver to Ackroyd.

Then he collected the coffee cups and withdrew.

My attention, diverted for a moment, came back to Ackroyd. He was staring like a man turned to stone at a long blue envelope. The other letters he had let drop to the ground.

"*Her writing,*" he said in a whisper. "She must have gone out and posted it last night, just before—before———"

He ripped open the envelope and drew out a thick enclosure. Then he looked up sharply.

"You're sure you shut the window?" he said.

"Quite sure," I said, surprised. "Why?"

"All this evening I've had a queer feeling of being watched, spied upon. What's that———?"

He turned sharply. So did I. We both had the impression of hearing the latch of the door give ever so slightly. I went across to it and opened it. There was no one there.

"Nerves," murmured Ackroyd to himself.

He unfolded the thick sheets of paper, and read aloud in a low voice.

"*My dear, my very dear Roger,—A life calls for a life. I see that—I saw it in your face this afternoon. So I am taking the only road open to me. I leave to you the punishment of the person who has made my life a hell upon earth for the last year. I would not tell you the name this afternoon, but I propose to write it to you now. I have no children or near relations to be spared, so do not fear publicity. If you can, Roger, my very dear Roger, forgive me the wrong I meant to do you, since when the time came, I could not do it after all....*"

Ackroyd, his finger on the sheet to turn it over, paused.

"Sheppard, forgive me, but I must read this alone," he said unsteadily. "It was meant for my eyes, and my eyes only."

He put the letter in the envelope and laid it on the table.

"Later, when I am alone."

"No," I cried impulsively, "read it now."

Ackroyd stared at me in some surprise.

"I beg your pardon," I said, reddening. "I do not mean read it aloud to me. But read it through whilst I am still here."

Ackroyd shook his head.

"No, I'd rather wait."

But for some reason, obscure to myself, I continued to urge him.

"At least, read the name of the man," I said.

Now Ackroyd is essentially pig-headed. The more you urge him to do a thing, the more determined he is not to do it. All my arguments were in vain.

The letter had been brought in at twenty minutes to nine. It was just on ten minutes to nine when I left him, the letter still unread. I hesitated with my hand on the door handle, looking back and wondering if there was anything I had left undone. I could think of nothing. With a shake of the head I passed out and closed the door behind me.

I was startled by seeing the figure of Parker close at hand. He looked embarrassed, and it occurred to me that he might have been listening at the door.

What a fat, smug, oily face the man had, and surely there was something decidedly shifty in his eye.

"Mr. Ackroyd particularly does not want to be disturbed," I said coldly. "He told me to tell you so."

"Quite so, sir. I—I fancied I heard the bell ring."

This was such a palpable untruth that I did not trouble to reply. Preceding me to the hall, Parker helped me on with my overcoat, and I stepped out into the night. The moon was overcast and everything seemed very dark and still. The village church clock chimed nine o'clock as I passed through the lodge gates. I turned to the left towards the village, and almost cannoned into a man coming in the opposite direction.

"This the way to Fernly Park, mister?" asked the stranger in a hoarse voice.

I looked at him. He was wearing a hat pulled down over his eyes, and his coat collar turned up. I could see little or nothing of his face, but he seemed a young fellow. The voice was rough and uneducated.

"These are the lodge gates here," I said.

"Thank you, mister." He paused, and then added, quite unnecessarily, "I'm a stranger in these parts, you see."

He went on, passing through the gates as I turned to look after him.

The odd thing was that his voice reminded me of some one's voice that I knew, but whose it was I could not think.

Ten minutes later I was at home once more. Caroline was full of curiosity to know why I had returned so early. I had to make up a slightly fictitious account of the evening in order to satisfy her, and I had an uneasy feeling that she saw through the transparent device.

At ten o'clock I rose, yawned, and suggested bed. Caroline acquiesced.

It was Friday night, and on Friday night I wind the clocks. I did it as usual, whilst Caroline satisfied herself that the servants had locked up the kitchen properly.

It was a quarter past ten as we went up the stairs. I had just reached the top when the telephone rang in the hall below.

"Mrs. Bates," said Caroline immediately.

"I'm afraid so," I said ruefully.

I ran down the stairs and took up the receiver.

"What?" I said. "*What?* Certainly, I'll come at once."

I ran upstairs, caught up my bag, and stuffed a few extra dressings into it.

"Parker telephoning," I shouted to Caroline, "from Fernly. They've just found Roger Ackroyd murdered."

CHAPTER V
MURDER

I GOT out the car in next to no time, and drove rapidly to Fernly. Jumping out, I pulled the bell impatiently. There was some delay in answering, and I rang again.

Then I heard the rattle of the chain and Parker, his impassivity of countenance quite unmoved, stood in the open doorway.

I pushed past him into the hall.

"Where is he?" I demanded sharply.

"I beg your pardon, sir?"

"Your master. Mr. Ackroyd. Don't stand there staring at me, man. Have you notified the police?"

"The police, sir? Did you say the police?" Parker stared at me as though I were a ghost.

"What's the matter with you, Parker? If, as you say, your master has been murdered——"

A gasp broke from Parker.

"The master? Murdered? Impossible, sir!"

It was my turn to stare.

"Didn't you telephone to me, not five minutes ago, and tell me that Mr. Ackroyd had been found murdered?"

"Me, sir? Oh! no indeed, sir. I wouldn't dream of doing such a thing."

"Do you mean to say it's all a hoax? That there's nothing the matter with Mr. Ackroyd?"

"Excuse me, sir, did the person telephoning use my name?"

"I'll give you the exact words I heard. '*Is that Dr. Sheppard? Parker, the butler at Fernly, speaking. Will you please come at once, sir. Mr. Ackroyd has been murdered.*'"

Parker and I stared at each other blankly.

"A very wicked joke to play, sir," he said at last, in a shocked tone. "Fancy saying a thing like that."

"Where is Mr. Ackroyd?" I asked suddenly.

"Still in the study, I fancy, sir. The ladies have gone to bed, and Major Blunt and Mr. Raymond are in the billiard room."

"I think I'll just look in and see him for a minute," I said. "I know he didn't want to be disturbed again, but this odd practical joke has made me uneasy. I'd just like to satisfy myself that he's all right."

"Quite so, sir. It makes me feel quite uneasy myself. If you don't object to my accompanying you as far as the door, sir——?"

"Not at all," I said. "Come along."

I passed through the door on the right, Parker on my heels, traversed the little lobby where a small flight of stairs led upstairs to Ackroyd's bedroom, and tapped on the study door.

There was no answer. I turned the handle, but the door was locked.

"Allow me, sir," said Parker.

Very nimbly, for a man of his build, he dropped on one knee and applied his eye to the keyhole.

"Key is in the lock all right, sir," he said, rising. "On the inside. Mr. Ackroyd must have locked himself in and possibly just dropped off to sleep."

I bent down and verified Parker's statement.

"It seems all right," I said, "but, all the same, Parker, I'm going to wake your master up. I shouldn't be satisfied to go home without hearing from his own lips that he's quite all right."

So saying, I rattled the handle and called out, "Ackroyd, Ackroyd, just a minute."

But still there was no answer. I glanced over my shoulder.

"I don't want to alarm the household," I said hesitatingly.

Parker went across and shut the door from the big hall through which we had come.

"I think that will be all right now, sir. The billiard room is at the other side of the house, and so are the kitchen quarters and the ladies' bedrooms."

I nodded comprehendingly. Then I banged once more frantically on the door, and stooping down, fairly bawled through the keyhole:—

"Ackroyd, Ackroyd! It's Sheppard. Let me in."

And still—silence. Not a sign of life from within the locked room. Parker and I glanced at each other.

"Look here, Parker," I said, "I'm going to break this door in—or rather, we are. I'll take the responsibility."

"If you say so, sir," said Parker, rather doubtfully.

"I do say so. I'm seriously alarmed about Mr. Ackroyd."

I looked round the small lobby and picked up a heavy oak chair. Parker and I held it between us and advanced to the assault. Once, twice, and three times we hurled it against the lock. At the third blow it gave, and we staggered into the room.

Ackroyd was sitting as I had left him in the arm-chair before the fire. His head had fallen sideways, and clearly visible, just below the collar of his coat, was a shining piece of twisted metalwork.

Parker and I advanced till we stood over the recumbent figure. I heard the butler draw in his breath with a sharp hiss.

"Stabbed from be'ind," he murmured. "'Orrible!"

He wiped his moist brow with his handkerchief, then stretched out a hand gingerly towards the hilt of the dagger.

"You mustn't touch that," I said sharply. "Go at once to the telephone and ring up the police station. Inform them of what has happened. Then tell Mr. Raymond and Major Blunt."

"Very good, sir."

Parker hurried away, still wiping his perspiring brow.

I did what little had to be done. I was careful not to disturb the position of the body, and not to handle the dagger at all. No object was to be attained by moving it. Ackroyd had clearly been dead some little time.

Then I heard young Raymond's voice, horror-stricken and incredulous, outside.

"What do you say? Oh! impossible! Where's the doctor?"

He appeared impetuously in the doorway, then stopped dead, his face very white. A hand put him aside, and Hector Blunt came past him into the room.

"My God!" said Raymond from behind him; "it's true, then."

Blunt came straight on till he reached the chair. He bent over the body, and I thought that, like Parker, he was going to lay hold of the dagger hilt. I drew him back with one hand.

"Nothing must be moved," I explained. "The police must see him exactly as he is now."

Blunt nodded in instant comprehension. His face was expressionless as ever, but I thought I detected signs of emotion beneath the stolid mask. Geoffrey Raymond had joined us now, and stood peering over Blunt's shoulder at the body.

"This is terrible," he said in a low voice.

He had regained his composure, but as he took off the pince-nez he habitually wore and polished them I observed that his hand was shaking.

"Robbery, I suppose," he said. "How did the fellow get in? Through the window? Has anything been taken?"

He went towards the desk.

"You think it's burglary?" I said slowly.

"What else could it be? There's no question of suicide, I suppose?"

"No man could stab himself in such a way," I said confidently. "It's murder right enough. But with what motive?"

"Roger hadn't an enemy in the world," said Blunt quietly. "Must have been burglars. But what was the thief after? Nothing seems to be disarranged?"

He looked round the room. Raymond was still sorting the papers on the desk.

"There seems nothing missing, and none of the drawers show signs of having been tampered with," the secretary observed at last. "It's very mysterious."

Blunt made a slight motion with his head.

"There are some letters on the floor here," he said.

I looked down. Three or four letters still lay where Ackroyd had dropped them earlier in the evening.

But the blue envelope containing Mrs. Ferrars's letter had disappeared. I half opened my mouth to speak, but at that moment the sound of a bell pealed through the house. There was a confused murmur of voices in the hall, and then Parker appeared with our local inspector and a police constable.

"Good evening, gentlemen," said the inspector. "I'm terribly sorry for this! A good kind gentleman like Mr. Ackroyd. The butler says it is murder. No possibility of accident or suicide, doctor?"

"None whatever," I said.

"Ah! A bad business."

He came and stood over the body.

"Been moved at all?" he asked sharply.

"Beyond making certain that life was extinct—an easy matter—I have not disturbed the body in any way."

"Ah! And everything points to the murderer having got clear away—for the moment, that is. Now then, let me hear all about it. Who found the body?"

I explained the circumstances carefully.

"A telephone message, you say? From the butler?"

"A message that I never sent," declared Parker earnestly. "I've not been near the telephone the whole evening. The others can bear me out that I haven't."

"Very odd, that. Did it sound like Parker's voice, doctor?"

"Well—I can't say I noticed. I took it for granted, you see."

"Naturally. Well, you got up here, broke in the door, and found poor Mr. Ackroyd like this. How long should you say he had been dead, doctor?"

"Half an hour at least—perhaps longer," I said.

"The door was locked on the inside, you say? What about the window?"

"I myself closed and bolted it earlier in the evening at Mr. Ackroyd's request."

The inspector strode across to it and threw back the curtains.

"Well, it's open now anyway," he remarked.

True enough, the window was open, the lower sash being raised to its fullest extent.

The inspector produced a pocket torch and flashed it along the sill outside.

"This is the way he went all right," he remarked, "*and* got in. See here."

In the light of the powerful torch, several clearly defined footmarks could be seen. They seemed to be those of shoes with rubber studs in the soles. One particularly clear one pointed inwards, another, slightly overlapping it, pointed outwards.

"Plain as a pikestaff," said the inspector. "Any valuables missing?"

Geoffrey Raymond shook his head.

"Not so that we can discover. Mr. Ackroyd never kept anything of particular value in this room."

"H'm," said the inspector. "Man found an open window. Climbed in, saw Mr. Ackroyd sitting there—maybe he'd fallen asleep. Man stabbed him from behind, then lost his nerve and made off. But he's left his tracks pretty clearly. We ought to get hold of *him* without much difficulty. No suspicious strangers been hanging about anywhere?"

"Oh!" I said suddenly.

"What is it, doctor?"

"I met a man this evening—just as I was turning out of the gate. He asked me the way to Fernly Park."

"What time would that be?"

"Just nine o'clock. I heard it chime the hour as I was turning out of the gate."

"Can you describe him?"

I did so to the best of my ability.

The inspector turned to the butler.

"Any one answering that description come to the front door?"

"No, sir. No one has been to the house at all this evening."

"What about the back?"

"I don't think so, sir, but I'll make inquiries."

He moved towards the door, but the inspector held up a large hand.

"No, thanks. I'll do my own inquiring. But first of all I want to fix the time a little more clearly. When was Mr. Ackroyd last seen alive?"

"Probably by me," I said, "when I left at—let me see—about ten minutes to nine. He told me that he didn't wish to be disturbed, and I repeated the order to Parker."

"Just so, sir," said Parker respectfully.

"Mr. Ackroyd was certainly alive at half-past nine," put in Raymond, "for I heard his voice in here talking."

"Who was he talking to?"

"That I don't know. Of course, at the time I took it for granted that it was Dr. Sheppard who was with him. I wanted to ask him a question about some papers I was engaged upon, but when I heard the voices I remembered that he had said he wanted to talk to Dr. Sheppard without being disturbed, and I went away again. But now it seems that the doctor had already left?"

I nodded.

"I was at home by a quarter-past nine," I said. "I didn't go out again until I received the telephone call."

"Who could have been with him at half-past nine?" queried the inspector. "It wasn't you, Mr.—er——"

"Major Blunt," I said.

"Major Hector Blunt?" asked the inspector, a respectful tone creeping into his voice.

Blunt merely jerked his head affirmatively.

"I think we've seen you down here before, sir," said the inspector. "I didn't recognize you for the moment, but you were staying with Mr. Ackroyd a year ago last May."

"June," corrected Blunt.

"Just so, June it was. Now, as I was saying, it wasn't you with Mr. Ackroyd at nine-thirty this evening?"

Blunt shook his head.

"Never saw him after dinner," he volunteered.

The inspector turned once more to Raymond.

"You didn't overhear any of the conversation going on, did you, sir?"

"I did catch just a fragment of it," said the secretary, "and, supposing as I did that it was Dr. Sheppard who was with Mr. Ackroyd, that fragment struck me as distinctly odd. As far as I can remember, the exact words were these. Mr. Ackroyd was speaking. 'The calls on my purse have been so frequent of late'—that is what he was saying—'of late, that I fear it is impossible for me to accede to your request....' I went away again at once, of course, so did not hear any more. But I rather wondered because Dr. Sheppard——"

"——Does not ask for loans for himself or subscriptions for others," I finished.

"A demand for money," said the inspector musingly. "It may be that here we have a very important clew." He turned to the butler. "You say, Parker, that nobody was admitted by the front door this evening?"

"That's what I say, sir."

"Then it seems almost certain that Mr. Ackroyd himself must have admitted this stranger. But I don't quite see——"

The inspector went into a kind of day-dream for some minutes.

"One thing's clear," he said at length, rousing himself from his absorption. "Mr. Ackroyd was alive and well at nine-thirty. That is the last moment at which he is known to have been alive."

Parker gave vent to an apologetic cough which brought the inspector's eyes on him at once.

"Well?" he said sharply.

"If you'll excuse me, sir, Miss Flora saw him after that."

"Miss Flora?"

"Yes, sir. About a quarter to ten that would be. It was after that that she told me Mr. Ackroyd wasn't to be disturbed again to-night."

"Did he send her to you with that message?"

"Not exactly, sir. I was bringing a tray with soda and whisky when Miss Flora, who was just coming out of this room, stopped me and said her uncle didn't want to be disturbed."

The inspector looked at the butler with rather closer attention than he had bestowed on him up to now.

"You'd already been told that Mr. Ackroyd didn't want to be disturbed, hadn't you?"

Parker began to stammer. His hands shook.

"Yes, sir. Yes, sir. Quite so, sir."

"And yet you were proposing to do so?"

"I'd forgotten, sir. At least I mean, I always bring the whisky and soda about that time, sir, and ask if there's anything more, and I thought—well, I was doing as usual without thinking."

It was at this moment that it began to dawn upon me that Parker was most suspiciously flustered. The man was shaking and twitching all over.

"H'm," said the inspector. "I must see Miss Ackroyd at once. For the moment we'll leave this room exactly as it is. I can return here after I've heard what Miss Ackroyd has to tell me. I shall just take the precaution of shutting and bolting the window."

This precaution accomplished, he led the way into the hall and we followed him. He paused a moment, as he glanced up at the little staircase, then spoke over his shoulder to the constable.

"Jones, you'd better stay here. Don't let any one go into that room."

Parker interposed deferentially.

"If you'll excuse me, sir. If you were to lock the door into the main hall, nobody could gain access to this part. That staircase leads only to Mr. Ackroyd's bedroom and bathroom. There is no communication with the other part of the house. There once was a door through, but Mr. Ackroyd had it blocked up. He liked to feel that his suite was entirely private."

To make things clear and explain the position, I have appended a rough sketch of the right-hand wing of the house. The small staircase leads, as Parker explained, to a big bedroom (made by two being knocked into one) and an adjoining bathroom and lavatory.

The inspector took in the position at a glance. We went through into the large hall and he locked the door behind him, slipping the key into his pocket. Then he gave the constable some low-voiced instructions, and the latter prepared to depart.

"We must get busy on those shoe tracks," explained the inspector. "But first of all, I must have a word with Miss Ackroyd. She was the last person to see her uncle alive. Does she know yet?"

Raymond shook his head.

"Well, no need to tell her for another five minutes. She can answer my questions better without being upset by knowing the truth about her uncle. Tell her there's been a burglary, and ask her if she would mind dressing and coming down to answer a few questions."

It was Raymond who went upstairs on this errand.

"Miss Ackroyd will be down in a minute," he said, when he returned. "I told her just what you suggested."

In less than five minutes Flora descended the staircase. She was wrapped in a pale pink silk kimono. She looked anxious and excited.

The inspector stepped forward.

"Good-evening, Miss Ackroyd," he said civilly. "We're afraid there's been an attempt at robbery, and we want you to help us. What's this room—the billiard room? Come in here and sit down."

Flora sat down composedly on the wide divan which ran the length of the wall, and looked up at the inspector.

"I don't quite understand. What has been stolen? What do you want me to tell you?"

"It's just this, Miss Ackroyd. Parker here says you came out of your uncle's study at about a quarter to ten. Is that right?"

"Quite right. I had been to say good-night to him."

"And the time is correct?"

"Well, it must have been about then. I can't say exactly. It might have been later."

"Was your uncle alone, or was there any one with him?"

"He was alone. Dr. Sheppard had gone."

"Did you happen to notice whether the window was open or shut?"

Flora shook her head.

"I can't say. The curtains were drawn."

"Exactly. And your uncle seemed quite as usual?"

"I think so."

"Do you mind telling us exactly what passed between you?"

Flora paused a minute, as though to collect her recollections.

"I went in and said, 'Good-night, uncle, I'm going to bed now. I'm tired to-night.' He gave a sort of grunt, and—I went over and kissed him, and he said something about my looking nice in the frock I had on, and then he told me to run away as he was busy. So I went."

"Did he ask specially not to be disturbed?"

"Oh! yes, I forgot. He said: 'Tell Parker I don't want anything more to-night, and that he's not to disturb me.' I met Parker just outside the door and gave him uncle's message."

"Just so," said the inspector.

"Won't you tell me what it is that has been stolen?"

"We're not quite—certain," said the inspector hesitatingly.

A wide look of alarm came into the girl's eyes. She started up.

"What is it? You're hiding something from me?"

Moving in his usual unobtrusive manner, Hector Blunt came between her and the inspector. She half stretched out her hand, and he took it in both of his, patting it as though she were a very small child, and she turned to him as though something in his stolid, rocklike demeanor promised comfort and safety.

"It's bad news, Flora," he said quietly. "Bad news for all of us. Your Uncle Roger——"

"Yes?"

"It will be a shock to you. Bound to be. Poor Roger's dead."

Flora drew away from him, her eyes dilating with horror.

"When?" she whispered. "When?"

"Very soon after you left him, I'm afraid," said Blunt gravely.

Flora raised her hand to her throat, gave a little cry, and I hurried to catch her as she fell. She had fainted, and Blunt and I carried her upstairs and laid her on her bed. Then I got him to wake Mrs. Ackroyd and tell her the news. Flora soon revived, and I brought her mother to her, telling her what to do for the girl. Then I hurried downstairs again.

CHAPTER VI
THE TUNISIAN DAGGER

I MET the inspector just coming from the door which led into the kitchen quarters.

"How's the young lady, doctor?"

"Coming round nicely. Her mother's with her."

"That's good. I've been questioning the servants. They all declare that no one has been to the back door to-night. Your description of that stranger was rather vague. Can't you give us something more definite to go upon?"

"I'm afraid not," I said regretfully. "It was a dark night, you see, and the fellow had his coat collar well pulled up and his hat squashed down over his eyes."

"H'm," said the inspector. "Looked as though he wanted to conceal his face. Sure it was no one you know?"

I replied in the negative, but not as decidedly as I might have done. I remembered my impression that the stranger's voice was not unfamiliar to me. I explained this rather haltingly to the inspector.

"It was a rough, uneducated voice, you say?"

I agreed, but it occurred to me that the roughness had been of an almost exaggerated quality. If, as the inspector thought, the man had wished to hide his face, he might equally well have tried to disguise his voice.

"Do you mind coming into the study with me again, doctor? There are one or two things I want to ask you."

I acquiesced. Inspector Davis unlocked the door of the lobby, we passed through, and he locked the door again behind him.

"We don't want to be disturbed," he said grimly. "And we don't want any eavesdropping either. What's all this about blackmail?"

"Blackmail!" I exclaimed, very much startled.

"Is it an effort of Parker's imagination? Or is there something in it?"

"If Parker heard anything about blackmail," I said slowly, "he must have been listening outside this door with his ear glued against the keyhole."

Davis nodded.

"Nothing more likely. You see, I've been instituting a few inquiries as to what Parker has been doing with himself this evening. To tell the truth, I didn't like his manner. The man knows something. When I began to question him, he got the wind up, and plumped out some garbled story of blackmail."

I took an instant decision.

"I'm rather glad you've brought the matter up," I said. "I've been trying to decide whether to make a clean breast of things or not. I'd already practically decided to tell you everything, but I was going to wait for a favorable opportunity. You might as well have it now."

And then and there I narrated the whole events of the evening as I have set them down here. The inspector listened keenly, occasionally interjecting a question.

"Most extraordinary story I ever heard," he said, when I had finished. "And you say that letter has completely disappeared? It looks bad—it looks very bad indeed. It gives us what we've been looking for—a motive for the murder."

I nodded.

"I realize that."

"You say that Mr. Ackroyd hinted at a suspicion he had that some member of his household was involved? Household's rather an elastic term."

"You don't think that Parker himself might be the man we're after?" I suggested.

"It looks very like it. He was obviously listening at the door when you came out. Then Miss Ackroyd came across him later bent on entering the study. Say he tried again when she was safely out of the way. He stabbed Ackroyd, locked the door on the inside, opened the window, and got out that way, and went round to a side door which he had previously left open. How's that?"

"There's only one thing against it," I said slowly. "If Ackroyd went on reading that letter as soon as I left, as he intended to do, I don't see him continuing to sit on here and turn things over in his mind for another hour. He'd have had Parker in at once, accused him then and there, and there would have been a fine old uproar. Remember, Ackroyd was a man of choleric temper."

"Mightn't have had time to go on with the letter just then," suggested the inspector. "We know some one was with him at half-past nine. If that visitor turned up as soon as you left, and after he went, Miss Ackroyd came in to say good-night—well, he wouldn't be able to go on with the letter until close upon ten o'clock."

"And the telephone call?"

"Parker sent that all right—perhaps before he thought of the locked door and open window. Then he changed his mind—or got in a panic—and decided to deny all knowledge of it. That was it, depend upon it."

"Ye-es," I said rather doubtfully.

"Anyway, we can find out the truth about the telephone call from the exchange. If it was put through from here, I don't see how any one else but Parker could have sent it. Depend upon it, he's our man. But keep it dark—we don't want to alarm him just yet, till we've got all the evidence. I'll see to it he doesn't give us the slip. To all appearances we'll be concentrating on your mysterious stranger."

He rose from where he had been sitting astride the chair belonging to the desk, and crossed over to the still form in the arm-chair.

"The weapon ought to give us a clew," he remarked, looking up. "It's something quite unique—a curio, I should think, by the look of it."

He bent down, surveying the handle attentively, and I heard him give a grunt of satisfaction. Then, very gingerly, he pressed his hands down below the hilt and drew the blade out from the wound. Still carrying it so as not to touch the handle, he placed it in a wide china mug which adorned the mantelpiece.

"Yes," he said, nodding at it. "Quite a work of art. There can't be many of them about."

It was indeed a beautiful object. A narrow, tapering blade, and a hilt of elaborately intertwined metals of curious and careful workmanship. He touched the blade gingerly with his finger, testing its sharpness, and made an appreciative grimace.

"Lord, what an edge," he exclaimed. "A child could drive that into a man—as easy as cutting butter. A dangerous sort of toy to have about."

"May I examine the body properly now?" I asked.

He nodded.

"Go ahead."

I made a thorough examination.

"Well?" said the inspector, when I had finished.

"I'll spare you the technical language," I said. "We'll keep that for the inquest. The blow was delivered by a right-handed man standing behind him, and death must have been instantaneous. By the expression on the dead man's face, I should say that the blow was quite unexpected. He probably died without knowing who his assailant was."

"Butlers can creep about as soft-footed as cats," said Inspector Davis. "There's not going to be much mystery about this crime. Take a look at the hilt of that dagger."

I took the look.

"I dare say they're not apparent to you, but I can see them clearly enough." He lowered his voice. "*Fingerprints!*"

He stood off a few steps to judge of his effect.

"Yes," I said mildly. "I guessed that."

I do not see why I should be supposed to be totally devoid of intelligence. After all, I read detective stories, and the newspapers, and am a man of quite average ability. If there had been toe marks on the dagger handle, now, that would have been quite a different thing. I would then have registered any amount of surprise and awe.

I think the inspector was annoyed with me for declining to get thrilled. He picked up the china mug and invited me to accompany him to the billiard room.

"I want to see if Mr. Raymond can tell us anything about this dagger," he explained.

Locking the outer door behind us again, we made our way to the billiard room, where we found Geoffrey Raymond. The inspector held up his exhibit.

"Ever seen this before, Mr. Raymond?"

"Why—I believe—I'm almost sure that is a curio given to Mr. Ackroyd by Major Blunt. It comes from Morocco—no, Tunis. So the crime was committed with that? What an extraordinary thing. It seems almost impossible, and yet there could hardly be two daggers the same. May I fetch Major Blunt?"

Without waiting for an answer, he hurried off.

"Nice young fellow that," said the inspector. "Something honest and ingenuous about him."

I agreed. In the two years that Geoffrey Raymond has been secretary to Ackroyd, I have never seen him ruffled or out of temper. And he has been, I know, a most efficient secretary.

In a minute or two Raymond returned, accompanied by Blunt.

"I was right," said Raymond excitedly. "It *is* the Tunisian dagger."

"Major Blunt hasn't looked at it yet," objected the inspector.

"Saw it the moment I came into the study," said the quiet man.

"You recognized it then?"

Blunt nodded.

"You said nothing about it," said the inspector suspiciously.

"Wrong moment," said Blunt. "Lot of harm done by blurting out things at the wrong time."

He returned the inspector's stare placidly enough.

The latter grunted at last and turned away. He brought the dagger over to Blunt.

"You're quite sure about it, sir. You identify it positively?"

"Absolutely. No doubt whatever."

"Where was this—er—curio usually kept? Can you tell me that, sir?"

It was the secretary who answered.

"In the silver table in the drawing-room."

"What?" I exclaimed.

The others looked at me.

"Yes, doctor?" said the inspector encouragingly.

"It's nothing."

"Yes, doctor?" said the inspector again, still more encouragingly.

"It's so trivial," I explained apologetically. "Only that when I arrived last night for dinner I heard the lid of the silver table being shut down in the drawing-room."

I saw profound skepticism and a trace of suspicion on the inspector's countenance.

"How did you know it was the silver table lid?"

I was forced to explain in detail—a long, tedious explanation which I would infinitely rather not have had to make.

The inspector heard me to the end.

"Was the dagger in its place when you were looking over the contents?" he asked.

"I don't know," I said. "I can't say I remember noticing it—but, of course, it may have been there all the time."

"We'd better get hold of the housekeeper," remarked the inspector, and pulled the bell.

A few minutes later Miss Russell, summoned by Parker, entered the room.

"I don't think I went near the silver table," she said, when the inspector had posed his question. "I was looking to see that all the flowers were fresh. Oh! yes, I remember now. The silver table was open—which it had no business to be, and I shut the lid down as I passed."

She looked at him aggressively.

"I see," said the inspector. "Can you tell me if this dagger was in its place then?"

Miss Russell looked at the weapon composedly.

"I can't say, I'm sure," she replied. "I didn't stop to look. I knew the family would be down any minute, and I wanted to get away."

"Thank you," said the inspector.

There was just a trace of hesitation in his manner, as though he would have liked to question her further, but Miss Russell clearly accepted the words as a dismissal, and glided from the room.

"Rather a Tartar, I should fancy, eh?" said the inspector, looking after her. "Let me see. This silver table is in front of one of the windows, I think you said, doctor?"

Raymond answered for me.

"Yes, the left-hand window."

"And the window was open?"

"They were both ajar."

"Well, I don't think we need go into the question much further. Somebody—I'll just say somebody—could get that dagger any time he liked, and exactly when he got it doesn't matter in the least. I'll be coming up in the morning with the chief constable, Mr. Raymond. Until then, I'll keep the key of that door. I want Colonel Melrose to see everything exactly as it is. I happen to know that he's dining out the other side of the county, and, I believe, staying the night...."

We watched the inspector take up the jar.

"I shall have to pack this carefully," he observed. "It's going to be an important piece of evidence in more ways than one."

A few minutes later as I came out of the billiard room with Raymond, the latter gave a low chuckle of amusement.

I felt the pressure of his hand on my arm, and followed the direction of his eyes. Inspector Davis seemed to be inviting Parker's opinion of a small pocket diary.

"A little obvious," murmured my companion. "So Parker is the suspect, is he? Shall we oblige Inspector Davis with a set of our fingerprints also?"

He took two cards from the card tray, wiped them with his silk handkerchief, then handed one to me and took the other himself. Then, with a grin, he handed them to the police inspector.

"Souvenirs," he said. "No. 1, Dr. Sheppard; No. 2, my humble self. One from Major Blunt will be forthcoming in the morning."

Youth is very buoyant. Even the brutal murder of his friend and employer could not dim Geoffrey Raymond's spirits for long. Perhaps that is as it should be. I do not know. I have lost the quality of resilience long since myself.

It was very late when I got back, and I hoped that Caroline would have gone to bed. I might have known better.

She had hot cocoa waiting for me, and whilst I drank it, she extracted the whole history of the evening from me. I said nothing of the blackmailing business, but contented myself with giving her the facts of the murder.

"The police suspect Parker," I said, as I rose to my feet and prepared to ascend to bed. "There seems a fairly clear case against him."

"Parker!" said my sister. "Fiddlesticks! That inspector must be a perfect fool. Parker indeed! Don't tell me."

With which obscure pronouncement we went up to bed.

CHAPTER VII
I LEARN MY NEIGHBOR'S PROFESSION

ON the following morning I hurried unforgivably over my round. My excuse can be that I had no very serious cases to attend. On my return Caroline came into the hall to greet me.

"Flora Ackroyd is here," she announced in an excited whisper.

"What?"

I concealed my surprise as best I could.

"She's very anxious to see you. She's been here half an hour."

Caroline led the way into our small sitting-room, and I followed.

Flora was sitting on the sofa by the window. She was in black and she sat nervously twisting her hands together. I was shocked by the sight of her face. All the color had faded away from it. But when she spoke her manner was as composed and resolute as possible.

"Dr. Sheppard, I have come to ask you to help me."

"Of course he'll help you, my dear," said Caroline.

I don't think Flora really wished Caroline to be present at the interview. She would, I am sure, have infinitely preferred to speak to me privately. But she also wanted to waste no time, so she made the best of it.

"I want you to come to The Larches with me."

"The Larches?" I queried, surprised.

"To see that funny little man?" exclaimed Caroline.

"Yes. You know who he is, don't you?"

"We fancied," I said, "that he might be a retired hairdresser."

Flora's blue eyes opened very wide.

"Why, he's Hercule Poirot! You know who I mean—the private detective. They say he's done the most wonderful things—just like detectives do in books. A year ago he retired and came to live down here. Uncle knew who he was, but he promised not to tell any one, because M. Poirot wanted to live quietly without being bothered by people."

"So that's who he is," I said slowly.

"You've heard of him, of course?"

"I'm rather an old fogey, as Caroline tells me," I said, "but I *have* just heard of him."

"Extraordinary!" commented Caroline.

I don't know what she was referring to—possibly her own failure to discover the truth.

"You want to go and see him?" I asked slowly. "Now why?"

"To get him to investigate this murder, of course," said Caroline sharply. "Don't be so stupid, James."

I was not really being stupid. Caroline does not always understand what I am driving at.

"You haven't got confidence in Inspector Davis?" I went on.

"Of course she hasn't," said Caroline. "I haven't either."

Any one would have thought it was Caroline's uncle who had been murdered.

"And how do you know he would take up the case?" I asked. "Remember he has retired from active work."

"That's just it," said Flora simply. "I've got to persuade him."

"You are sure you are doing wisely?" I asked gravely.

"Of course she is," said Caroline. "I'll go with her myself if she likes."

"I'd rather the doctor came with me if you don't mind, Miss Sheppard," said Flora.

She knows the value of being direct on certain occasions. Any hints would certainly have been wasted on Caroline.

"You see," she explained, following directness with tact, "Dr. Sheppard being the doctor, and having found the body, he would be able to give all the details to M. Poirot."

"Yes," said Caroline grudgingly, "I see that."

I took a turn or two up and down the room.

"Flora," I said gravely, "be guided by me. I advise you not to drag this detective into the case."

Flora sprang to her feet. The color rushed into her cheeks.

"I know why you say that," she cried. "But it's exactly for that reason I'm so anxious to go. You're afraid! But I'm not. I know Ralph better than you do."

"Ralph," said Caroline. "What has Ralph got to do with it?"

Neither of us heeded her.

"Ralph may be weak," continued Flora. "He may have done foolish things in the past—wicked things even—but he wouldn't murder any one."

"No, no," I exclaimed. "I never thought it of him."

"Then why did you go to the Three Boars last night?" demanded Flora, "on your way home—after uncle's body was found?"

I was momentarily silenced. I had hoped that that visit of mine would remain unnoticed.

"How did you know about that?" I countered.

"I went there this morning," said Flora. "I heard from the servants that Ralph was staying there——"

I interrupted her.

"You had no idea that he was in King's Abbot?"

"No. I was astounded. I couldn't understand it. I went there and asked for him. They told me, what I suppose they told you last night, that he went out at about nine o'clock yesterday evening—and—and never came back."

Her eyes met mine defiantly, and as though answering something in my look, she burst out:—

"Well, why shouldn't he? He might have gone—anywhere. He may even have gone back to London."

"Leaving his luggage behind?" I asked gently.

Flora stamped her foot.

"I don't care. There must be a simple explanation."

"And that's why you want to go to Hercule Poirot? Isn't it better to leave things as they are? The police don't suspect Ralph in the least, remember. They're working on quite another tack."

"But that's just *it*," cried the girl. "They *do* suspect him. A man from Cranchester turned up this morning—Inspector Raglan, a horrid, weaselly little man. I found he had been to the Three Boars this morning before me. They told me all about his having been there, and the questions he had asked. He must think Ralph did it."

"That's a change of mind from last night, if so," I said slowly. "He doesn't believe in Davis's theory that it was Parker then?"

"Parker indeed," said my sister, and snorted.

Flora came forward and laid her hand on my arm.

"Oh! Dr. Sheppard, let us go at once to this M. Poirot. He will find out the truth."

"My dear Flora," I said gently, laying my hand on hers. "Are you quite sure it is the truth we want?"

She looked at me, nodding her head gravely.

"You're not sure," she said. "I am. I know Ralph better than you do."

"Of course he didn't do it," said Caroline, who had been keeping silent with great difficulty. "Ralph may be extravagant, but he's a dear boy, and has the nicest manners."

I wanted to tell Caroline that large numbers of murderers have had nice manners, but the presence of Flora restrained me. Since the girl was determined, I was forced to give in to her and we started at once, getting away before my sister was able to fire off any more pronouncements beginning with her favorite words, "Of course."

An old woman with an immense Breton cap opened the door of The Larches to us. M. Poirot was at home, it seemed.

We were ushered into a little sitting-room arranged with formal precision, and there, after the lapse of a minute or so, my friend of yesterday came to us.

"Monsieur le docteur," he said, smiling. "Mademoiselle."

He bowed to Flora.

"Perhaps," I began, "you have heard of the tragedy which occurred last night."

His face grew grave.

"But certainly I have heard. It is horrible. I offer mademoiselle all my sympathy. In what way can I serve you?"

"Miss Ackroyd," I said, "wants you to—to——"

"To find the murderer," said Flora in a clear voice.

"I see," said the little man. "But the police will do that, will they not?"

"They might make a mistake," said Flora. "They are on their way to make a mistake now, I think. Please, M. Poirot, won't you help us? If—if it is a question of money——"

Poirot held up his hand.

"Not that, I beg of you, mademoiselle. Not that I do not care for money." His eyes showed a momentary twinkle. "Money, it means much to me and always has done. No, if I go into this, you must understand one thing clearly. *I shall go through with it to the end.* The good dog, he does not leave the scent, remember! You may wish that, after all, you had left it to the local police."

"I want the truth," said Flora, looking him straight in the eyes.

"All the truth?"

"All the truth."

"Then I accept," said the little man quietly. "And I hope you will not regret those words. Now, tell me all the circumstances."

"Dr. Sheppard had better tell you," said Flora. "He knows more than I do."

Thus enjoined, I plunged into a careful narrative, embodying all the facts I have previously set down. Poirot listened carefully, inserting a question here and there, but for the most part sitting in silence, his eyes on the ceiling.

I brought my story to a close with the departure of the inspector and myself from Fernly Park the previous night.

"And now," said Flora, as I finished, "tell him all about Ralph."

I hesitated, but her imperious glance drove me on.

"You went to this inn—this Three Boars—last night on your way home?" asked Poirot, as I brought my tale to a close. "Now exactly why was that?"

I paused a moment to choose my words carefully.

"I thought some one ought to inform the young man of his uncle's death. It occurred to me after I had left Fernly that possibly no one but myself and Mr. Ackroyd were aware that he was staying in the village."

Poirot nodded.

"Quite so. That was your only motive in going there, eh?"

"That was my only motive," I said stiffly.

"It was not to—shall we say—reassure yourself about *ce jeune homme*?"

"Reassure myself?"

"I think, M. le docteur, that you know very well what I mean, though you pretend not to do so. I suggest that it would have been a relief to you if you had found that Captain Paton had been at home all the evening."

"Not at all," I said sharply.

The little detective shook his head at me gravely.

"You have not the trust in me of Miss Flora," he said. "But no matter. What we have to look at is this—Captain Paton is missing, under circumstances which call for an explanation. I will not hide from you that the matter looks grave. Still, it may admit of a perfectly simple explanation."

"That's just what I keep saying," cried Flora eagerly.

Poirot touched no more upon that theme. Instead he suggested an immediate visit to the local police. He thought it better for Flora to return home, and for me to be the one to accompany him there and introduce him to the officer in charge of the case.

We carried out this plan forthwith. We found Inspector Davis outside the police station looking very glum indeed. With him was Colonel Melrose, the Chief Constable, and another man whom, from Flora's description of "weaselly," I had no difficulty in recognizing as Inspector Raglan from Cranchester.

I know Melrose fairly well, and I introduced Poirot to him and explained the situation. The chief constable was clearly vexed, and Inspector Raglan looked as black as thunder. Davis, however, seemed slightly exhilarated by the sight of his superior officer's annoyance.

"The case is going to be plain as a pikestaff," said Raglan. "Not the least need for amateurs to come butting in. You'd think any fool would have seen the way things were last night, and then we shouldn't have lost twelve hours."

He directed a vengeful glance at poor Davis, who received it with perfect stolidity.

"Mr. Ackroyd's family must, of course, do what they see fit," said Colonel Melrose. "But we cannot have the official investigation hampered in any way. I know M. Poirot's great reputation, of course," he added courteously.

"The police can't advertise themselves, worse luck," said Raglan.

It was Poirot who saved the situation.

"It is true that I have retired from the world," he said. "I never intended to take up a case again. Above all things, I have a horror of publicity. I must beg, that in the case of my being able to contribute something to the solution of the mystery, my name may not be mentioned."

Inspector Raglan's face lightened a little.

"I've heard of some very remarkable successes of yours," observed the colonel, thawing.

"I have had much experience," said Poirot quietly. "But most of my successes have been obtained by the aid of the police. I admire enormously your English police. If Inspector Raglan permits me to assist him, I shall be both honored and flattered."

The inspector's countenance became still more gracious.

Colonel Melrose drew me aside.

"From all I hear, this little fellow's done some really remarkable things," he murmured. "We're naturally anxious not to have to call in Scotland Yard. Raglan seems very sure of himself, but I'm not quite certain that I agree with him. You see, I—er—know the parties concerned better than he does. This fellow doesn't seem out after kudos, does he? Would work in with us unobtrusively, eh?"

"To the greater glory of Inspector Raglan," I said solemnly.

"Well, well," said Colonel Melrose breezily in a louder voice, "we must put you wise to the latest developments, M. Poirot."

"I thank you," said Poirot. "My friend, Dr. Sheppard, said something of the butler being suspected?"

"That's all bunkum," said Raglan instantly. "These high-class servants get in such a funk that they act suspiciously for nothing at all."

"The fingerprints?" I hinted.

"Nothing like Parker's." He gave a faint smile, and added: "And yours and Mr. Raymond's don't fit either, doctor."

"What about those of Captain Ralph Paton?" asked Poirot quietly.

I felt a secret admiration for the way he took the bull by the horns. I saw a look of respect creep into the inspector's eye.

"I see you don't let the grass grow under your feet, Mr. Poirot. It will be a pleasure to work with you, I'm sure. We're going to take that young gentleman's fingerprints as soon as we can lay hands upon him."

"I can't help thinking you're mistaken, inspector," said Colonel Melrose warmly. "I've known Ralph Paton from a boy upward. He'd never stoop to murder."

"Maybe not," said the inspector tonelessly.

"What have you got against him?" I asked.

"Went out just on nine o'clock last night. Was seen in neighborhood of Fernly Park somewhere about nine-thirty. Not been seen since. Believed to be in serious money difficulties. I've got a pair of his shoes here—shoes with rubber studs in them. He had two pairs, almost exactly alike. I'm going up now to compare them with those footmarks. The constable is up there seeing that no one tampers with them."

"We'll go at once," said Colonel Melrose. "You and M. Poirot will accompany us, will you not?"

We assented, and all drove up in the colonel's car. The inspector was anxious to get at once to the footmarks, and asked to be put down at the lodge. About half-way up the drive, on the right, a path branched off which led round to the terrace and the window of Ackroyd's study.

"Would you like to go with the inspector, M. Poirot?" asked the chief constable, "or would you prefer to examine the study?"

Poirot chose the latter alternative. Parker opened the door to us. His manner was smug and deferential, and he seemed to have recovered from his panic of the night before.

Colonel Melrose took a key from his pocket, and unlocking the door which led into the lobby, he ushered us through into the study.

"Except for the removal of the body, M. Poirot, this room is exactly as it was last night."

"And the body was found—where?"

As precisely as possible, I described Ackroyd's position. The arm-chair still stood in front of the fire.

Poirot went and sat down in it.

"The blue letter you speak of, where was it when you left the room?"

"Mr. Ackroyd had laid it down on this little table at his right hand."

Poirot nodded.

"Except for that, everything was in its place?"

"Yes, I think so."

"Colonel Melrose, would you be so extremely obliging as to sit down in this chair a minute. I thank you. Now, M. le docteur, will you kindly indicate to me the exact position of the dagger?"

I did so, whilst the little man stood in the doorway.

"The hilt of the dagger was plainly visible from the door then. Both you and Parker could see it at once?"

"Yes."

Poirot went next to the window.

"The electric light was on, of course, when you discovered the body?" he asked over his shoulder.

I assented, and joined him where he was studying the marks on the window-sill.

"The rubber studs are the same pattern as those in Captain Paton's shoes," he said quietly.

Then he came back once more to the middle of the room. His eye traveled round, searching everything in the room with a quick, trained glance.

"Are you a man of good observation, Dr. Sheppard?" he asked at last.

"I think so," I said, surprised.

"There was a fire in the grate, I see. When you broke the door down and found Mr. Ackroyd dead, how was the fire? Was it low?"

I gave a vexed laugh.

"I—I really can't say. I didn't notice. Perhaps Mr. Raymond or Major Blunt——"

The little man opposite me shook his head with a faint smile.

"One must always proceed with method. I made an error of judgment in asking you that question. To each man his own knowledge. You could tell me the details of the patient's appearance—nothing there would escape you. If I wanted information about the papers on that desk, Mr. Raymond would have noticed anything there was to see. To find out about the fire, I must ask the man whose business it is to observe such things. You permit——"

He moved swiftly to the fireplace and rang the bell.

After a lapse of a minute or two Parker appeared.

"The bell rang, sir," he said hesitatingly.

"Come in, Parker," said Colonel Melrose. "This gentleman wants to ask you something."

Parker transferred a respectful attention to Poirot.

"Parker," said the little man, "when you broke down the door with Dr. Sheppard last night, and found your master dead, what was the state of the fire?"

Parker replied without a pause.

"It had burned very low, sir. It was almost out."

"Ah!" said Poirot. The exclamation sounded almost triumphant. He went on:—

"Look round you, my good Parker. Is this room exactly as it was then?"

The butler's eye swept round. It came to rest on the windows.

"The curtains were drawn, sir, and the electric light was on."

Poirot nodded approval.

"Anything else?"

"Yes, sir, this chair was drawn out a little more."

He indicated a big grandfather chair to the left of the door between it and the window. I append a plan of the room with the chair in question marked with an X.

"Just show me," said Poirot.

The butler drew the chair in question out a good two feet from the wall, turning it so that the seat faced the door.

"*Voilà ce qui est curieux*," murmured Poirot. "No one would want to sit in a chair in such a position, I fancy. Now who pushed it back into place again, I wonder? Did you, my friend?"

"No, sir," said Parker. "I was too upset with seeing the master and all."

Poirot looked across at me.

"Did you, doctor?"

I shook my head.

"It was back in position when I arrived with the police, sir," put in Parker. "I'm sure of that."

"Curious," said Poirot again.

"Raymond or Blunt must have pushed it back," I suggested. "Surely it isn't important?"

"It is completely unimportant," said Poirot. "That is why it is so interesting," he added softly.

"Excuse me a minute," said Colonel Melrose. He left the room with Parker.

"Do you think Parker is speaking the truth?" I asked.

"About the chair, yes. Otherwise I do not know. You will find, M. le docteur, if you have much to do with cases of this kind, that they all resemble each other in one thing."

"What is that?" I asked curiously.

"Every one concerned in them has something to hide."

"Have I?" I asked, smiling.

Poirot looked at me attentively.

"I think you have," he said quietly.

"But——"

"Have you told me everything known to you about this young man Paton?" He smiled as I grew red. "Oh! do not fear. I will not press you. I shall learn it in good time."

"I wish you'd tell me something of your methods," I said hastily, to cover my confusion. "The point about the fire, for instance?"

"Oh! that was very simple. You leave Mr. Ackroyd at—ten minutes to nine, was it not?"

"Yes, exactly, I should say."

"The window is then closed and bolted and the door unlocked. At a quarter past ten when the body is discovered, the door is locked and the window is open. Who opened it? Clearly only Mr. Ackroyd himself could have done so, and for one of two reasons. Either because the room became unbearably hot (but since the fire was nearly out and there was a sharp drop in temperature last night, that cannot be the reason), or because he admitted some one that way. And if he admitted some one that way, it must have been some one well known to him, since he had previously shown himself uneasy on the subject of that same window."

"It sounds very simple," I said.

"Everything is simple, if you arrange the facts methodically. We are concerned now with the personality of the person who was with him at nine-thirty last night. Everything goes to show that that was the individual admitted by the window, and though Mr. Ackroyd was seen alive later by Miss Flora, we cannot approach a solution of the mystery until we know who that visitor was. The window may have been left open after his departure and so afforded entrance to the murderer, or the same person may have returned a second time. Ah! here is the colonel who returns."

Colonel Melrose entered with an animated manner.

"That telephone call has been traced at last," he said. "It did not come from here. It was put through to Dr. Sheppard at 10.15 last night from a public call office at King's Abbot station. And at 10.23 the night mail leaves for Liverpool."

CHAPTER VIII
INSPECTOR RAGLAN IS CONFIDENT

WE looked at each other.

"You'll have inquiries made at the station, of course?" I said.

"Naturally, but I'm not over sanguine as to the result. You know what that station is like."

I did. King's Abbot is a mere village, but its station happens to be an important junction. Most of the big expresses stop there, and trains are shunted, re-sorted, and made up. It has two or three public telephone boxes. At that time of night three local trains come in close upon each other, to catch the connection with the express for the north which comes in at 10.19 and leaves at 10.23. The whole place is in a bustle, and the chances of one particular person being noticed telephoning or getting into the express are very small indeed.

"But why telephone at all?" demanded Melrose. "That is what I find so extraordinary. There seems no rhyme or reason in the thing."

Poirot carefully straightened a china ornament on one of the bookcases.

"Be sure there was a reason," he said over his shoulder.

"But what reason could it be?"

"When we know that, we shall know everything. This case is very curious and very interesting."

There was something almost indescribable in the way he said those last words. I felt that he was looking at the case from some peculiar angle of his own, and what he saw I could not tell.

He went to the window and stood there, looking out.

"You say it was nine o'clock, Dr. Sheppard, when you met this stranger outside the gate?"

He asked the question without turning round.

"Yes," I replied. "I heard the church clock chime the hour."

"How long would it take him to reach the house—to reach this window, for instance?"

"Five minutes at the outside. Two or three minutes only if he took the path at the right of the drive and came straight here."

"But to do that he would have to know the way. How can I explain myself?—it would mean that he had been here before—that he knew his surroundings."

"That is true," replied Colonel Melrose.

"We could find out, doubtless, if Mr. Ackroyd had received any strangers during the past week?"

"Young Raymond could tell us that," I said.

"Or Parker," suggested Colonel Melrose.

"*Ou tous les deux*," suggested Poirot, smiling.

Colonel Melrose went in search of Raymond, and I rang the bell once more for Parker.

Colonel Melrose returned almost immediately, accompanied by the young secretary, whom he introduced to Poirot. Geoffrey Raymond was fresh and debonair as ever. He seemed surprised and delighted to make Poirot's acquaintance.

"No idea you'd been living among us incognito, M. Poirot," he said. "It will be a great privilege to watch you at work——Hallo, what's this?"

Poirot had been standing just to the left of the door. Now he moved aside suddenly, and I saw that while my back was turned he must have swiftly drawn out the arm-chair till it stood in the position Parker had indicated.

"Want me to sit in the chair whilst you take a blood test?" asked Raymond good-humoredly. "What's the idea?"

"M. Raymond, this chair was pulled out—so—last night when Mr. Ackroyd was found killed. Some one moved it back again into place. Did you do so?"

The secretary's reply came without a second's hesitation.

"No, indeed I didn't. I don't even remember that it was in that position, but it must have been if you say so. Anyway, somebody else must have moved it back to its proper place. Have they destroyed a clew in doing so? Too bad!"

"It is of no consequence," said the detective. "Of no consequence whatever. What I really want to ask you is this, M. Raymond: Did any stranger come to see Mr. Ackroyd during this past week?"

The secretary reflected for a minute or two, knitting his brows, and during the pause Parker appeared in answer to the bell.

"No," said Raymond at last. "I can't remember any one. Can you, Parker?"

"I beg your pardon, sir?"

"Any stranger coming to see Mr. Ackroyd this week?"

The butler reflected for a minute or two.

"There was the young man who came on Wednesday, sir," he said at last. "From Curtis and Troute, I understood he was."

Raymond moved this aside with an impatient hand.

"Oh! yes, I remember, but that is not the kind of stranger this gentleman means." He turned to Poirot. "Mr. Ackroyd had some idea of purchasing a dictaphone," he explained. "It would have enabled us to get through a lot more work in a limited time. The firm in question sent down their representative, but nothing came of it. Mr. Ackroyd did not make up his mind to purchase."

Poirot turned to the butler.

"Can you describe this young man to me, my good Parker?"

46

"He was fair-haired, sir, and short. Very neatly dressed in a blue serge suit. A very presentable young man, sir, for his station in life."

Poirot turned to me.

"The man you met outside the gate, doctor, was tall, was he not?"

"Yes," I said. "Somewhere about six feet, I should say."

"There is nothing in that, then," declared the Belgian. "I thank you, Parker."

The butler spoke to Raymond.

"Mr. Hammond has just arrived, sir," he said. "He is anxious to know if he can be of any service, and he would be glad to have a word with you."

"I'll come at once," said the young man. He hurried out. Poirot looked inquiringly at the chief constable.

"The family solicitor, M. Poirot," said the latter.

"It is a busy time for this young M. Raymond," murmured M. Poirot. "He has the air efficient, that one."

"I believe Mr. Ackroyd considered him a most able secretary."

"He has been here—how long?"

"Just on two years, I fancy."

"His duties he fulfills punctiliously. Of that I am sure. In what manner does he amuse himself? Does he go in for *le sport*?"

"Private secretaries haven't much time for that sort of thing," said Colonel Melrose, smiling. "Raymond plays golf, I believe. And tennis in the summer time."

"He does not attend the courses—I should say the running of the horses?"

"Race meetings? No, I don't think he's interested in racing."

Poirot nodded and seemed to lose interest. He glanced slowly round the study.

"I have seen, I think, all that there is to be seen here."

I, too, looked round.

"If those walls could speak," I murmured.

Poirot shook his head.

"A tongue is not enough," he said. "They would have to have also eyes and ears. But do not be too sure that these dead things"—he touched the top of the bookcase as he spoke—"are always dumb. To me they speak sometimes—chairs, tables—they have their message!"

He turned away towards the door.

"What message?" I cried. "What have they said to you to-day?"

He looked over his shoulder and raised one eyebrow quizzically.

"An opened window," he said. "A locked door. A chair that apparently moved itself. To all three I say, 'Why?' and I find no answer."

He shook his head, puffed out his chest, and stood blinking at us. He looked ridiculously full of his own importance. It crossed my mind to wonder whether he was really any good as a detective. Had his big reputation been built up on a series of lucky chances?

I think the same thought must have occurred to Colonel Melrose, for he frowned.

"Anything more you want to see, M. Poirot?" he inquired brusquely.

"You would perhaps be so kind as to show me the silver table from which the weapon was taken? After that, I will trespass on your kindness no longer."

We went to the drawing-room, but on the way the constable waylaid the colonel, and after a muttered conversation the latter excused himself and left us together. I showed Poirot the silver table, and after raising the lid once or twice and letting it fall, he pushed open the window and stepped out on the terrace. I followed him.

Inspector Raglan had just turned the corner of the house, and was coming towards us. His face looked grim and satisfied.

"So there you are, M. Poirot," he said. "Well, this isn't going to be much of a case. I'm sorry, too. A nice enough young fellow gone wrong."

Poirot's face fell, and he spoke very mildly.

"I'm afraid I shall not be able to be of much aid to you, then?"

"Next time, perhaps," said the inspector soothingly. "Though we don't have murders every day in this quiet little corner of the world."

Poirot's gaze took on an admiring quality.

"You have been of a marvelous promptness," he observed. "How exactly did you go to work, if I may ask?"

"Certainly," said the inspector. "To begin with—method. That's what I always say—method!"

"Ah!" cried the other. "That, too, is my watchword. Method, order, and the little gray cells."

"The cells?" said the inspector, staring.

"The little gray cells of the brain," explained the Belgian.

"Oh, of course; well, we all use them, I suppose."

"In a greater or lesser degree," murmured Poirot. "And there are, too, differences in quality. Then there is the psychology of a crime. One must study that."

"Ah!" said the inspector, "you've been bitten with all this psychoanalysis stuff? Now, I'm a plain man——"

"Mrs. Raglan would not agree, I am sure, to that," said Poirot, making him a little bow.

Inspector Raglan, a little taken aback, bowed.

"You don't understand," he said, grinning broadly. "Lord, what a lot of difference language makes. I'm telling you how I set to work. First of all, method. Mr. Ackroyd was last seen alive at a quarter to ten by his niece, Miss Flora Ackroyd. That's fact number one, isn't it?"

"If you say so."

"Well, it is. At half-past ten, the doctor here says that Mr. Ackroyd has been dead at least half an hour. You stick to that, doctor?"

"Certainly," I said. "Half an hour or longer."

"Very good. That gives us exactly a quarter of an hour in which the crime must have been committed. I make a list of every one in the house, and work through it, setting down opposite their names where they were and what they were doing between the hour of 9.45 and 10 p.m."

He handed a sheet of paper to Poirot. I read it over his shoulder. It ran as follows, written in a neat script:—

Major Blunt.—In billiard room with Mr. Raymond. (Latter confirms.)
Mr. Raymond.—Billiard room. (See above.)

Mrs. Ackroyd.—*9.45 watching billiard match. Went up to bed 9.55. (Raymond and Blunt watched her up staircase.)*
Miss Ackroyd.—*Went straight from her uncle's room upstairs. (Confirmed by Parker, also housemaid, Elsie Dale.)*
Servants:—
Parker.—*Went straight to butler's pantry. (Confirmed by housekeeper, Miss Russell, who came down to speak to him about something at 9.47, and remained at least ten minutes.)*
Miss Russell.—*As above. Spoke to housemaid, Elsie Dale, upstairs at 9.45.*
Ursula Bourne (parlormaid).—*In her own room until 9.55. Then in Servants' Hall.*
Mrs. Cooper (cook).—*In Servants' Hall.*
Gladys Jones (second housemaid).—*In Servants' Hall.*
Elsie Dale.—*Upstairs in bedroom. Seen there by Miss Russell and Miss Flora Ackroyd.*
Mary Thripp (kitchenmaid).—*Servants' Hall.*

"The cook has been here seven years, the parlormaid eighteen months, and Parker just over a year. The others are new. Except for something fishy about Parker, they all seem quite all right."

"A very complete list," said Poirot, handing it back to him. "I am quite sure that Parker did not do the murder," he added gravely.

"So is my sister," I struck in. "And she's usually right." Nobody paid any attention to my interpolation.

"That disposes pretty effectually of the household," continued the inspector. "Now we come to a very grave point. The woman at the lodge—Mary Black—was pulling the curtains last night when she saw Ralph Paton turn in at the gate and go up towards the house."

"She is sure of that?" I asked sharply.

"Quite sure. She knows him well by sight. He went past very quickly and turned off by the path to the right, which is a short cut to the terrace."

"And what time was that?" asked Poirot, who had sat with an immovable face.

"Exactly twenty-five minutes past nine," said the inspector gravely.

There was a silence. Then the inspector spoke again.

"It's all clear enough. It fits in without a flaw. At twenty-five minutes past nine, Captain Paton is seen passing the lodge; at nine-thirty or thereabouts, Mr. Geoffrey Raymond hears some one in here asking for money and Mr. Ackroyd refusing. What happens next? Captain Paton leaves the same way—through the window. He walks along the terrace, angry and baffled. He comes to the open drawing-room window. Say it's now a quarter to ten. Miss Flora Ackroyd is saying good-night to her uncle. Major Blunt, Mr. Raymond, and Mrs. Ackroyd are in the billiard room. The drawing-room is empty. He steals in, takes the dagger from the silver table, and returns to the study window. He slips off his shoes, climbs in, and—well, I don't need to go into details. Then he slips out again and goes off. Hadn't the nerve to go back to the inn. He makes for the station, rings up from there——"

"Why?" said Poirot softly.

I jumped at the interruption. The little man was leaning forward. His eyes shone with a queer green light.

For a moment Inspector Raglan was taken aback by the question.

"It's difficult to say exactly why he did that," he said at last. "But murderers do funny things. You'd know that if you were in the police force. The cleverest of them make stupid mistakes sometimes. But come along and I'll show you those footprints."

We followed him round the corner of the terrace to the study window. At a word from Raglan a police constable produced the shoes which had been obtained from the local inn.

The inspector laid them over the marks.

"They're the same," he said confidently. "That is to say, they're not the same pair that actually made these prints. He went away in those. This is a pair just like them, but older—see how the studs are worn down."

"Surely a great many people wear shoes with rubber studs in them?" asked Poirot.

"That's so, of course," said the inspector. "I shouldn't put so much stress on the footmarks if it wasn't for everything else."

"A very foolish young man, Captain Ralph Paton," said Poirot thoughtfully. "To leave so much evidence of his presence."

"Ah! well," said the inspector, "it was a dry, fine night, you know. He left no prints on the terrace or on the graveled path. But, unluckily for him, a spring must have welled up just lately at the end of the path from the drive. See here."

A small graveled path joined the terrace a few feet away. In one spot, a few yards from its termination, the ground was wet and boggy. Crossing this wet place there were again the marks of footsteps, and amongst them the shoes with rubber studs.

Poirot followed the path on a little way, the inspector by his side.

"You noticed the women's footprints?" he said suddenly.

The inspector laughed.

"Naturally. But several different women have walked this way—and men as well. It's a regular short cut to the house, you see. It would be impossible to sort out all the footsteps. After all, it's the ones on the window-sill that are really important."

Poirot nodded.

"It's no good going farther," said the inspector, as we came in view of the drive. "It's all graveled again here, and hard as it can be."

Again Poirot nodded, but his eyes were fixed on a small garden house—a kind of superior summer-house. It was a little to the left of the path ahead of us, and a graveled walk ran up to it.

Poirot lingered about until the inspector had gone back towards the house. Then he looked at me.

"You must have indeed been sent from the good God to replace my friend Hastings," he said, with a twinkle. "I observe that you do not quit my side. How say you, Dr. Sheppard, shall we investigate that summer-house? It interests me."

He went up to the door and opened it. Inside, the place was almost dark. There were one or two rustic seats, a croquet set, and some folded deck-chairs.

I was startled to observe my new friend. He had dropped to his hands and knees and was crawling about the floor. Every now and then he shook his head as though not satisfied. Finally, he sat back on his heels.

"Nothing," he murmured. "Well, perhaps it was not to be expected. But it would have meant so much——"

He broke off, stiffening all over. Then he stretched out his hand to one of the rustic chairs. He detached something from one side of it.

"What is it?" I cried. "What have you found?"

He smiled, unclosing his hand so that I should see what lay in the palm of it. A scrap of stiff white cambric.

I took it from him, looked at it curiously, and then handed it back.

"What do you make of it, eh, my friend?" he asked, eyeing me keenly.

"A scrap torn from a handkerchief," I suggested, shrugging my shoulders.

He made another dart and picked up a small quill—a goose quill by the look of it.

"And that?" he cried triumphantly. "What do you make of that?"

I only stared.

He slipped the quill into his pocket, and looked again at the scrap of white stuff.

"A fragment of a handkerchief?" he mused. "Perhaps you are right. But remember this—*a good laundry does not starch a handkerchief.*"

He nodded at me triumphantly, then he put away the scrap carefully in his pocket-book.

CHAPTER IX
THE GOLDFISH POND

WE walked back to the house together. There was no sign of the inspector. Poirot paused on the terrace and stood with his back to the house, slowly turning his head from side to side.

"*Une belle propriété,*" he said at last appreciatively. "Who inherits it?"

His words gave me almost a shock. It is an odd thing, but until that moment the question of inheritance had never come into my head. Poirot watched me keenly.

"It is a new idea to you, that," he said at last. "You had not thought of it before—eh?"

"No," I said truthfully. "I wish I had."

He looked at me again curiously.

"I wonder just what you mean by that," he said thoughtfully. "Ah! no," as I was about to speak. "*Inutile!* You would not tell me your real thought."

"Every one has something to hide," I quoted, smiling.

"Exactly."

"You still believe that?"

"More than ever, my friend. But it is not easy to hide things from Hercule Poirot. He has a knack of finding out."

He descended the steps of the Dutch garden as he spoke.

"Let us walk a little," he said over his shoulder. "The air is pleasant to-day."

I followed him. He led me down a path to the left enclosed in yew hedges. A walk led down the middle, bordered each side with formal flower beds, and at the end was a round paved recess with a seat and a pond of goldfish. Instead of pursuing the path to the end, Poirot took another which wound up the side of a wooded slope. In one spot the trees had been cleared away, and a seat had been put. Sitting there one had a splendid view over the countryside, and one looked right down on the paved recess and the goldfish pond.

"England is very beautiful," said Poirot, his eyes straying over the prospect. Then he smiled. "And so are English girls," he said in a lower tone. "Hush, my friend, and look at the pretty picture below us."

It was then that I saw Flora. She was moving along the path we had just left and she was humming a little snatch of song. Her step was more dancing than walking, and in spite of her black dress, there was nothing but joy in her whole attitude. She gave a sudden pirouette on her toes, and her black draperies swung out. At the same time she flung her head back and laughed outright.

As she did so a man stepped out from the trees. It was Hector Blunt.

The girl started. Her expression changed a little.

"How you startled me—I didn't see you."

Blunt said nothing, but stood looking at her for a minute or two in silence.

"What I like about you," said Flora, with a touch of malice, "is your cheery conversation."

I fancy that at that Blunt reddened under his tan. His voice, when he spoke, sounded different—it had a curious sort of humility in it.

"Never was much of a fellow for talking. Not even when I was young."

"That was a very long time ago, I suppose," said Flora gravely.

I caught the undercurrent of laughter in her voice, but I don't think Blunt did.

"Yes," he said simply, "it was."

"How does it feel to be Methuselah?" asked Flora.

This time the laughter was more apparent, but Blunt was following out an idea of his own.

"Remember the Johnny who sold his soul to the devil? In return for being made young again? There's an opera about it."

"Faust, you mean?"

"That's the beggar. Rum story. Some of us would do it if we could."

"Any one would think you were creaking at the joints to hear you talk," cried Flora, half vexed, half amused.

Blunt said nothing for a minute or two. Then he looked away from Flora into the middle distance and observed to an adjacent tree trunk that it was about time he got back to Africa.

"Are you going on another expedition—shooting things?"

"Expect so. Usually do, you know—shoot things, I mean."

"You shot that head in the hall, didn't you?"

Blunt nodded. Then he jerked out, going rather red, as he did so:—

"Care for some decent skins any time? If so, I could get 'em for you."

"Oh! please do," cried Flora. "Will you really? You won't forget?"

"I shan't forget," said Hector Blunt.

He added, in a sudden burst of communicativeness:—

"Time I went. I'm no good in this sort of life. Haven't got the manners for it. I'm a rough fellow, no use in society. Never remember the things one's expected to say. Yes, time I went."

"But you're not going at once," cried Flora. "Not—not while we're in all this trouble. Oh! please. If you go——"

She turned away a little.

"You want me to stay?" asked Blunt.

He spoke deliberately but quite simply.

"We all——"

"I meant you personally," said Blunt, with directness.

Flora turned slowly back again and met his eyes.

"I want you to stay," she said, "if—if that makes any difference."

"It makes all the difference," said Blunt.

There was a moment's silence. They sat down on the stone seat by the goldfish pond. It seemed as though neither of them knew quite what to say next.

"It—it's such a lovely morning," said Flora at last. "You know, I can't help feeling happy, in spite—in spite of everything. That's awful, I suppose?"

"Quite natural," said Blunt. "Never saw your uncle until two years ago, did you? Can't be expected to grieve very much. Much better to have no humbug about it."

"There's something awfully consoling about you," said Flora. "You make things so simple."

"Things are simple as a rule," said the big game hunter.

"Not always," said Flora.

Her voice had lowered itself, and I saw Blunt turn and look at her, bringing his eyes back from (apparently) the coast of Africa to do so. He evidently put his own construction on her change of tone, for he said, after a minute or two, in rather an abrupt manner:—

"I say, you know, you mustn't worry. About that young chap, I mean. Inspector's an ass. Everybody knows—utterly absurd to think he could have done it. Man from outside. Burglar chap. That's the only possible solution."

Flora turned to look at him.

"You really think so?"

"Don't you?" said Blunt quickly.

"I—oh, yes, of course."

Another silence, and then Flora burst out:—

"I'm—I'll tell you why I felt so happy this morning. However heartless you think me, I'd rather tell you. It's because the lawyer has been—Mr. Hammond. He told us about the will. Uncle Roger has left me twenty thousand pounds. Think of it—twenty thousand beautiful pounds."

Blunt looked surprised.

"Does it mean so much to you?"

"Mean much to me? Why, it's everything. Freedom—life—no more scheming and scraping and lying——"

"Lying?" said Blunt, sharply interrupting.

Flora seemed taken aback for a minute.

"You know what I mean," she said uncertainly. "Pretending to be thankful for all the nasty castoff things rich relations give you. Last year's coats and skirts and hats."

"Don't know much about ladies' clothes; should have said you were always very well turned out."

"It's cost me something, though," said Flora in a low voice. "Don't let's talk of horrid things. I'm so happy. I'm free. Free to do what I like. Free not to——"

She stopped suddenly.

"Not to what?" asked Blunt quickly.

"I forget now. Nothing important."

Blunt had a stick in his hand, and he thrust it into the pond, poking at something.

"What are you doing, Major Blunt?"

"There's something bright down there. Wondered what it was—looks like a gold brooch. Now I've stirred up the mud and it's gone."

"Perhaps it's a crown," suggested Flora. "Like the one Mélisande saw in the water."

"Mélisande," said Blunt reflectively—"she's in an opera, isn't she?"

"Yes, you seem to know a lot about operas."

"People take me sometimes," said Blunt sadly. "Funny idea of pleasure—worse racket than the natives make with their tom-toms."

Flora laughed.

"I remember Mélisande," continued Blunt, "married an old chap old enough to be her father."

He threw a small piece of flint into the goldfish pond. Then, with a change of manner, he turned to Flora.

"Miss Ackroyd, can I do anything? About Paton, I mean. I know how dreadfully anxious you must be."

"Thank you," said Flora in a cold voice. "There is really nothing to be done. Ralph will be all right. I've got hold of the most wonderful detective in the world, and he's going to find out all about it."

For some time I had felt uneasy as to our position. We were not exactly eavesdropping, since the two in the garden below had only to lift their heads to see us. Nevertheless, I should have drawn attention to our presence before now, had not my companion put a warning pressure on my arm. Clearly he wished me to remain silent.

But now he rose briskly to his feet, clearing his throat.

"I demand pardon," he cried. "I cannot allow mademoiselle thus extravagantly to compliment me, and not draw attention to my presence. They say the listener hears no good of himself, but that is not the case this time. To spare my blushes, I must join you and apologize."

He hurried down the path with me close behind him, and joined the others by the pond.

"This is M. Hercule Poirot," said Flora. "I expect you've heard of him."

Poirot bowed.

"I know Major Blunt by reputation," he said politely. "I am glad to have encountered you, monsieur. I am in need of some information that you can give me."

Blunt looked at him inquiringly.

"When did you last see M. Ackroyd alive?"

"At dinner."

"And you neither saw nor heard anything of him after that?"

"Didn't see him. Heard his voice."

"How was that?"

"I strolled out on the terrace——"

"Pardon me, what time was this?"

"About half-past nine. I was walking up and down smoking in front of the drawing-room window. I heard Ackroyd talking in his study——"

Poirot stooped and removed a microscopic weed.

"Surely you couldn't hear voices in the study from that part of the terrace," he murmured.

He was not looking at Blunt, but I was, and to my intense surprise, I saw the latter flush.

"Went as far as the corner," he explained unwillingly.

"Ah! indeed?" said Poirot.

In the mildest manner he conveyed an impression that more was wanted.

"Thought I saw—a woman disappearing into the bushes. Just a gleam of white, you know. Must have been mistaken. It was while I was standing at the corner of the terrace that I heard Ackroyd's voice speaking to that secretary of his."

"Speaking to Mr. Geoffrey Raymond?"

"Yes—that's what I supposed at the time. Seems I was wrong."

"Mr. Ackroyd didn't address him by name?"

"Oh, no."

"Then, if I may ask, why did you think——?"

Blunt explained laboriously.

"Took it for granted that it *would* be Raymond, because he had said just before I came out that he was taking some papers to Ackroyd. Never thought of it being anybody else."

"Can you remember what the words you heard were?"

"Afraid I can't. Something quite ordinary and unimportant. Only caught a scrap of it. I was thinking of something else at the time."

"It is of no importance," murmured Poirot. "Did you move a chair back against the wall when you went into the study after the body was discovered?"

"Chair? No—why should I?"

Poirot shrugged his shoulders but did not answer. He turned to Flora.

"There is one thing I should like to know from you, mademoiselle. When you were examining the things in the silver table with Dr. Sheppard, was the dagger in its place, or was it not?"

Flora's chin shot up.

"Inspector Raglan has been asking me that," she said resentfully. "I've told him, and I'll tell you. I'm perfectly certain the dagger was *not* there. He thinks it was and that Ralph sneaked it later in the evening. And—and he doesn't believe me. He thinks I'm saying it to—to shield Ralph."

"And aren't you?" I asked gravely.

Flora stamped her foot.

"You, too, Dr. Sheppard! Oh! it's too bad."

Poirot tactfully made a diversion.

"It is true what I heard you say, Major Blunt. There is something that glitters in this pond. Let us see if I can reach it."

He knelt down by the pond, baring his arm to the elbow, and lowered it in very slowly, so as not to disturb the bottom of the pond. But in spite of all his precautions the mud eddied and swirled, and he was forced to draw his arm out again empty-handed.

He gazed ruefully at the mud upon his arm. I offered him my handkerchief, which he accepted with fervent protestations of thanks. Blunt looked at his watch.

"Nearly lunch time," he said. "We'd better be getting back to the house."

"You will lunch with us, M. Poirot?" asked Flora. "I should like you to meet my mother. She is—very fond of Ralph."

The little man bowed.

"I shall be delighted, mademoiselle."

"And you will stay, too, won't you, Dr. Sheppard?"

I hesitated.

"Oh, do!"

I wanted to, so I accepted the invitation without further ceremony.

We set out towards the house, Flora and Blunt walking ahead.

"What hair," said Poirot to me in a low tone, nodding towards Flora. "The real gold! They will make a pretty couple. She and the dark, handsome Captain Paton. Will they not?"

I looked at him inquiringly, but he began to fuss about a few microscopic drops of water on his coat sleeve. The man reminded me in some ways of a cat. His green eyes and his finicking habits.

"And all for nothing, too," I said sympathetically. "I wonder what it was in the pond?"

"Would you like to see?" asked Poirot.

I stared at him. He nodded.

"My good friend," he said gently and reproachfully, "Hercule Poirot does not run the risk of disarranging his costume without being sure of attaining his object. To do so would be ridiculous and absurd. I am never ridiculous."

"But you brought your hand out empty," I objected.

"There are times when it is necessary to have discretion. Do you tell your patients everything—everything, doctor? I think not. Nor do you tell your excellent sister everything either, is it not so? Before showing my empty hand, I dropped what it contained into my other hand. You shall see what that was."

He held out his left hand, palm open. On it lay a little circlet of gold. A woman's wedding ring.

I took it from him.

"Look inside," commanded Poirot.

I did so. Inside was an inscription in fine writing:—

From R., March 13th.

I looked at Poirot, but he was busy inspecting his appearance in a tiny pocket glass. He paid particular attention to his mustaches, and none at all to me. I saw that he did not intend to be communicative.

CHAPTER X
THE PARLORMAID

WE found Mrs. Ackroyd in the hall. With her was a small dried-up little man, with an aggressive chin and sharp gray eyes, and "lawyer" written all over him.

"Mr. Hammond is staying to lunch with us," said Mrs. Ackroyd. "You know Major Blunt, Mr. Hammond? And dear Dr. Sheppard—also a close friend of poor Roger's. And, let me see———"

She paused, surveying Hercule Poirot in some perplexity.

"This is M. Poirot, mother," said Flora. "I told you about him this morning."

"Oh! yes," said Mrs. Ackroyd vaguely. "Of course, my dear, of course. He is to find Ralph, is he not?"

"He is to find out who killed uncle," said Flora.

"Oh! my dear," cried her mother. "Please! My poor nerves. I am a wreck this morning, a positive wreck. Such a dreadful thing to happen. I can't help feeling that it must have been an accident of some kind. Roger was so fond of handling queer curios. His hand must have slipped, or something."

This theory was received in polite silence. I saw Poirot edge up to the lawyer, and speak to him in a confidential undertone. They moved aside into the embrasure of the window. I joined them—then hesitated.

"Perhaps I'm intruding," I said.

"Not at all," cried Poirot heartily. "You and I, M. le docteur, we investigate this affair side by side. Without you I should be lost. I desire a little information from the good Mr. Hammond."

"You are acting on behalf of Captain Ralph Paton, I understand," said the lawyer cautiously.

Poirot shook his head.

"Not so. I am acting in the interests of justice. Miss Ackroyd has asked me to investigate the death of her uncle."

Mr. Hammond seemed slightly taken aback.

"I cannot seriously believe that Captain Paton can be concerned in this crime," he said, "however strong the circumstantial evidence against him may be. The mere fact that he was hard pressed for money———"

"Was he hard pressed for money?" interpolated Poirot quickly.

The lawyer shrugged his shoulders.

"It was a chronic condition with Ralph Paton," he said dryly. "Money went through his hands like water. He was always applying to his stepfather."

"Had he done so of late? During the last year, for instance?"

"I cannot say. Mr. Ackroyd did not mention the fact to me."

"I comprehend. Mr. Hammond, I take it that you are acquainted with the provisions of Mr. Ackroyd's will?"

"Certainly. That is my principal business here to-day."

"Then, seeing that I am acting for Miss Ackroyd, you will not object to telling me the terms of that will?"

"They are quite simple. Shorn of legal phraseology, and after paying certain legacies and bequests——"

"Such as——?" interrupted Poirot.

Mr. Hammond seemed a little surprised.

"A thousand pounds to his housekeeper, Miss Russell; fifty pounds to the cook, Emma Cooper; five hundred pounds to his secretary, Mr. Geoffrey Raymond. Then to various hospitals——"

Poirot held up his hand.

"Ah! the charitable bequests, they interest me not."

"Quite so. The income on ten thousand pounds' worth of shares to be paid to Mrs. Cecil Ackroyd during her lifetime. Miss Flora Ackroyd inherits twenty thousand pounds outright. The residue—including this property, and the shares in Ackroyd and Son—to his adopted son, Ralph Paton."

"Mr. Ackroyd possessed a large fortune?"

"A very large fortune. Captain Paton will be an exceedingly wealthy young man."

There was a silence. Poirot and the lawyer looked at each other.

"Mr. Hammond," came Mrs. Ackroyd's voice plaintively from the fireplace.

The lawyer answered the summons. Poirot took my arm and drew me right into the window.

"Regard the irises," he remarked in rather a loud voice. "Magnificent, are they not? A straight and pleasing effect."

At the same time I felt the pressure of his hand on my arm, and he added in a low tone:—

"Do you really wish to aid me? To take part in this investigation?"

"Yes, indeed," I said eagerly. "There's nothing I should like better. You don't know what a dull old fogey's life I lead. Never anything out of the ordinary."

"Good, we will be colleagues then. In a minute or two I fancy Major Blunt will join us. He is not happy with the good mamma. Now there are some things I want to know—but I do not wish to seem to want to know them. You comprehend? So it will be your part to ask the questions."

"What questions do you want me to ask?" I asked apprehensively.

"I want you to introduce the name of Mrs. Ferrars."

"Yes?"

"Speak of her in a natural fashion. Ask him if he was down here when her husband died. You understand the kind of thing I mean. And while he replies, watch his face without seeming to watch it. *C'est compris?*"

There was no time for more, for at that minute, as Poirot had prophesied, Blunt left the others in his abrupt fashion and came over to us.

I suggested strolling on the terrace, and he acquiesced. Poirot stayed behind.

I stopped to examine a late rose.

"How things change in the course of a day or so," I observed. "I was up here last Wednesday, I remember, walking up and down this same terrace. Ackroyd was with me—full of spirits. And now—three days later—Ackroyd's dead, poor fellow, Mrs. Ferrars's dead—you knew her, didn't you? But of course you did."

Blunt nodded his head.

"Had you seen her since you'd been down this time?"

"Went with Ackroyd to call. Last Tuesday, think it was. Fascinating woman—but something queer about her. Deep—one would never know what she was up to."

I looked into his steady gray eyes. Nothing there surely. I went on:—

"I suppose you'd met her before."

"Last time I was here—she and her husband had just come here to live." He paused a minute and then added: "Rum thing, she had changed a lot between then and now."

"How—changed?" I asked.

"Looked ten years older."

"Were you down here when her husband died?" I asked, trying to make the question sound as casual as possible.

"No. From all I heard it would be a good riddance. Uncharitable, perhaps, but the truth."

I agreed.

"Ashley Ferrars was by no means a pattern husband," I said cautiously.

"Blackguard, I thought," said Blunt.

"No," I said, "only a man with more money than was good for him."

"Oh! money! All the troubles in the world can be put down to money—or the lack of it."

"Which has been your particular trouble?" I asked.

"I've enough for what I want. I'm one of the lucky ones."

"Indeed."

"I'm not too flush just now, as a matter of fact. Came into a legacy a year ago, and like a fool let myself be persuaded into putting it into some wild-cat scheme."

I sympathized, and narrated my own similar trouble.

Then the gong pealed out, and we all went in to lunch. Poirot drew me back a little.

"*Eh! bien?*"

"He's all right," I said. "I'm sure of it."

"Nothing—disturbing?"

"He had a legacy just a year ago," I said. "But why not? Why shouldn't he? I'll swear the man is perfectly square and aboveboard."

"Without doubt, without doubt," said Poirot soothingly. "Do not upset yourself."

He spoke as though to a fractious child.

We all trooped into the dining-room. It seemed incredible that less than twenty-four hours had passed since I last sat at that table.

Afterwards, Mrs. Ackroyd took me aside and sat down with me on a sofa.

"I can't help feeling a little hurt," she murmured, producing a handkerchief of the kind obviously not meant to be cried into. "Hurt, I mean, by Roger's lack of confidence in me. That twenty thousand pounds ought to have been left to *me*—not to Flora. A mother could be trusted to safeguard the interests of her child. A lack of trust, I call it."

"You forget, Mrs. Ackroyd," I said, "Flora was Ackroyd's own niece, a blood relation. It would have been different had you been his sister instead of his sister-in-law."

"As poor Cecil's widow, I think my feelings ought to have been considered," said the lady, touching her eye-lashes gingerly with the handkerchief. "But Roger was always most peculiar—not to say *mean*—about money matters. It has been a most difficult position for both Flora and myself. He did not even give the poor child an allowance. He would pay her bills, you know, and even that with a good deal of reluctance and asking what she wanted all those fal-lals for—so like a man—but—now I've forgotten what it was I was going to say! Oh, yes, not a penny we could call our own, you know. Flora resented it—yes, I must say she resented it—very strongly. Though devoted to her uncle, of course. But any girl would have resented it. Yes, I must say Roger had very strange ideas about money. He wouldn't even buy new face towels, though I told him the old ones were in holes. And then," proceeded Mrs. Ackroyd, with a sudden leap highly characteristic of her conversation, "to leave all that money—a thousand pounds—fancy, a thousand pounds!—to that woman."

"What woman?"

"That Russell woman. Something very queer about her, and so I've always said. But Roger wouldn't hear a word against her. Said she was a woman of great force of character, and that he admired and respected her. He was always going on about her rectitude and independence and moral worth. *I* think there's something fishy about her. She was certainly doing her best to marry Roger. But I soon put a stop to that. She's always hated me. Naturally. *I* saw through her."

I began to wonder if there was any chance of stemming Mrs. Ackroyd's eloquence, and getting away.

Mr. Hammond provided the necessary diversion by coming up to say good-by. I seized my chance and rose also.

"About the inquest," I said. "Where would you prefer it to be held. Here, or at the Three Boars?"

Mrs. Ackroyd stared at me with a dropped jaw.

"The inquest?" she asked, the picture of consternation. "But surely there won't have to be an inquest?"

Mr. Hammond gave a dry little cough and murmured, "Inevitable. Under the circumstances," in two short little barks.

"But surely Dr. Sheppard can arrange———"

"There are limits to my powers of arrangement," I said dryly.

"If his death was an accident———"

"He was murdered, Mrs. Ackroyd," I said brutally.

She gave a little cry.

"No theory of accident will hold water for a minute."

Mrs. Ackroyd looked at me in distress. I had no patience with what I thought was her silly fear of unpleasantness.

"If there's an inquest, I—I shan't have to answer questions and all that, shall I?" she asked.

"I don't know what will be necessary," I answered. "I imagine Mr. Raymond will take the brunt of it off you. He knows all the circumstances, and can give formal evidence of identification."

The lawyer assented with a little bow.

"I really don't think there is anything to dread, Mrs. Ackroyd," he said. "You will be spared all unpleasantness. Now, as to the question of money, have you all you need for the present? I mean," he added, as she looked at him inquiringly, "ready money. Cash, you know. If not, I can arrange to let you have whatever you require."

"That ought to be all right," said Raymond, who was standing by. "Mr. Ackroyd cashed a cheque for a hundred pounds yesterday."

"A hundred pounds?"

"Yes. For wages and other expenses due to-day. At the moment it is still intact."

"Where is this money? In his desk?"

"No, he always kept his cash in his bedroom. In an old collar-box, to be accurate. Funny idea, wasn't it?"

"I think," said the lawyer, "we ought to make sure the money is there before I leave."

"Certainly," agreed the secretary. "I'll take you up now.... Oh! I forgot. The door's locked."

Inquiry from Parker elicited the information that Inspector Raglan was in the housekeeper's room asking a few supplementary questions. A few minutes later the inspector joined the party in the hall, bringing the key with him. He unlocked the door and we passed into the lobby and up the small staircase. At the top of the stairs the door into Ackroyd's bedroom stood open. Inside the room it was dark, the curtains were drawn, and the bed was turned down just as it had been last night. The inspector drew the curtains, letting in the sunlight, and Geoffrey Raymond went to the top drawer of a rosewood bureau.

"He kept his money like that, in an unlocked drawer. Just fancy," commented the inspector.

The secretary flushed a little.

"Mr. Ackroyd had perfect faith in the honesty of all the servants," he said hotly.

"Oh! quite so," said the inspector hastily.

Raymond opened the drawer, took out a round leather collar-box from the back of it, and opening it, drew out a thick wallet.

"Here is the money," he said, taking out a fat roll of notes. "You will find the hundred intact, I know, for Mr. Ackroyd put it in the collar-box in my presence last night when he was dressing for dinner, and of course it has not been touched since."

Mr. Hammond took the roll from him and counted it. He looked up sharply.

"A hundred pounds, you said. But there is only sixty here."

Raymond stared at him.

"Impossible," he cried, springing forward. Taking the notes from the other's hand, he counted them aloud.

Mr. Hammond had been right. The total amounted to sixty pounds.

"But—I can't understand it," cried the secretary, bewildered.

Poirot asked a question.

"You saw Mr. Ackroyd put this money away last night when he was dressing for dinner? You are sure he had not paid away any of it already?"

"I'm sure he hadn't. He even said, 'I don't want to take a hundred pounds down to dinner with me. Too bulgy.'"

"Then the affair is very simple," remarked Poirot. "Either he paid out that forty pounds sometime last evening, or else it has been stolen."

"That's the matter in a nutshell," agreed the inspector. He turned to Mrs. Ackroyd. "Which of the servants would come in here yesterday evening?"

"I suppose the housemaid would turn down the bed."

"Who is she? What do you know about her?"

"She's not been here very long," said Mrs. Ackroyd. "But she's a nice ordinary country girl."

"I think we ought to clear this matter up," said the inspector. "If Mr. Ackroyd paid that money away himself, it may have a bearing on the mystery of the crime. The other servants all right, as far as you know?"

"Oh, I think so."

"Not missed anything before?"

"No."

"None of them leaving, or anything like that?"

"The parlormaid is leaving."

"When?"

"She gave notice yesterday, I believe."

"To you?"

"Oh, no. *I* have nothing to do with the servants. Miss Russell attends to the household matters."

The inspector remained lost in thought for a minute or two. Then he nodded his head and remarked, "I think I'd better have a word with Miss Russell, and I'll see the girl Dale as well."

Poirot and I accompanied him to the housekeeper's room. Miss Russell received us with her usual sang-froid.

Elsie Dale had been at Fernly five months. A nice girl, quick at her duties, and most respectable. Good references. The last girl in the world to take anything not belonging to her.

What about the parlormaid?

"She, too, was a most superior girl. Very quiet and ladylike. An excellent worker."

"Then why is she leaving?" asked the inspector.

Miss Russell pursed up her lips.

"It was none of my doing. I understand Mr. Ackroyd found fault with her yesterday afternoon. It was her duty to do the study, and she disarranged some of the papers on his desk, I believe. He was very annoyed about it, and she gave notice. At least, that is what I understood from her, but perhaps you'd like to see her yourselves?"

The inspector assented. I had already noticed the girl when she was waiting on us at lunch. A tall girl, with a lot of brown hair rolled tightly away at the back of her neck, and very steady gray eyes. She came in answer to the housekeeper's summons, and stood very straight with those same gray eyes fixed on us.

"You are Ursula Bourne?" asked the inspector.

"Yes, sir."

"I understand you are leaving?"

"Yes, sir."

"Why is that?"

"I disarranged some papers on Mr. Ackroyd's desk. He was very angry about it, and I said I had better leave. He told me to go as soon as possible."

"Were you in Mr. Ackroyd's bedroom at all last night? Tidying up or anything?"

"No, sir. That is Elsie's work. I never went near that part of the house."

"I must tell you, my girl, that a large sum of money is missing from Mr. Ackroyd's room."

At last I saw her roused. A wave of color swept over her face.

"I know nothing about any money. If you think I took it, and that that is why Mr. Ackroyd dismissed me, you are wrong."

"I'm not accusing you of taking it, my girl," said the inspector. "Don't flare up so."

The girl looked at him coldly.

"You can search my things if you like," she said disdainfully. "But you won't find anything."

Poirot suddenly interposed.

"It was yesterday afternoon that Mr. Ackroyd dismissed you—or you dismissed yourself, was it not?" he asked.

The girl nodded.

"How long did the interview last?"

"The interview?"

"Yes, the interview between you and Mr. Ackroyd in the study?"

"I—I don't know."

"Twenty minutes? Half an hour?"

"Something like that."

"Not longer?"

"Not longer than half an hour, certainly."

"Thank you, mademoiselle."

I looked curiously at him. He was rearranging a few objects on the table, setting them straight with precise fingers. His eyes were shining.

"That'll do," said the inspector.

Ursula Bourne disappeared. The inspector turned to Miss Russell.

"How long has she been here? Have you got a copy of the reference you had with her?"

Without answering the first question, Miss Russell moved to an adjacent bureau, opened one of the drawers, and took out a handful of letters clipped together with a patent fastener. She selected one and handed it to the inspector.

"H'm," said he. "Reads all right. Mrs. Richard Folliott, Marby Grange, Marby. Who's this woman?"

"Quite good county people," said Miss Russell.

"Well," said the inspector, handing it back, "let's have a look at the other one, Elsie Dale."

Elsie Dale was a big fair girl, with a pleasant but slightly stupid face. She answered our questions readily enough, and showed much distress and concern at the loss of the money.

"I don't think there's anything wrong with her," observed the inspector, after he had dismissed her.

"What about Parker?"

Miss Russell pursed her lips together and made no reply.

"I've a feeling there's something wrong about that man," the inspector continued thoughtfully. "The trouble is that I don't quite see when he got his opportunity. He'd be busy with his duties immediately after dinner, and he's got a pretty good alibi all through the evening. I know, for I've been devoting particular attention to it. Well, thank you very much, Miss Russell. We'll leave things as they are for the present. It's highly probable Mr. Ackroyd paid that money away himself."

The housekeeper bade us a dry good-afternoon, and we took our leave.

I left the house with Poirot.

"I wonder," I said, breaking the silence, "what the papers the girl disarranged could have been for Ackroyd to have got into such a state about them? I wonder if there is any clew there to the mystery."

"The secretary said there were no papers of particular importance on the desk," said Poirot quietly.

"Yes, but———" I paused.

"It strikes you as odd that Ackroyd should have flown into a rage about so trivial a matter?"

"Yes, it does rather."

"But was it a trivial matter?"

"Of course," I admitted, "we don't know what those papers may have been. But Raymond certainly said———"

"Leave M. Raymond out of it for a minute. What did you think of that girl?"

"Which girl? The parlormaid?"

"Yes, the parlormaid. Ursula Bourne."

"She seemed a nice girl," I said hesitatingly.

Poirot repeated my words, but whereas I had laid a slight stress on the fourth word, he put it on the second.

"She *seemed* a nice girl—yes."

Then, after a minute's silence, he took something from his pocket and handed it to me.

"See, my friend, I will show you something. Look there."

The paper he had handed me was that compiled by the inspector and given by him to Poirot that morning. Following the pointing finger, I saw a small cross marked in pencil opposite the name Ursula Bourne.

"You may not have noticed it at the time, my good friend, but there was one person on this list whose alibi had no kind of confirmation. Ursula Bourne."

"You don't think———"

"Dr. Sheppard, I dare to think anything. Ursula Bourne may have killed Mr. Ackroyd, but I confess I can see no motive for her doing so. Can you?"

He looked at me very hard—so hard that I felt uncomfortable.

"Can you?" he repeated.

"No motive whatsoever," I said firmly.

His gaze relaxed. He frowned and murmured to himself:—

"Since the blackmailer was a man, it follows that she cannot be the blackmailer, then——"

I coughed.

"As far as that goes——" I began doubtfully.

He spun round on me.

"What? What are you going to say?"

"Nothing. Nothing. Only that, strictly speaking, Mrs. Ferrars in her letter mentioned a *person*—she didn't actually specify a man. But we took it for granted, Ackroyd and I, that it *was* a man."

Poirot did not seem to be listening to me. He was muttering to himself again.

"But then it is possible after all—yes, certainly it is possible—but then—ah! I must rearrange my ideas. Method, order; never have I needed them more. Everything must fit in—in its appointed place—otherwise I am on the wrong tack."

He broke off, and whirled round upon me again.

"Where is Marby?"

"It's on the other side of Cranchester."

"How far away?"

"Oh!—fourteen miles, perhaps."

"Would it be possible for you to go there? To-morrow, say?"

"To-morrow? Let me see, that's Sunday. Yes, I could arrange it. What do you want me to do there?"

"See this Mrs. Folliott. Find out all you can about Ursula Bourne."

"Very well. But—I don't much care for the job."

"It is not the time to make difficulties. A man's life may hang on this."

"Poor Ralph," I said with a sigh. "You believe him to be innocent, though?"

Poirot looked at me very gravely.

"Do you want to know the truth?"

"Of course."

"Then you shall have it. My friend, everything points to the assumption that he is guilty."

"What!" I exclaimed.

Poirot nodded.

"Yes, that stupid inspector—for he is stupid—has everything pointing his way. I seek for the truth—and the truth leads me every time to Ralph Paton. Motive, opportunity, means. But I will leave no stone unturned. I promised Mademoiselle Flora. And she was very sure, that little one. But very sure indeed."

CHAPTER XI
POIROT PAYS A CALL

I WAS slightly nervous when I rang the bell at Marby Grange the following afternoon. I wondered very much what Poirot expected to find out. He had entrusted the job to me. Why? Was it because, as in the case of questioning Major Blunt, he wished to remain in the background? The wish, intelligible in the first case, seemed to me quite meaningless here.

My meditations were interrupted by the advent of a smart parlormaid.

Yes, Mrs. Folliott was at home. I was ushered into a big drawing-room, and looked round me curiously as I waited for the mistress of the house. A large bare room, some good bits of old china, and some beautiful etchings, shabby covers and curtains. A lady's room in every sense of the term.

I turned from the inspection of a Bartolozzi on the wall as Mrs. Folliott came into the room. She was a tall woman, with untidy brown hair, and a very winning smile.

"Dr. Sheppard," she said hesitatingly.

"That is my name," I replied. "I must apologize for calling upon you like this, but I wanted some information about a parlormaid previously employed by you, Ursula Bourne."

With the utterance of the name the smile vanished from her face, and all the cordiality froze out of her manner. She looked uncomfortable and ill at ease.

"Ursula Bourne?" she said hesitatingly.

"Yes," I said. "Perhaps you don't remember the name?"

"Oh, yes, of course. I—I remember perfectly."

"She left you just over a year ago, I understand?"

"Yes. Yes, she did. That is quite right."

"And you were satisfied with her whilst she was with you? How long was she with you, by the way?"

"Oh! a year or two—I can't remember exactly how long. She—she is very capable. I'm sure you will find her quite satisfactory. I didn't know she was leaving Fernly. I hadn't the least idea of it."

"Can you tell me anything about her?" I asked.

"Anything about her?"

"Yes, where she comes from, who her people are—that sort of thing?"

Mrs. Folliott's face wore more than ever its frozen look.

"I don't know at all."

"Who was she with before she came to you?"

"I'm afraid I don't remember."

There was a spark of anger now underlying her nervousness. She flung up her head in a gesture that was vaguely familiar.

"Is it really necessary to ask all these questions?"

"Not at all," I said, with an air of surprise and a tinge of apology in my manner. "I had no idea you would mind answering them. I am very sorry."

Her anger left her and she became confused again.

"Oh! I don't mind answering them. I assure you I don't. Why should I? It—it just seemed a little odd, you know. That's all. A little odd."

One advantage of being a medical practitioner is that you can usually tell when people are lying to you. I should have known from Mrs. Folliott's manner, if from nothing else, that she did mind answering my questions—minded intensely. She was thoroughly uncomfortable and upset, and there was plainly some mystery in the background. I judged her to be a woman quite unused to deception of any kind, and consequently rendered acutely uneasy when forced to practice it. A child could have seen through her.

But it was also clear that she had no intention of telling me anything further. Whatever the mystery centering around Ursula Bourne might be, I was not going to learn it through Mrs. Folliott.

Defeated, I apologized once more for disturbing her, took my hat and departed.

I went to see a couple of patients and arrived home about six o'clock. Caroline was sitting beside the wreck of tea things. She had that look of suppressed exultation on her face which I know only too well. It is a sure sign with her, of either the getting or the giving of information. I wondered which it had been.

"I've had a very interesting afternoon," began Caroline as I dropped into my own particular easy chair, and stretched out my feet to the inviting blaze in the fireplace.

"Have you?" I asked. "Miss Ganett drop in to tea?"

Miss Ganett is one of the chief of our newsmongers.

"Guess again," said Caroline with intense complacency.

I guessed several times, working slowly through all the members of Caroline's Intelligence Corps. My sister received each guess with a triumphant shake of the head. In the end she volunteered the information herself.

"M. Poirot!" she said. "Now what do you think of that?"

I thought a good many things of it, but I was careful not to say them to Caroline.

"Why did he come?" I asked.

"To see me, of course. He said that knowing my brother so well, he hoped he might be permitted to make the acquaintance of his charming sister—your charming sister, I've got mixed up, but you know what I mean."

"What did he talk about?" I asked.

"He told me a lot about himself and his cases. You know that Prince Paul of Mauretania—the one who's just married a dancer?"

"Yes?"

"I saw a most intriguing paragraph about her in Society Snippets the other day, hinting that she was really a Russian Grand Duchess—one of the Czar's daughters who managed to escape from the Bolsheviks. Well, it seems that M. Poirot solved a baffling murder mystery that threatened to involve them both. Prince Paul was beside himself with gratitude."

"Did he give him an emerald tie pin the size of a plover's egg?" I inquired sarcastically.

"He didn't mention it. Why?"

"Nothing," I said. "I thought it was always done. It is in detective fiction anyway. The super detective always has his rooms littered with rubies and pearls and emeralds from grateful Royal clients."

"It's very interesting to hear about these things from the inside," said my sister complacently.

It would be—to Caroline. I could not but admire the ingenuity of M. Hercule Poirot, who had selected unerringly the case of all others that would most appeal to an elderly maiden lady living in a small village.

"Did he tell you if the dancer was really a Grand Duchess?" I inquired.

"He was not at liberty to speak," said Caroline importantly.

I wondered how far Poirot had strained the truth in talking to Caroline—probably not at all. He had conveyed his innuendoes by means of his eyebrows and his shoulders.

"And after all this," I remarked, "I suppose you were ready to eat out of his hand."

"Don't be coarse, James. I don't know where you get these vulgar expressions from."

"Probably from my only link with the outside world—my patients. Unfortunately my practice does not lie amongst Royal princes and interesting Russian émigrés."

Caroline pushed her spectacles up and looked at me.

"You seem very grumpy, James. It must be your liver. A blue pill, I think, to-night."

To see me in my own home, you would never imagine that I was a doctor of medicine. Caroline does the home prescribing both for herself and me.

"Damn my liver," I said irritably. "Did you talk about the murder at all?"

"Well, naturally, James. What else is there to talk about locally? I was able to set M. Poirot right upon several points. He was very grateful to me. He said I had the makings of a born detective in me—and a wonderful psychological insight into human nature."

Caroline was exactly like a cat that is full to overflowing with rich cream. She was positively purring.

"He talked a lot about the little gray cells of the brain, and of their functions. His own, he says, are of the first quality."

"He would say so," I remarked bitterly. "Modesty is certainly not his middle name."

"I wish you would not be so horribly American, James. He thought it very important that Ralph should be found as soon as possible, and induced to come forward and give an account of himself. He says that his disappearance will produce a very unfortunate impression at the inquest."

"And what did you say to that?"

"I agreed with him," said Caroline importantly. "And I was able to tell him the way people were already talking about it."

"Caroline," I said sharply, "did you tell M. Poirot what you overheard in the wood that day?"

"I did," said Caroline complacently.

I got up and began to walk about.

"You realize what you're doing, I hope," I jerked out. "You're putting a halter round Ralph Paton's neck as surely as you're sitting in that chair."

"Not at all," said Caroline, quite unruffled. "I was surprised *you* hadn't told him."

"I took very good care not to," I said. "I'm fond of that boy."

"So am I. That's why I say you're talking nonsense. I don't believe Ralph did it, and so the truth can't hurt him, and we ought to give M. Poirot all the help we can. Why, think, very likely Ralph was out with that identical girl on the night of the murder, and if so, he's got a perfect alibi."

"If he's got a perfect alibi," I retorted, "why doesn't he come forward and say so?"

"Might get the girl into trouble," said Caroline sapiently. "But if M. Poirot gets hold of her, and puts it to her as her duty, she'll come forward of her own accord and clear Ralph."

"You seem to have invented a romantic fairy story of your own," I said. "You read too many trashy novels, Caroline. I've always told you so."

I dropped into my chair again.

"Did Poirot ask you any more questions?" I inquired.

"Only about the patients you had that morning."

"The patients?" I demanded, unbelievingly.

"Yes, your surgery patients. How many and who they were?"

"Do you mean to say you were able to tell him that?" I demanded.

Caroline is really amazing.

"Why not?" asked my sister triumphantly. "I can see the path up to the surgery door perfectly from this window. And I've got an excellent memory, James. Much better than yours, let me tell you."

"I'm sure you have," I murmured mechanically.

My sister went on, checking the names on her fingers.

"There was old Mrs. Bennett, and that boy from the farm with the bad finger, Dolly Grice to have a needle out of her finger; that American steward off the liner. Let me see—that's four. Yes, and old George Evans with his ulcer. And lastly——"

She paused significantly.

"Well?"

Caroline brought out her climax triumphantly. She hissed in the most approved style—aided by the fortunate number of s's at her disposal.

"*Miss Russell!*"

She sat back in her chair and looked at me meaningly, and when Caroline looks at you meaningly, it is impossible to miss it.

"I don't know what you mean," I said, quite untruthfully. "Why shouldn't Miss Russell consult me about her bad knee?"

"Bad knee," said Caroline. "Fiddlesticks! No more bad knee than you and I. She was after something else."

"What?" I asked.

Caroline had to admit that she didn't know.

"But depend upon it, that was what he was trying to get at, M. Poirot, I mean. There's something fishy about that woman, and he knows it."

"Precisely the remark Mrs. Ackroyd made to me yesterday," I said. "That there was something fishy about Miss Russell."

"Ah!" said Caroline darkly, "Mrs. Ackroyd! There's another!"

"Another what?"

Caroline refused to explain her remarks. She merely nodded her head several times, rolled up her knitting, and went upstairs to don the high mauve silk blouse and the gold locket which she calls dressing for dinner.

I stayed there staring into the fire and thinking over Caroline's words. Had Poirot really come to gain information about Miss Russell, or was it only Caroline's tortuous mind that interpreted everything according to her own ideas?

There had certainly been nothing in Miss Russell's manner that morning to arouse suspicion. At least——

I remembered her persistent conversation on the subject of drug-taking and from that she had led the conversation to poisons and poisoning. But there was nothing in that. Ackroyd had not been poisoned. Still, it was odd....

I heard Caroline's voice, rather acid in note, calling from the top of the stairs.

"James, you will be late for dinner."

I put some coal on the fire and went upstairs obediently.

It is well at any price to have peace in the home.

CHAPTER XII
ROUND THE TABLE

A JOINT inquest was held on Monday.

I do not propose to give the proceedings in detail. To do so would only be to go over the same ground again and again. By arrangement with the police, very little was allowed to come out. I gave evidence as to the cause of Ackroyd's death and the probable time. The absence of Ralph Paton was commented on by the coroner, but not unduly stressed.

Afterwards, Poirot and I had a few words with Inspector Raglan. The inspector was very grave.

"It looks bad, Mr. Poirot," he said. "I'm trying to judge the thing fair and square. I'm a local man, and I've seen Captain Paton many times in Cranchester. I'm not wanting him to be the guilty one—but it's bad whichever way you look at it. If he's innocent, why doesn't he come forward? We've got evidence against him, but it's just possible that that evidence could be explained away. Then why doesn't he give an explanation?"

A lot more lay behind the inspector's words than I knew at the time. Ralph's description had been wired to every port and railway station in England. The police everywhere were on the alert. His rooms in town were watched, and any houses he had been known to be in the habit of frequenting. With such a *cordon* it seemed impossible that Ralph should be able to evade detection. He had no luggage, and, as far as any one knew, no money.

"I can't find any one who saw him at the station that night," continued the inspector. "And yet he's well known down here, and you'd think somebody would have noticed him. There's no news from Liverpool either."

"You think he went to Liverpool?" queried Poirot.

"Well, it's on the cards. That telephone message from the station, just three minutes before the Liverpool express left—there ought to be something in that."

"Unless it was deliberately intended to throw you off the scent. That might just possibly be the point of the telephone message."

"That's an idea," said the inspector eagerly. "Do you really think that's the explanation of the telephone call?"

"My friend," said Poirot gravely, "I do not know. But I will tell you this: I believe that when we find the explanation of that telephone call we shall find the explanation of the murder."

"You said something like that before, I remember," I observed, looking at him curiously.

Poirot nodded.

"I always come back to it," he said seriously.

"It seems to me utterly irrelevant," I declared.

"I wouldn't say that," demurred the inspector. "But I must confess I think Mr. Poirot here harps on it a little too much. We've better clews than that. The fingerprints on the dagger, for instance."

Poirot became suddenly very foreign in manner, as he often did when excited over anything.

"M. l'Inspecteur," he said, "beware of the blind—the blind—*comment dire?*—the little street that has no end to it."

Inspector Raglan stared, but I was quicker.

"You mean a blind alley?" I said.

"That is it—the blind street that leads nowhere. So it may be with those fingerprints—they may lead you nowhere."

"I don't see how that can well be," said the police officer. "I suppose you're hinting that they're faked? I've read of such things being done, though I can't say I've ever come across it in my experience. But fake or true—they're bound to lead *somewhere*."

Poirot merely shrugged his shoulders, flinging out his arms wide.

The inspector then showed us various enlarged photographs of the fingerprints, and proceeded to become technical on the subject of loops and whorls.

"Come now," he said at last, annoyed by Poirot's detached manner, "you've got to admit that those prints were made by some one who was in the house that night?"

"*Bien entendu,*" said Poirot, nodding his head.

"Well, I've taken the prints of every member of the household, every one, mind you, from the old lady down to the kitchenmaid."

I don't think Mrs. Ackroyd would enjoy being referred to as the old lady. She must spend a considerable amount on cosmetics.

"Every one's," repeated the inspector fussily.

"Including mine," I said dryly.

"Very well. None of them correspond. That leaves us two alternatives. Ralph Paton, or the mysterious stranger the doctor here tells us about. When we get hold of those two——"

"Much valuable time may have been lost," broke in Poirot.

"I don't quite get you, Mr. Poirot?"

"You have taken the prints of every one in the house, you say," murmured Poirot. "Is that the exact truth you are telling me there, M. l'Inspecteur?"

"Certainly."

"Without overlooking any one?"

"Without overlooking any one."

"The quick or the dead?"

For a moment the inspector looked bewildered at what he took to be a religious observation. Then he reacted slowly.

"You mean——"

"The dead, M. l'Inspecteur."

The inspector still took a minute or two to understand.

"I am suggesting," said Poirot placidly, "that the fingerprints on the dagger handle are those of Mr. Ackroyd himself. It is an easy matter to verify. His body is still available."

"But why? What would be the point of it? You're surely not suggesting suicide, Mr. Poirot?"

"Ah! no. My theory is that the murderer wore gloves or wrapped something round his hand. After the blow was struck, he picked up the victim's hand and closed it round the dagger handle."

"But why?"

Poirot shrugged his shoulders again.

"To make a confusing case even more confusing."

"Well," said the inspector, "I'll look into it. What gave you the idea in the first place?"

"When you were so kind as to show me the dagger and draw attention to the fingerprints. I know very little of loops and whorls—see, I confess my ignorance frankly. But it did occur to me that the position of the prints was somewhat awkward. Not so would I have held a dagger in order to strike. Naturally, with the right hand brought up over the shoulder backwards, it would have been difficult to put it in exactly the right position."

Inspector Raglan stared at the little man. Poirot, with an air of great unconcern, flecked a speck of dust from his coat sleeve.

"Well," said the inspector, "it's an idea. I'll look into it all right, but don't you be disappointed if nothing comes of it."

He endeavored to make his tone kindly and patronizing. Poirot watched him go off. Then he turned to me with twinkling eyes.

"Another time," he observed, "I must be more careful of his *amour propre*. And now that we are left to our own devices, what do you think, my good friend, of a little reunion of the family?"

The "little reunion," as Poirot called it, took place about half an hour later. We sat round the table in the dining-room at Fernly—Poirot at the head of the table, like the chairman of some ghastly board meeting. The servants were not present, so we were six in all. Mrs. Ackroyd, Flora, Major Blunt, young Raymond, Poirot, and myself.

When every one was assembled, Poirot rose and bowed.

"Messieurs, mesdames, I have called you together for a certain purpose." He paused. "To begin with, I want to make a very special plea to mademoiselle."

"To me?" said Flora.

"Mademoiselle, you are engaged to Captain Ralph Paton. If any one is in his confidence, you are. I beg you, most earnestly, if you know of his whereabouts, to persuade him to come forward. One little minute"—as Flora raised her head to speak—"say nothing till you have well reflected. Mademoiselle, his position grows daily more dangerous. If he had come forward at once, no matter how damning the facts, he might have had a chance of explaining them away. But this silence—this flight—what can it mean? Surely only one thing, knowledge of guilt. Mademoiselle, if you really believe in his innocence, persuade him to come forward before it is too late."

Flora's face had gone very white.

"Too late!" she repeated, very low.

Poirot leant forward, looking at her.

"See now, mademoiselle," he said very gently, "it is Papa Poirot who asks you this. The old Papa Poirot who has much knowledge and much experience. I would not seek to entrap you, mademoiselle. Will you not trust me—and tell me where Ralph Paton is hiding?"

The girl rose, and stood facing him.

"M. Poirot," she said in a clear voice, "I swear to you—swear solemnly—that I have no idea where Ralph is, and that I have neither seen him nor heard from him either on the day of—of the murder, or since."

She sat down again. Poirot gazed at her in silence for a minute or two, then he brought his hand down on the table with a sharp rap.

"*Bien!* That is that," he said. His face hardened. "Now I appeal to these others who sit round this table, Mrs. Ackroyd, Major Blunt, Dr. Sheppard, Mr. Raymond. You are all friends and intimates of the missing man. If you know where Ralph Paton is hiding, speak out."

There was a long silence. Poirot looked to each in turn.

"I beg of you," he said in a low voice, "speak out."

But still there was silence, broken at last by Mrs. Ackroyd.

"I must say," she observed in a plaintive voice, "that Ralph's absence is most peculiar—most peculiar indeed. Not to come forward at such a time. It looks, you know, as though there were something *behind* it. I can't help thinking, Flora dear, that it was a very fortunate thing your engagement was never formally announced."

"Mother!" cried Flora angrily.

"Providence," declared Mrs. Ackroyd. "I have a devout belief in Providence—a divinity that shapes our ends, as Shakespeare's beautiful line runs."

"Surely you don't make the Almighty directly responsible for thick ankles, Mrs. Ackroyd, do you?" asked Geoffrey Raymond, his irresponsible laugh ringing out.

His idea was, I think, to loosen the tension, but Mrs. Ackroyd threw him a glance of reproach and took out her handkerchief.

"Flora has been saved a terrible amount of notoriety and unpleasantness. Not for a moment that I think dear Ralph had anything to do with poor Roger's death. I *don't* think so. But then I have a trusting heart—I always have had, ever since a child. I am loath to believe the worst of any one. But, of course, one must remember that Ralph was in several air raids as a young boy. The results are apparent long after, sometimes, they say. People are not responsible for their actions in the least. They lose control, you know, without being able to help it."

"Mother," cried Flora, "you don't think Ralph did it?"

"Come, Mrs. Ackroyd," said Blunt.

"I don't know what to think," said Mrs. Ackroyd tearfully. "It's all very upsetting. What would happen to the estate, I wonder, if Ralph were found guilty?"

Raymond pushed his chair away from the table violently. Major Blunt remained very quiet, looking thoughtfully at her. "Like shell-shock, you know," said Mrs. Ackroyd obstinately, "and I dare say Roger kept him very short of money—with the best intentions, of course. I can see you are all against me, but I do think it is very odd that Ralph has not come forward, and I must say I am thankful Flora's engagement was never announced formally."

"It will be to-morrow," said Flora in a clear voice.

"Flora!" cried her mother, aghast.

Flora had turned to the secretary.

"Will you send the announcement to the *Morning Post* and the *Times*, please, Mr. Raymond."

"If you are sure that it is wise, Miss Ackroyd," he replied gravely.

She turned impulsively to Blunt.

"You understand," she said. "What else can I do? As things are, I must stand by Ralph. Don't you see that I must?"

She looked very searchingly at him, and after a long pause he nodded abruptly.

Mrs. Ackroyd burst out into shrill protests. Flora remained unmoved. Then Raymond spoke.

"I appreciate your motives, Miss Ackroyd. But don't you think you're being rather precipitate? Wait a day or two."

"To-morrow," said Flora, in a clear voice. "It's no good, mother, going on like this. Whatever else I am, I'm not disloyal to my friends."

"M. Poirot," Mrs. Ackroyd appealed tearfully, "can't you say anything at all?"

"Nothing to be said," interpolated Blunt. "She's doing the right thing. I'll stand by her through thick and thin."

Flora held out her hand to him.

"Thank you, Major Blunt," she said.

"Mademoiselle," said Poirot, "will you let an old man congratulate you on your courage and your loyalty? And will you not misunderstand me if I ask you—ask you most solemnly—to postpone the announcement you speak of for at least two days more?"

Flora hesitated.

"I ask it in Ralph Paton's interests as much as in yours, mademoiselle. You frown. You do not see how that can be. But I assure you that it is so. *Pas de blagues*. You put the case into my hands—you must not hamper me now."

Flora paused a few minutes before replying.

"I do not like it," she said at last, "but I will do what you say."

She sat down again at the table.

"And now, messieurs et mesdames," said Poirot rapidly, "I will continue with what I was about to say. Understand this, I mean to arrive at the truth. The truth, however ugly in itself, is always curious and beautiful to the seeker after it. I am much aged, my powers may not be what they were." Here he clearly expected a contradiction. "In all probability this is the last case I shall ever investigate. But

Hercule Poirot does not end with a failure. Messieurs et mesdames, I tell you, I mean to *know*. And I shall know—in spite of you all."

He brought out the last words provocatively, hurling them in our face as it were. I think we all flinched back a little, excepting Geoffrey Raymond, who remained good humored and imperturbable as usual.

"How do you mean—in spite of us all?" he asked, with slightly raised eyebrows.

"But—just that, monsieur. Every one of you in this room is concealing something from me." He raised his hand as a faint murmur of protest arose. "Yes, yes, I know what I am saying. It may be something unimportant—trivial—which is supposed to have no bearing on the case, but there it is. *Each one of you has something to hide.* Come, now, am I right?"

His glance, challenging and accusing, swept round the table. And every pair of eyes dropped before his. Yes, mine as well.

"I am answered," said Poirot, with a curious laugh. He got up from his seat. "I appeal to you all. Tell me the truth—the whole truth." There was a silence. "Will no one speak?"

He gave the same short laugh again.

"*C'est dommage,*" he said, and went out.

CHAPTER XIII
THE GOOSE QUILL

THAT evening, at Poirot's request, I went over to his house after dinner. Caroline saw me depart with visible reluctance. I think she would have liked to have accompanied me.

Poirot greeted me hospitably. He had placed a bottle of Irish whisky (which I detest) on a small table, with a soda water siphon and a glass. He himself was engaged in brewing hot chocolate. It was a favorite beverage of his, I discovered later.

He inquired politely after my sister, whom he declared to be a most interesting woman.

"I'm afraid you've been giving her a swelled head," I said dryly. "What about Sunday afternoon?"

He laughed and twinkled.

"I always like to employ the expert," he remarked obscurely, but he refused to explain the remark.

"You got all the local gossip anyway," I remarked. "True, and untrue."

"And a great deal of valuable information," he added quietly.

"Such as——?"

He shook his head.

"Why not have told me the truth?" he countered. "In a place like this, all Ralph Paton's doings were bound to be known. If your sister had not happened to pass through the wood that day somebody else would have done so."

"I suppose they would," I said grumpily. "What about this interest of yours in my patients?"

Again he twinkled.

"Only one of them, doctor. Only one of them."

"The last?" I hazarded.

"I find Miss Russell a study of the most interesting," he said evasively.

"Do you agree with my sister and Mrs. Ackroyd that there is something fishy about her?" I asked.

"Eh? What do you say—fishy?"

I explained to the best of my ability.

"And they say that, do they?"

"Didn't my sister convey as much to you yesterday afternoon?"

"*C'est possible.*"

"For no reason whatever," I declared.

"*Les femmes*," generalized Poirot. "They are marvelous! They invent haphazard—and by miracle they are right. Not that it is that, really. Women observe subconsciously a thousand little details, without knowing that they are doing so. Their subconscious mind adds these little things together—and they call the result intuition. Me, I am very skilled in psychology. I know these things."

He swelled his chest out importantly, looking so ridiculous, that I found it difficult not to burst out laughing. Then he took a small sip of his chocolate, and carefully wiped his mustache.

"I wish you'd tell me," I burst out, "what you really think of it all?"

He put down his cup.

"You wish that?"

"I do."

"You have seen what I have seen. Should not our ideas be the same?"

"I'm afraid you're laughing at me," I said stiffly. "Of course, I've no experience of matters of this kind."

Poirot smiled at me indulgently.

"You are like the little child who wants to know the way the engine works. You wish to see the affair, not as the family doctor sees it, but with the eye of a detective who knows and cares for no one—to whom they are all strangers and all equally liable to suspicion."

"You put it very well," I said.

"So I give you then, a little lecture. The first thing is to get a clear history of what happened that evening—always bearing in mind that the person who speaks may be lying."

I raised my eyebrows.

"Rather a suspicious attitude."

"But necessary—I assure you, necessary. Now first—Dr. Sheppard leaves the house at ten minutes to nine. How do I know that?"

"Because I told you so."

"But you might not be speaking the truth—or the watch you went by might be wrong. But Parker also says that you left the house at ten minutes to nine. So we accept that statement and pass on. At nine o'clock you run into a man—and here we come to what we will call the Romance of the Mysterious Stranger—just outside the Park gates. How do I know that that is so?"

"I told you so," I began again, but Poirot interrupted me with a gesture of impatience.

"Ah! but it is that you are a little stupid to-night, my friend. *You* know that it is so—but how am *I* to know? *Eh bien*, I am able to tell you that the Mysterious Stranger was not a hallucination on your part, because the maid of a Miss Ganett met him a few minutes before you did, and of her too he inquired the way to Fernly Park. We accept his presence, therefore, and we can be fairly sure of two things about him—that he was a stranger to the neighborhood, and that whatever his object in going to Fernly, there was no great secrecy about it, since he twice asked the way there."

"Yes," I said, "I see that."

"Now I have made it my business to find out more about this man. He had a drink at the Three Boars, I learn, and the barmaid there says that he spoke with an American accent and mentioned having just come over from the States. Did it strike you that he had an American accent?"

"Yes, I think he had," I said, after a minute or two, during which I cast my mind back; "but a very slight one."

"*Précisément.* There is also this which, you will remember, I picked up in the summer-house?"

He held out to me the little quill. I looked at it curiously. Then a memory of something I had read stirred in me.

Poirot, who had been watching my face, nodded.

"Yes, heroin 'snow.' Drug-takers carry it like this, and sniff it up the nose."

"Diamorphine hydrochloride," I murmured mechanically.

"This method of taking the drug is very common on the other side. Another proof, if we wanted one, that the man came from Canada or the States."

"What first attracted your attention to that summer-house?" I asked curiously.

"My friend the inspector took it for granted that any one using that path did so as a short cut to the house, but as soon as I saw the summer-house, I realized that the same path would be taken by any one using the summer-house as a rendezvous. Now it seems fairly certain that the stranger came neither to the front nor to the back door. Then did some one from the house go out and meet him? If so, what could be a more convenient place than that little summer-house? I searched it with the hope that I might find some clew inside. I found two, the scrap of cambric and the quill."

"And the scrap of cambric?" I asked curiously. "What about that?"

Poirot raised his eyebrows.

"You do not use your little gray cells," he remarked dryly. "The scrap of starched cambric should be obvious."

"Not very obvious to me." I changed the subject. "Anyway," I said, "this man went to the summer-house to meet somebody. Who was that somebody?"

"Exactly the question," said Poirot. "You will remember that Mrs. Ackroyd and her daughter came over from Canada to live here?"

"Is that what you meant to-day when you accused them of hiding the truth?"

"Perhaps. Now another point. What did you think of the parlormaid's story?"

"What story?"

"The story of her dismissal. Does it take half an hour to dismiss a servant? Was the story of those important papers a likely one? And remember, though she says she was in her bedroom from nine-thirty until ten o'clock, there is no one to confirm her statement."

"You bewilder me," I said.

"To me it grows clearer. But tell me now your own ideas and theories."

I drew a piece of paper from my pocket.

"I just scribbled down a few suggestions," I said apologetically.

"But excellent—you have method. Let us hear them."

I read out in a somewhat embarrassed voice.

"To begin with, one must look at the thing logically——"

"Just what my poor Hastings used to say," interrupted Poirot, "but alas! he never did so."

"*Point No. 1.*—Mr. Ackroyd was heard talking to some one at half-past nine.

"*Point No. 2.*—At some time during the evening Ralph Paton must have come in through the window, as evidenced by the prints of his shoes.

"*Point No. 3.*—Mr. Ackroyd was nervous that evening, and would only have admitted some one he knew.

"*Point No. 4.*—The person with Mr. Ackroyd at nine-thirty was asking for money. We know Ralph Paton was in a scrape.

"*These four points go to show that the person with Mr. Ackroyd at nine-thirty was Ralph Paton. But we know that Mr. Ackroyd was alive at a quarter to ten, therefore it was not Ralph who killed him. Ralph left the window open. Afterwards the murderer came in that way.*"

"And who was the murderer?" inquired Poirot.

"The American stranger. He may have been in league with Parker, and possibly in Parker we have the man who blackmailed Mrs. Ferrars. If so, Parker may have heard enough to realize the game was up, have told his accomplice so, and the latter did the crime with the dagger which Parker gave him."

"It is a theory that," admitted Poirot. "Decidedly you have cells of a kind. But it leaves a good deal unaccounted for."

"Such as——?"

"The telephone call, the pushed-out chair——"

"Do you really think the latter important?" I interrupted.

"Perhaps not," admitted my friend. "It may have been pulled out by accident, and Raymond or Blunt may have shoved it into place unconsciously under the stress of emotion. Then there is the missing forty pounds."

"Given by Ackroyd to Ralph," I suggested. "He may have reconsidered his first refusal."

"That still leaves one thing unexplained?"

"What?"

"Why was Blunt so certain in his own mind that it was Raymond with Mr. Ackroyd at nine-thirty?"

"He explained that," I said.

"You think so? I will not press the point. Tell me instead, what were Ralph Paton's reasons for disappearing?"

"That's rather more difficult," I said slowly. "I shall have to speak as a medical man. Ralph's nerves must have gone phut! If he suddenly found out that his uncle had been murdered within a few minutes of his leaving him—after, perhaps, a rather stormy interview—well, he might get the wind up and clear right out. Men have been known to do that—act guiltily when they're perfectly innocent."

"Yes, that is true," said Poirot. "But we must not lose sight of one thing."

"I know what you're going to say," I remarked: "motive. Ralph Paton inherits a great fortune by his uncle's death."

"That is one motive," agreed Poirot.

"One?"

"*Mais oui*. Do you realize that there are three separate motives staring us in the face. Somebody certainly stole the blue envelope and its contents. That is one motive. Blackmail! Ralph Paton may have been the man who blackmailed Mrs. Ferrars. Remember, as far as Hammond knew, Ralph Paton had not applied to his uncle for help of late. That looks as though he were being supplied with money elsewhere. Then there is the fact that he was in some—how do you say—scrape?—which he feared might get to his uncle's ears. And finally there is the one you have just mentioned."

"Dear me," I said, rather taken aback. "The case does seem black against him."

"Does it?" said Poirot. "That is where we disagree, you and I. Three motives—it is almost too much. I am inclined to believe that, after all, Ralph Paton is innocent."

CHAPTER XIV
MRS. ACKROYD

AFTER the evening talk I have just chronicled, the affair seemed to me to enter on a different phase. The whole thing can be divided into two parts, each clear and distinct from the other. Part I. ranges from Ackroyd's death on the Friday evening to the following Monday night. It is the straight-forward narrative of what occurred, as presented to Hercule Poirot. I was at Poirot's elbow the whole time. I saw what he saw. I tried my best to read his mind. As I know now, I failed in this latter task. Though Poirot showed me all his discoveries—as, for instance, the gold wedding-ring—he held back the vital and yet logical impressions that he formed. As I came to know later, this secrecy was characteristic of him. He would throw out hints and suggestions, but beyond that he would not go.

As I say, up till the Monday evening, my narrative might have been that of Poirot himself. I played Watson to his Sherlock. But after Monday our ways diverged. Poirot was busy on his own account. I got to hear of what he was doing, because, in King's Abbot, you get to hear of everything, but he did not take me into his confidence beforehand. And I, too, had my own preoccupations.

On looking back, the thing that strikes me most is the piecemeal character of this period. Every one had a hand in the elucidation of the mystery. It was rather like a jig-saw puzzle to which every one contributed their own little piece of knowledge or discovery. But their task ended there. To Poirot alone belongs the renown of fitting those pieces into their correct place.

Some of the incidents seemed at the time irrelevant and unmeaning. There was, for instance, the question of the black boots. But that comes later.... To take things strictly in chronological order, I must begin with the summons from Mrs. Ackroyd.

She sent for me early on Tuesday morning, and since the summons sounded an urgent one, I hastened there, expecting to find her *in extremis*.

The lady was in bed. So much did she concede to the etiquette of the situation. She gave me her bony hand, and indicated a chair drawn up to the bedside.

"Well, Mrs. Ackroyd," I said, "and what's the matter with you?"

I spoke with that kind of spurious geniality which seems to be expected of general practitioners.

"I'm prostrated," said Mrs. Ackroyd in a faint voice. "Absolutely prostrated. It's the shock of poor Roger's death. They say these things often aren't felt at the *time*, you know. It's the reaction afterwards."

It is a pity that a doctor is precluded by his profession from being able sometimes to say what he really thinks.

I would have given anything to be able to answer "Bunkum!"

Instead, I suggested a tonic. Mrs. Ackroyd accepted the tonic. One move in the game seemed now to be concluded. Not for a moment did I imagine that I had been sent for because of the shock occasioned by Ackroyd's death. But Mrs. Ackroyd is totally incapable of pursuing a straight-forward course on any subject. She always approaches her object by tortuous means. I wondered very much why it was she had sent for me.

"And then that scene—yesterday," continued my patient.

She paused as though expecting me to take up a cue.

"What scene?"

"Doctor, how can you? Have you forgotten? That dreadful little Frenchman—or Belgian—or whatever he is. Bullying us all like he did. It has quite upset me. Coming on top of Roger's death."

"I'm very sorry, Mrs. Ackroyd," I said.

"I don't know what he meant—shouting at us like he did. I should hope I know my duty too well to *dream* of concealing anything. I have given the police *every* assistance in my power."

Mrs. Ackroyd paused, and I said, "Quite so." I was beginning to have a glimmering of what all the trouble was about.

"No one can say that I have failed in my duty," continued Mrs. Ackroyd. "I am sure Inspector Raglan is perfectly satisfied. Why should this little upstart of a foreigner make a fuss? A most ridiculous-looking creature he is too—just like a comic Frenchman in a revue. I can't think why Flora insisted on bringing him into the case. She never said a word to me about it. Just went off and did it on her own. Flora is too independent. I am a woman of the world and her mother. She should have come to me for advice first."

I listened to all this in silence.

"What does he think? That's what I want to know. Does he actually imagine I'm hiding something? He—he—positively *accused* me yesterday."

I shrugged my shoulders.

"It is surely of no consequence, Mrs. Ackroyd," I said. "Since you are not concealing anything, any remarks he may have made do not apply to you."

Mrs. Ackroyd went off at a tangent, after her usual fashion.

"Servants are so tiresome," she said. "They gossip, and talk amongst themselves. And then it gets round—and all the time there's probably nothing in it at all."

"Have the servants been talking?" I asked. "What about?"

Mrs. Ackroyd cast a very shrewd glance at me. It quite threw me off my balance.

"I was sure *you'd* know, doctor, if any one did. You were with M. Poirot all the time, weren't you?"

"I was."

"Then of course you know. It was that girl, Ursula Bourne, wasn't it? Naturally—she's leaving. She *would* want to make all the trouble she could. Spiteful, that's what they are. They're all alike. Now, you being there, doctor, you must know exactly what she did say? I'm most anxious that no wrong impression should get about. After all, you don't repeat every little detail to the police, do you? There are family matters sometimes—nothing to do with the question of the murder. But if the girl was spiteful, she may have made out all sorts of things."

I was shrewd enough to see that a very real anxiety lay behind these outpourings. Poirot had been justified in his premises. Of the six people round the table yesterday, Mrs. Ackroyd at least had had something to hide. It was for me to discover what that something might be.

"If I were you, Mrs. Ackroyd," I said brusquely, "I should make a clean breast of things."

She gave a little scream.

"Oh! doctor, how can you be so abrupt. It sounds as though—as though——And I can explain everything so simply."

"Then why not do so," I suggested.

Mrs. Ackroyd took out a frilled handkerchief, and became tearful.

"I thought, doctor, that you might put it to M. Poirot—explain it, you know—because it's so difficult for a foreigner to see our point of view. And you don't know—nobody could know—what I've had to contend with. A martyrdom—a long martyrdom. That's what my life has been. I don't like to speak ill of the dead—but there it is. Not the smallest bill, but it had all to be gone over—just as though Roger had had a few miserly hundreds a year instead of being (as Mr. Hammond told me yesterday) one of the wealthiest men in these parts."

Mrs. Ackroyd paused to dab her eyes with the frilled handkerchief.

"Yes," I said encouragingly. "You were talking about bills?"

"Those dreadful bills. And some I didn't like to show Roger at all. They were things a man wouldn't understand. He would have said the things weren't necessary. And of course they mounted up, you know, and they kept coming in——"

She looked at me appealingly, as though asking me to condole with her on this striking peculiarity.

"It's a habit they have," I agreed.

"And the tone altered—became quite abusive. I assure you, doctor, I was becoming a nervous wreck. I couldn't sleep at nights. And a dreadful fluttering round the heart. And then I got a letter from a Scotch gentleman—as a matter of fact there were two letters—both Scotch gentlemen. Mr. Bruce MacPherson was one, and the other were Colin MacDonald. Quite a coincidence."

"Hardly that," I said dryly. "They are usually Scotch gentlemen, but I suspect a Semitic strain in their ancestry."

"Ten pounds to ten thousand on note of hand alone," murmured Mrs. Ackroyd reminiscently. "I wrote to one of them, but it seemed there were difficulties."

She paused.

I gathered that we were just coming to delicate ground. I have never known any one more difficult to bring to the point.

"You see," murmured Mrs. Ackroyd, "it's all a question of expectations, isn't it? Testamentary expectations. And though, of course, I expected that Roger would provide for me, I didn't *know*. I thought that if only I could glance over a copy of his will—not in any sense of vulgar prying—but just so that I could make my own arrangements."

She glanced sideways at me. The position was now very delicate indeed. Fortunately words, ingeniously used, will serve to mask the ugliness of naked facts.

"I could only tell this to you, dear Dr. Sheppard," said Mrs. Ackroyd rapidly. "I can trust you not to misjudge me, and to represent the matter in the right light to M. Poirot. It was on Friday afternoon——"

She came to a stop and swallowed uncertainly.

"Yes," I repeated encouragingly. "On Friday afternoon. Well?"

"Every one was out, or so I thought. And I went into Roger's study—I had some real reason for going there—I mean, there was nothing underhand about it. And as I saw all the papers heaped on the desk, it just came to me, like a flash: 'I wonder if Roger keeps his will in one of the drawers of the desk.' I'm so impulsive, always was, from a child. I do things on the spur of the moment. He'd left his keys—very careless of him—in the lock of the top drawer."

"I see," I said helpfully. "So you searched the desk. Did you find the will?"

Mrs. Ackroyd gave a little scream, and I realized that I had not been sufficiently diplomatic.

"How dreadful it sounds. But it wasn't at all like that really."

"Of course it wasn't," I said hastily. "You must forgive my unfortunate way of putting things."

"You see, men are so peculiar. In dear Roger's place, I should not have objected to revealing the provisions of my will. But men are so secretive. One is forced to adopt little subterfuges in self-defence."

"And the result of the little subterfuge?" I asked.

"That's just what I'm telling you. As I got to the bottom drawer, Bourne came in. Most awkward. Of course I shut the drawer and stood up, and I called her attention to a few specks of dust on the surface. But I didn't like the way she looked—quite respectful in manner, but a very nasty light in her eyes. Almost contemptuous, if you know what I mean. I never have liked that girl very much. She's a good servant, and she says Ma'am, and doesn't object to wearing caps and aprons (which I declare to you a lot of them do nowadays), and she can say 'Not at home' without scruples if she has to answer the door instead of Parker, and she doesn't have those peculiar gurgling noises inside which so many parlormaids seem to have when they wait at table——Let me see, where was I?"

"You were saying, that in spite of several valuable qualities, you never liked Bourne."

"No more I do. She's—odd. There's something different about her from the others. Too well educated, that's my opinion. You can't tell who are ladies and who aren't nowadays."

"And what happened next?" I asked.

"Nothing. At least, Roger came in. And I thought he was out for a walk. And he said: 'What's all this?' and I said, 'Nothing. I just came in to fetch *Punch*.' And I took *Punch* and went out with it. Bourne stayed behind. I heard her asking Roger if she could speak to him for a minute. I went straight up to my room, to lie down. I was very upset."

There was a pause.

"You will explain to M. Poirot, won't you? You can see for yourself what a trivial matter the whole thing was. But, of course, when he was so stern about concealing things, I thought of this at once. Bourne may have made some extraordinary story out of it, but you can explain, can't you?"

"That is all?" I said. "You have told me everything?"

"Ye-es," said Mrs. Ackroyd. "Oh! yes," she added firmly.

But I had noted the momentary hesitation, and I knew that there was still something she was keeping back. It was nothing less than a flash of sheer genius that prompted me to ask the question I did.

"Mrs. Ackroyd," I said, "was it you who left the silver table open?"

I had my answer in the blush of guilt that even rouge and powder could not conceal.

"How did you know?" she whispered.

"It was you, then?"

"Yes—I—you see—there were one or two pieces of old silver—very interesting. I had been reading up the subject and there was an illustration of quite a small piece which had fetched an immense sum at Christy's. It looked to me just the same as the one in the silver table. I thought I would take it up to London with me when I went—and—and have it valued. Then if it really was a valuable piece, just think what a charming surprise it would have been for Roger?"

I refrained from comments, accepting Mrs. Ackroyd's story on its merits. I even forbore to ask her why it was necessary to abstract what she wanted in such a surreptitious manner.

"Why did you leave the lid open?" I asked. "Did you forget?"

"I was startled," said Mrs. Ackroyd. "I heard footsteps coming along the terrace outside. I hastened out of the room and just got up the stairs before Parker opened the front door to you."

"That must have been Miss Russell," I said thoughtfully. Mrs. Ackroyd had revealed to me one fact that was extremely interesting. Whether her designs upon Ackroyd's silver had been strictly honorable I neither knew nor cared. What did interest me was the fact that Miss Russell must have entered the drawing-room by the window, and that I had not been wrong when I judged her to be out of breath with running. Where had she been? I thought of the summer-house and the scrap of cambric.

"I wonder if Miss Russell has her handkerchiefs starched!" I exclaimed on the spur of the moment.

Mrs. Ackroyd's start recalled me to myself, and I rose.

"You think you can explain to M. Poirot?" she asked anxiously.

"Oh, certainly. Absolutely."

I got away at last, after being forced to listen to more justifications of her conduct.

The parlormaid was in the hall, and it was she who helped me on with my overcoat. I observed her more closely than I had done heretofore. It was clear that she had been crying.

"How is it," I asked, "that you told us that Mr. Ackroyd sent for you on Friday to his study? I hear now that it was *you* who asked to speak to *him*?"

For a minute the girl's eyes dropped before mine.

Then she spoke.

"I meant to leave in any case," she said uncertainly.

I said no more. She opened the front door for me. Just as I was passing out, she said suddenly in a low voice:—

"Excuse me, sir, is there any news of Captain Paton?"

I shook my head, looking at her inquiringly.

"He ought to come back," she said. "Indeed—indeed he ought to come back."

She was looking at me with appealing eyes.

"Does no one know where he is?" she asked.

"Do you?" I said sharply.

She shook her head.

"No, indeed. I know nothing. But any one who was a friend to him would tell him this: he ought to come back."

I lingered, thinking that perhaps the girl would say more. Her next question surprised me.

"When do they think the murder was done? Just before ten o'clock?"

"That is the idea," I said. "Between a quarter to ten and the hour."

"Not earlier? Not before a quarter to ten?"

I looked at her attentively. She was so clearly eager for a reply in the affirmative.

"That's out of the question," I said. "Miss Ackroyd saw her uncle alive at a quarter to ten."

She turned away, and her whole figure seemed to droop.

"A handsome girl," I said to myself as I drove off. "An exceedingly handsome girl."

Caroline was at home. She had had a visit from Poirot and was very pleased and important about it.

"I am helping him with the case," she explained.

I felt rather uneasy. Caroline is bad enough as it is. What will she be like with her detective instincts encouraged?

"Are you going round the neighborhood looking for Ralph Paton's mysterious girl?" I inquired.

84

"I might do that on my own account," said Caroline. "No, this is a special thing M. Poirot wants me to find out for him."

"What is it?" I asked.

"He wants to know whether Ralph Paton's boots were black or brown," said Caroline with tremendous solemnity.

I stared at her. I see now that I was unbelievably stupid about these boots. I failed altogether to grasp the point.

"They were brown shoes," I said. "I saw them."

"Not shoes, James, boots. M. Poirot wants to know whether a pair of boots Ralph had with him at the hotel were brown or black. A lot hangs on it."

Call me dense if you like. I didn't see.

"And how are you going to find out?" I asked.

Caroline said there would be no difficulty about that. Our Annie's dearest friend was Miss Ganett's maid, Clara. And Clara was walking out with the boots at the Three Boars. The whole thing was simplicity itself, and by the aid of Miss Ganett, who coöperated loyally, at once giving Clara leave of absence, the matter was rushed through at express speed.

It was when we were sitting down to lunch that Caroline remarked, with would-be unconcern:—

"About those boots of Ralph Paton's."

"Well," I said, "what about them?"

"M. Poirot thought they were probably brown. He was wrong. They're black."

And Caroline nodded her head several times. She evidently felt that she had scored a point over Poirot.

I did not answer. I was puzzling over what the color of a pair of Ralph Paton's boots had to do with the case.

CHAPTER XV
GEOFFREY RAYMOND

I WAS to have a further proof that day of the success of Poirot's tactics. That challenge of his had been a subtle touch born of his knowledge of human nature. A mixture of fear and guilt had wrung the truth from Mrs. Ackroyd. She was the first to react.

That afternoon when I returned from seeing my patients, Caroline told me that Geoffrey Raymond had just left.

"Did he want to see me?" I asked, as I hung up my coat in the hall.

Caroline was hovering by my elbow.

"It was M. Poirot he wanted to see," she said. "He'd just come from The Larches. M. Poirot was out. Mr. Raymond thought that he might be here, or that you might know where he was."

"I haven't the least idea."

"I tried to make him wait," said Caroline, "but he said he would call back at The Larches in half an hour, and went away down the village. A great pity, because M. Poirot came in practically the minute after he left."

"Came in here?"

"No, to his own house."

"How do you know?"

"The side window," said Caroline briefly.

It seemed to me that we had now exhausted the topic. Caroline thought otherwise.

"Aren't you going across?"

"Across where?"

"To The Larches, of course."

"My dear Caroline," I said, "what for?"

"Mr. Raymond wanted to see him very particularly," said Caroline. "You might hear what it's all about."

I raised my eyebrows.

"Curiosity is not my besetting sin," I remarked coldly. "I can exist comfortably without knowing exactly what my neighbors are doing and thinking."

"Stuff and nonsense, James," said my sister. "You want to know just as much as I do. You're not so honest, that's all. You always have to pretend."

"Really, Caroline," I said, and retired into my surgery.

Ten minutes later Caroline tapped at the door and entered. In her hand she held what seemed to be a pot of jam.

"I wonder, James," she said, "if you would mind taking this pot of medlar jelly across to M. Poirot? I promised it to him. He has never tasted any home-made medlar jelly."

"Why can't Annie go?" I asked coldly.

"She's doing some mending. I can't spare her."

Caroline and I looked at each other.

"Very well," I said, rising. "But if I take the beastly thing, I shall just leave it at the door. You understand that?"

My sister raised her eyebrows.

"Naturally," she said. "Who suggested you should do anything else?"

The honors were with Caroline.

"If you *do* happen to see M. Poirot," she said, as I opened the front door, "you might tell him about the boots."

It was a most subtle parting shot. I wanted dreadfully to understand the enigma of the boots. When the old lady with the Breton cap opened the door to me, I found myself asking if M. Poirot was in, quite automatically.

Poirot sprang up to meet me, with every appearance of pleasure.

"Sit down, my good friend," he said. "The big chair? This small one? The room is not too hot, no?"

I thought it was stifling, but refrained from saying so. The windows were closed, and a large fire burned in the grate.

"The English people, they have a mania for the fresh air," declared Poirot. "The big air, it is all very well outside, where it belongs. Why admit it to the house? But let us not discuss such banalities. You have something for me, yes?"

"Two things," I said. "First—this—from my sister."

I handed over the pot of medlar jelly.

"How kind of Mademoiselle Caroline. She has remembered her promise. And the second thing?"

"Information—of a kind."

And I told him of my interview with Mrs. Ackroyd. He listened with interest, but not much excitement.

"It clears the ground," he said thoughtfully. "And it has a certain value as confirming the evidence of the housekeeper. She said, you remember, that she found the silver table lid open and closed it down in passing."

"What about her statement that she went into the drawing-room to see if the flowers were fresh?"

"Ah! we never took that very seriously, did we, my friend? It was patently an excuse, trumped up in a hurry, by a woman who felt it urgent to explain her presence—which, by the way, you would probably never have thought of questioning. I considered it possible that her agitation might arise from the fact that she had been tampering with the silver table, but I think now that we must look for another cause."

"Yes," I said. "Whom did she go out to meet? And why?"

"You think she went to meet some one?"

"I do."

Poirot nodded.

"So do I," he said thoughtfully.

There was a pause.

"By the way," I said, "I've got a message for you from my sister. Ralph Paton's boots were black, not brown."

I was watching him closely as I gave the message, and I fancied that I saw a momentary flicker of discomposure. If so, it passed almost immediately.

"She is absolutely positive they are not brown?"

"Absolutely."

"Ah!" said Poirot regretfully. "That is a pity."

And he seemed quite crestfallen.

He entered into no explanations, but at once started a new subject of conversation.

"The housekeeper, Miss Russell, who came to consult you on that Friday morning—is it indiscreet to ask what passed at the interview—apart from the medical details, I mean?"

"Not at all," I said. "When the professional part of the conversation was over, we talked for a few minutes about poisons, and the ease or difficulty of detecting them, and about drug-taking and drug-takers."

"With special reference to cocaine?" asked Poirot.

"How did you know?" I asked, somewhat surprised.

For answer, the little man rose and crossed the room to where newspapers were filed. He brought me a copy of the *Daily Budget*, dated Friday, 16th September, and showed me an article dealing with the smuggling of cocaine. It was a somewhat lurid article, written with an eye to picturesque effect.

"That is what put cocaine into her head, my friend," he said.

I would have catechized him further, for I did not quite understand his meaning, but at that moment the door opened and Geoffrey Raymond was announced.

He came in fresh and debonair as ever, and greeted us both.

"How are you, doctor? M. Poirot, this is the second time I've been here this morning. I was anxious to catch you."

"Perhaps I'd better be off," I suggested rather awkwardly.

"Not on my account, doctor. No, it's just this," he went on, seating himself at a wave of invitation from Poirot, "I've got a confession to make."

"*En verité*?" said Poirot, with an air of polite interest.

"Oh, it's of no consequence, really. But, as a matter of fact, my conscience has been pricking me ever since yesterday afternoon. You accused us all of keeping back something, M. Poirot. I plead guilty. I've had something up my sleeve."

"And what is that, M. Raymond?"

"As I say, it's nothing of consequence—just this. I was in debt—badly, and that legacy came in the nick of time. Five hundred pounds puts me on my feet again with a little to spare."

He smiled at us both with that engaging frankness that made him such a likable youngster.

"You know how it is. Suspicious looking policeman—don't like to admit you were hard up for money—think it will look bad to them. But I was a fool, really, because Blunt and I were in the billiard room from a quarter to ten onwards, so I've got a watertight alibi and nothing to fear. Still, when you thundered out that stuff about concealing things, I felt a nasty prick of conscience, and I thought I'd like to get it off my mind."

He got up again and stood smiling at us.

"You are a very wise young man," said Poirot, nodding at him with approval. "See you, when I know that any one is hiding things from me, I suspect that the thing hidden may be something very bad indeed. You have done well."

"I'm glad I'm cleared from suspicion," laughed Raymond. "I'll be off now."

"So that is that," I remarked, as the door closed behind the young secretary.

"Yes," agreed Poirot. "A mere bagatelle—but if he had not been in the billiard room—who knows? After all, many crimes have been committed for the sake of less than five hundred pounds. It all depends on what sum is sufficient to break a man. A question of the relativity, is it not so? Have you reflected, my friend, that many people in that house stood to benefit by Mr. Ackroyd's death? Mrs. Ackroyd, Miss Flora, young Mr. Raymond, the housekeeper, Miss Russell. Only one, in fact, does not, Major Blunt."

His tone in uttering that name was so peculiar that I looked up, puzzled.

"I don't quite understand you?" I said.

"Two of the people I accused have given me the truth."

"You think Major Blunt has something to conceal also?"

"As for that," remarked Poirot nonchalantly, "there is a saying, is there not, that Englishmen conceal only one thing—their love? And Major Blunt, I should say, is not good at concealments."

"Sometimes," I said, "I wonder if we haven't rather jumped to conclusions on one point."

"What is that?"

"We've assumed that the blackmailer of Mrs. Ferrars is necessarily the murderer of Mr. Ackroyd. Mightn't we be mistaken?"

Poirot nodded energetically.

"Very good. Very good indeed. I wondered if that idea would come to you. Of course it is possible. But we must remember one point. The letter disappeared. Still, that, as you say, may not necessarily mean that the murderer took it. When you first found the body, Parker may have abstracted the letter unnoticed by you."

"Parker?"

"Yes, Parker. I always come back to Parker—not as the murderer—no, he did not commit the murder; but who is more suitable than he as the mysterious scoundrel who terrorized Mrs. Ferrars? He may have got his information about Mr. Ferrars's death from one of the King's Paddock servants. At any rate, he is more likely to have come upon it than a casual guest such as Blunt, for instance."

"Parker might have taken the letter," I admitted. "It wasn't till later that I noticed it was gone."

"How much later? After Blunt and Raymond were in the room, or before?"

"I can't remember," I said slowly. "I think it was before—no, afterwards. Yes, I'm almost sure it was afterwards."

"That widens the field to three," said Poirot thoughtfully. "But Parker is the most likely. It is in my mind to try a little experiment with Parker. How say you, my friend, will you accompany me to Fernly?"

I acquiesced, and we set out at once. Poirot asked to see Miss Ackroyd, and presently Flora came to us.

"Mademoiselle Flora," said Poirot, "I have to confide in you a little secret. I am not yet satisfied of the innocence of Parker. I propose to make a little experiment with your assistance. I want to reconstruct some of his actions on that night. But we must think of something to tell him—ah! I have it. I wish to satisfy myself as to whether voices in the little lobby could have been heard outside on the terrace. Now, ring for Parker, if you will be so good."

I did so, and presently the butler appeared, suave as ever.

"You rang, sir?"

"Yes, my good Parker. I have in mind a little experiment. I have placed Major Blunt on the terrace outside the study window. I want to see if any one there could have heard the voices of Miss Ackroyd and yourself in the lobby that night. I want to enact that little scene over again. Perhaps you would fetch the tray or whatever it was you were carrying?"

Parker vanished, and we repaired to the lobby outside the study door. Presently we heard a chink in the outer hall, and Parker appeared in the doorway carrying a tray with a siphon, a decanter of whisky, and two glasses on it.

"One moment," cried Poirot, raising his hand and seemingly very excited. "We must have everything in order. Just as it occurred. It is a little method of mine."

"A foreign custom, sir," said Parker. "Reconstruction of the crime they call it, do they not?"

He was quite imperturbable as he stood there politely waiting on Poirot's orders.

"Ah! he knows something, the good Parker," cried Poirot. "He has read of these things. Now, I beg you, let us have everything of the most exact. You came from the outer hall—so. Mademoiselle was—where?"

"Here," said Flora, taking up her stand just outside the study door.

"Quite right, sir," said Parker.

"I had just closed the door," continued Flora.

"Yes, miss," agreed Parker. "Your hand was still on the handle as it is now."

"Then *allez*," said Poirot. "Play me the little comedy."

Flora stood with her hand on the door handle, and Parker came stepping through the door from the hall, bearing the tray.

He stopped just inside the door. Flora spoke.

"Oh! Parker. Mr. Ackroyd doesn't want to be disturbed again to-night."

"Is that right?" she added in an undertone.

"To the best of my recollection, Miss Flora," said Parker, "but I fancy you used the word evening instead of night." Then, raising his voice in a somewhat theatrical fashion: "Very good, miss. Shall I lock up as usual?"

"Yes, please."

Parker retired through the door, Flora followed him, and started to ascend the main staircase.

"Is that enough?" she asked over her shoulder.

"Admirable," declared the little man, rubbing his hands. "By the way, Parker, are you sure there were two glasses on the tray that evening? Who was the second one for?"

"I always bring two glasses, sir," said Parker. "Is there anything further?"

"Nothing. I thank you."

Parker withdrew, dignified to the last.

Poirot stood in the middle of the hall frowning. Flora came down and joined us.

"Has your experiment been successful?" she asked. "I don't quite understand, you know——"

Poirot smiled admiringly at her.

"It is not necessary that you should," he said. "But tell me, were there indeed two glasses on Parker's tray that night?"

Flora wrinkled her brows a minute.

"I really can't remember," she said. "I think there were. Is—is that the object of your experiment?"

Poirot took her hand and patted it.

"Put it this way," he said. "I am always interested to see if people will speak the truth."

"And did Parker speak the truth?"

"I rather think he did," said Poirot thoughtfully.

A few minutes later saw us retracing our steps to the village.

"What was the point of that question about the glasses?" I asked curiously.

Poirot shrugged his shoulders.

"One must say something," he remarked. "That particular question did as well as any other."

I stared at him.

"At any rate, my friend," he said more seriously, "I know now something I wanted to know. Let us leave it at that."

CHAPTER XVI
AN EVENING AT MAH JONG

THAT night we had a little Mah Jong party. This kind of simple entertainment is very popular in King's Abbot. The guests arrive in goloshes and waterproofs after dinner. They partake of coffee and later of cake, sandwiches, and tea.

On this particular night our guests were Miss Ganett and Colonel Carter, who lives near the church. A good deal of gossip is handed round at these evenings, sometimes seriously interfering with the game in progress. We used to play bridge—chatty bridge of the worst description. We find Mah Jong much more peaceful. The irritated demand as to why on earth your partner did not lead a certain card is entirely done away with, and though we still express criticisms frankly, there is not the same acrimonious spirit.

"Very cold evening, eh, Sheppard?" said Colonel Carter, standing with his back to the fire. Caroline had taken Miss Ganett to her own room, and was there assisting her to disentangle herself from her many wraps. "Reminds me of the Afghan passes."

"Indeed?" I said politely.

"Very mysterious business this about poor Ackroyd," continued the colonel, accepting a cup of coffee. "A deuce of a lot behind it—that's what I say. Between you and me, Sheppard, I've heard the word blackmail mentioned!"

The colonel gave me the look which might be tabulated "one man of the world to another."

"A woman in it, no doubt," he said. "Depend upon it, a woman in it."

Caroline and Miss Ganett joined us at this minute. Miss Ganett drank coffee whilst Caroline got out the Mah Jong box and poured out the tiles upon the table.

"Washing the tiles," said the colonel facetiously. "That's right—washing the tiles, as we used to say in the Shanghai Club."

It is the private opinion of both Caroline and myself that Colonel Carter has never been in the Shanghai Club in his life. More, that he has never been farther east than India, where he juggled with tins of bully beef and plum and apple jam during the Great War. But the colonel is determinedly military, and in King's Abbot we permit people to indulge their little idiosyncrasies freely.

"Shall we begin?" said Caroline.

We sat round the table. For some five minutes there was complete silence, owing to the fact that there is tremendous secret competition amongst us as to who can build their wall quickest.

"Go on, James," said Caroline at last. "You're East Wind."

I discarded a tile. A round or two proceeded, broken by the monotonous remarks of "Three Bamboos," "Two Circles," "Pung," and frequently from Miss Ganett "Unpung," owing to that lady's habit of too hastily claiming tiles to which she had no right.

"I saw Flora Ackroyd this morning," said Miss Ganett. "Pung—no—Unpung. I made a mistake."

"Four Circles," said Caroline. "Where did you see her?"

"She didn't see *me*," said Miss Ganett, with that tremendous significance only to be met with in small villages.

"Ah!" said Caroline interestedly. "Chow."

"I believe," said Miss Ganett, temporarily diverted, "that it's the right thing nowadays to say 'Chee' not 'Chow.'"

"Nonsense," said Caroline. "I have always said '*Chow*.'"

"In the Shanghai Club," said Colonel Carter, "they say '*Chow*.'"

Miss Ganett retired, crushed.

"What were you saying about Flora Ackroyd?" asked Caroline, after a moment or two devoted to the game. "Was she with any one?"

"Very much so," said Miss Ganett.

The eyes of the two ladies met, and seemed to exchange information.

"Really," said Caroline interestedly. "Is that it? Well, it doesn't surprise me in the least."

"We're waiting for you to discard, Miss Caroline," said the colonel. He sometimes affects the pose of the bluff male, intent on the game and indifferent to gossip. But nobody is deceived.

"If you ask me," said Miss Ganett. ("Was that a Bamboo you discarded, dear? Oh! no, I see now—it was a Circle.) As I was saying, if you ask me, Flora's been exceedingly lucky. Exceedingly lucky she's been."

"How's that, Miss Ganett?" asked the colonel. "I'll Pung that Green Dragon. How do you make out that Miss Flora's been lucky? Very charming girl and all that, I know."

"I mayn't know very much about crime," said Miss Ganett, with the air of one who knows everything there is to know, "but I can tell you one thing. The first question that's always asked is 'Who last saw the deceased alive?' And the person who did is regarded with suspicion. Now, Flora Ackroyd last saw her uncle alive. It might have looked very nasty for her—very nasty indeed. It's my opinion—and I give it for what it's worth, that Ralph Paton is staying away on her account, to draw suspicion away from her."

"Come, now," I protested mildly, "you surely can't suggest that a young girl like Flora Ackroyd is capable of stabbing her uncle in cold blood?"

"Well, I don't know," said Miss Ganett. "I've just been reading a book from the library about the underworld of Paris, and it says that some of the worst women criminals are young girls with the faces of angels."

"That's in France," said Caroline instantly.

"Just so," said the colonel. "Now, I'll tell you a very curious thing—a story that was going round the Bazaars in India...."

The colonel's story was one of interminable length, and of curiously little interest. A thing that happened in India many years ago cannot compare for a moment with an event that took place in King's Abbot the day before yesterday.

It was Caroline who brought the colonel's story to a close by fortunately going Mah Jong. After the slight unpleasantness always occasioned by my corrections of Caroline's somewhat faulty arithmetic, we started a new hand.

"East Wind passes," said Caroline. "I've got an idea of my own about Ralph Paton. Three Characters. But I'm keeping it to myself for the present."

"Are you, dear?" said Miss Ganett. "Chow—I mean Pung."

"Yes," said Caroline firmly.

"Was it all right about the boots?" asked Miss Ganett. "Their being black, I mean?"

"Quite all right," said Caroline.

"What was the point, do you think?" asked Miss Ganett.

Caroline pursed up her lips, and shook her head with an air of knowing all about it.

"Pung," said Miss Ganett. "No—Unpung. I suppose that now the doctor's in with M. Poirot he knows all the secrets?"

"Far from it," I said.

"James is so modest," said Caroline. "Ah! a concealed Kong."

The colonel gave vent to a whistle. For the moment gossip was forgotten.

"Your own wind, too," he said. "*And* you've got two Pungs of Dragons. We must be careful. Miss Caroline's out for a big hand."

We played for some minutes with no irrelevant conversation.

"This M. Poirot now," said Colonel Carter, "is he really such a great detective?"

"The greatest the world has ever known," said Caroline solemnly. "He had to come here incognito to avoid publicity."

"Chow," said Miss Ganett. "Quite wonderful for our little village, I'm sure. By the way, Clara—my maid, you know—is great friends with Elsie, the housemaid at Fernly, and what do you think Elsie told her? That there's been a lot of money stolen, and it's her opinion—Elsie's—I mean, that the parlormaid had something to do with it. She's leaving at the month, and she's crying a good deal at night. If you ask me, the girl is very likely in league with a *gang*. She's always been a queer girl—she's not friends with any of the girls round here. She goes off by herself on her days out—very unnatural, I call it, and most suspicious. I asked her once to come to our Girls' Friendly Evenings, but she refused, and then I asked her a few questions about her home and her family—all that sort of thing, and I'm bound to say I considered her manner most impertinent. Outwardly very respectful—but she shut me up in the most barefaced way."

Miss Ganett stopped for breath, and the colonel, who was totally uninterested in the servant question, remarked that in the Shanghai Club brisk play was the invariable rule.

We had a round of brisk play.

"That Miss Russell," said Caroline. "She came here pretending to consult James on Friday morning. It's my opinion she wanted to see where the poisons were kept. Five Characters."

"Chow," said Miss Ganett. "What an extraordinary idea? I wonder if you can be right."

"Talking of poisons," said the colonel. "Eh—what? Haven't I discarded? Oh! Eight Bamboos."

"Mah Jong!" said Miss Ganett.

Caroline was very much annoyed.

"One Red Dragon," she said regretfully, "and I should have had a hand of three doubles."

"I've had two Red Dragons all the time," I mentioned.

"So exactly like you, James," said Caroline reproachfully. "You've no conception of the spirit of the game."

I myself thought I had played rather cleverly. I should have had to pay Caroline an enormous amount if she had gone Mah Jong. Miss Ganett's Mah Jong was of the poorest variety possible, as Caroline did not fail to point out to her.

East Wind passed, and we started a new hand in silence.

"What I was going to tell you just now was this," said Caroline.

"Yes?" said Miss Ganett encouragingly.

"My idea about Ralph Paton, I mean."

"Yes, dear," said Miss Ganett, still more encouragingly. "Chow!"

"It's a sign of weakness to Chow so early," said Caroline severely. "You should go for a big hand."

"I know," said Miss Ganett. "You were saying—about Ralph Paton, you know?"

"Yes. Well, I've a pretty shrewd idea where he is."

We all stopped to stare at her.

"This is very interesting, Miss Caroline," said Colonel Carter. "All your own idea, eh?"

"Well, not exactly. I'll tell you about it. You know that big map of the county we have in the hall?"

We all said Yes.

"As M. Poirot was going out the other day, he stopped and looked at it, and he made some remark—I can't remember exactly what it was. Something about Cranchester being the only big town anywhere near us—which is true, of course. But after he had gone—it came to me suddenly."

"What came to you?"

"His meaning. Of course Ralph is in Cranchester."

It was at that moment that I knocked down the rack that held my pieces. My sister immediately reproved me for clumsiness, but half-heartedly. She was intent on her theory.

"Cranchester, Miss Caroline?" said Colonel Carter. "Surely not Cranchester! It's so near."

"That's exactly it," cried Caroline triumphantly. "It seems quite clear by now that he didn't get away from here by train. He must simply have walked into Cranchester. And I believe he's there still. No one would dream of his being so near at hand."

I pointed out several objections to the theory, but when once Caroline has got something firmly into her head, nothing dislodges it.

"And you think M. Poirot has the same idea," said Miss Ganett thoughtfully. "It's a curious coincidence, but I was out for a walk this afternoon on the Cranchester road, and he passed me in a car coming from that direction."

We all looked at each other.

"Why, dear me," said Miss Ganett suddenly, "I'm Mah Jong all the time, and I never noticed it."

Caroline's attention was distracted from her own inventive exercises. She pointed out to Miss Ganett that a hand consisting of mixed suits and too many Chows was hardly worth going Mah Jong on. Miss Ganett listened imperturbably and collected her counters.

"Yes, dear, I know what you mean," she said. "But it rather depends on what kind of a hand you have to start with, doesn't it?"

"You'll never get the big hands if you don't go for them," urged Caroline.

"Well, we must all play our own way, mustn't we?" said Miss Ganett. She looked down at her counters. "After all, I'm up, so far."

Caroline, who was considerably down, said nothing.

East Wind passed, and we set to once more. Annie brought in the tea things. Caroline and Miss Ganett were both slightly ruffled as is often the case during one of these festive evenings.

"If you would only play a leetle quicker, dear," said Caroline, as Miss Ganett hesitated over her discard. "The Chinese put down the tiles so quickly it sounds like little birds pattering."

For some few minutes we played like the Chinese.

"You haven't contributed much to the sum of information, Sheppard," said Colonel Carter genially. "You're a sly dog. Hand in glove with the great detective, and not a hint as to the way things are going."

"James is an extraordinary creature," said Caroline. "He can *not* bring himself to part with information."

She looked at me with some disfavor.

"I assure you," I said, "that I don't know anything. Poirot keeps his own counsel."

"Wise man," said the colonel with a chuckle. "He doesn't give himself away. But they're wonderful fellows, these foreign detectives. Up to all sorts of dodges, I believe."

"Pung," said Miss Ganett, in a tone of quiet triumph. "And Mah Jong."

The situation became more strained. It was annoyance at Miss Ganett's going Mah Jong for the third time running which prompted Caroline to say to me as we built a fresh wall:—

"You are too tiresome, James. You sit there like a dead head, and say nothing at all!"

"But, my dear," I protested, "I have really nothing to say—that is, of the kind you mean."

"Nonsense," said Caroline, as she sorted her hand. "You *must* know something interesting."

I did not answer for a moment. I was overwhelmed and intoxicated. I had read of there being such a thing as the Perfect Winning—going Mah Jong on one's original hand. I had never hoped to hold the hand myself.

With suppressed triumph I laid my hand face upwards on the table.

"As they say in the Shanghai Club," I remarked, "Tin-ho—the Perfect Winning!"

The colonel's eyes nearly bulged out of his head.

"Upon my soul," he said. "What an extraordinary thing. I never saw that happen before!"

It was then that I went on, goaded by Caroline's gibes, and rendered reckless by my triumph.

"And as to anything interesting," I said. "What about a gold wedding ring with a date and 'From R.' inside."

I pass over the scene that followed. I was made to say exactly where this treasure was found. I was made to reveal the date.

"March 13th," said Caroline. "Just six months ago. Ah!"

Out of the babel of excited suggestions and suppositions three theories were evolved:—

1. That of Colonel Carter: that Ralph was secretly married to Flora. The first or most simple solution.

2. That of Miss Ganett: that Roger Ackroyd had been secretly married to Mrs. Ferrars.

3. That of my sister: that Roger Ackroyd had married his housekeeper, Miss Russell.

A fourth or super-theory was propounded by Caroline later as we went up to bed.

"Mark my words," she said suddenly, "I shouldn't be at all surprised if Geoffrey Raymond and Flora weren't married."

"Surely it would be 'From G,' not 'From R' then," I suggested.

"You never know. Some girls call men by their surnames. And you heard what Miss Ganett said this evening—about Flora's carryings on."

Strictly speaking, I had not heard Miss Ganett say anything of the kind, but I respected Caroline's knowledge of innuendoes.

"How about Hector Blunt," I hinted. "If it's anybody——"

"Nonsense," said Caroline. "I dare say he admires her—may even be in love with her. But depend upon it a girl isn't going to fall in love with a man old enough to be her father when there's a good-looking young secretary about. She may encourage Major Blunt just as a blind. Girls are very artful. But there's one thing I *do* tell you, James Sheppard. Flora Ackroyd does not care a penny piece for Ralph Paton, and never has. You can take it from me."

I took it from her meekly.

CHAPTER XVII
PARKER

IT occurred to me the next morning that under the exhilaration produced by Tin-ho, or the Perfect Winning, I might have been slightly indiscreet. True, Poirot had not asked me to keep the discovery of the ring to myself. On the other hand, he had said nothing about it whilst at Fernly, and as far as I knew, I was the only person aware that it had been found. I felt distinctly guilty. The fact was by now spreading through King's Abbot like wildfire. I was expecting wholesale reproaches from Poirot any minute.

The joint funeral of Mrs. Ferrars and Roger Ackroyd was fixed for eleven o'clock. It was a melancholy and impressive ceremony. All the party from Fernly were there.

After it was over, Poirot, who had also been present, took me by the arm, and invited me to accompany him back to The Larches. He was looking very grave, and

I feared that my indiscretion of the night before had got round to his ears. But it soon transpired that his thoughts were occupied by something of a totally different nature.

"See you," he said. "We must act. With your help I propose to examine a witness. We will question him, we will put such fear into him that the truth is bound to come out."

"What witness are you talking of?" I asked, very much surprised.

"Parker!" said Poirot. "I asked him to be at my house this morning at twelve o'clock. He should await us there at this very minute."

"What do you think," I ventured, glancing sideways at his face.

"I know this—that I am not satisfied."

"You think that it was he who blackmailed Mrs. Ferrars?"

"Either that, or——"

"Well?" I said, after waiting a minute or two.

"My friend, I will say this to you—I hope it was he."

The gravity of his manner, and something indefinable that tinged it, reduced me to silence.

On arrival at The Larches, we were informed that Parker was already there awaiting our return. As we entered the room, the butler rose respectfully.

"Good morning, Parker," said Poirot pleasantly. "One instant, I pray of you."

He removed his overcoat and gloves.

"Allow me, sir," said Parker, and sprang forward to assist him. He deposited the articles neatly on a chair by the door. Poirot watched him with approval.

"Thank you, my good Parker," he said. "Take a seat, will you not? What I have to say may take some time."

Parker seated himself with an apologetic bend of the head.

"Now what do you think I asked you to come here for this morning—eh?"

Parker coughed.

"I understood, sir, that you wished to ask me a few questions about my late master—private like."

"*Précisément*," said Poirot, beaming. "Have you made many experiments in blackmail?"

"Sir!"

The butler sprang to his feet.

"Do not excite yourself," said Poirot placidly. "Do not play the farce of the honest, injured man. You know all there is to know about the blackmail, is it not so?"

"Sir, I—I've never—never been——"

"Insulted," suggested Poirot, "in such a way before. Then why, my excellent Parker, were you so anxious to overhear the conversation in Mr. Ackroyd's study the other evening, after you had caught the word blackmail?"

"I wasn't—I——"

"Who was your last master?" rapped out Poirot suddenly.

"My last master?"

"Yes, the master you were with before you came to Mr. Ackroyd."

"A Major Ellerby, sir——"

Poirot took the words out of his mouth.

"Just so, Major Ellerby. Major Ellerby was addicted to drugs, was he not? You traveled about with him. When he was in Bermuda there was some trouble—a man was killed. Major Ellerby was partly responsible. It was hushed up. But you knew about it. How much did Major Ellerby pay you to keep your mouth shut?"

Parker was staring at him open-mouthed. The man had gone to pieces, his cheeks shook flabbily.

"You see, me, I have made inquiries," said Poirot pleasantly. "It is as I say. You got a good sum then as blackmail, and Major Ellerby went on paying you until he died. Now I want to hear about your latest experiment."

Parker still stared.

"It is useless to deny. Hercule Poirot *knows*. It is so, what I have said about Major Ellerby, is it not?"

As though against his will, Parker nodded reluctantly once. His face was ashen pale.

"But I never hurt a hair of Mr. Ackroyd's head," he moaned. "Honest to God, sir, I didn't. I've been afraid of this coming all the time. And I tell you I didn't—I didn't kill him."

His voice rose almost to a scream.

"I am inclined to believe you, my friend," said Poirot. "You have not the nerve—the courage. But I must have the truth."

"I'll tell you anything, sir, anything you want to know. It's true that I tried to listen that night. A word or two I heard made me curious. And Mr. Ackroyd's wanting not to be disturbed, and shutting himself up with the doctor the way he did. It's God's own truth what I told the police. I heard the word blackmail, sir, and well——"

He paused.

"You thought there might be something in it for you?" suggested Poirot smoothly.

"Well—well, yes, I did, sir. I thought that if Mr. Ackroyd was being blackmailed, why shouldn't I have a share of the pickings?"

A very curious expression passed over Poirot's face. He leaned forward.

"Had you any reason to suppose before that night that Mr. Ackroyd was being blackmailed?"

"No, indeed, sir. It was a great surprise to me. Such a regular gentleman in all his habits."

"How much did you overhear?"

"Not very much, sir. There seemed what I might call a spite against me. Of course I had to attend to my duties in the pantry. And when I did creep along once or twice to the study it was no use. The first time Dr. Sheppard came out and almost caught me in the act, and another time Mr. Raymond passed me in the big hall and went that way, so I knew it was no use; and when I went with the tray, Miss Flora headed me off."

Poirot stared for a long time at the man, as if to test his sincerity. Parker returned his gaze earnestly.

"I hope you believe me, sir. I've been afraid all along the police would rake up that old business with Major Ellerby and be suspicious of me in consequence."

"*Eh bien*," said Poirot at last. "I am disposed to believe you. But there is one thing I must request of you—to show me your bank-book. You have a bank-book, I presume?"

"Yes, sir, as a matter of fact, I have it with me now."

With no sign of confusion, he produced it from his pocket. Poirot took the slim, green-covered book and perused the entries.

"Ah! I perceive you have purchased £500 of National Savings Certificates this year?"

"Yes, sir. I have already over a thousand pounds saved—the result of my connection with—er—my late master, Major Ellerby. And I have had quite a little flutter on some horses this year—very successful. If you remember, sir, a rank outsider won the Jubilee. I was fortunate enough to back it—£20."

Poirot handed him back the book.

"I will wish you good-morning. I believe that you have told me the truth. If you have not—so much the worse for you, my friend."

When Parker had departed, Poirot picked up his overcoat once more.

"Going out again?" I asked.

"Yes, we will pay a little visit to the good M. Hammond."

"You believe Parker's story?"

"It is credible enough on the face of it. It seems clear that—unless he is a very good actor indeed—he genuinely believes it was Ackroyd himself who was the victim of blackmail. If so, he knows nothing at all about the Mrs. Ferrars business."

"Then in that case—who——"

"*Précisément!* Who? But our visit to M. Hammond will accomplish one purpose. It will either clear Parker completely or else——"

"Well?"

"I fall into the bad habit of leaving my sentences unfinished this morning," said Poirot apologetically. "You must bear with me."

"By the way," I said, rather sheepishly, "I've got a confession to make. I'm afraid I have inadvertently let out something about that ring."

"What ring?"

"The ring you found in the goldfish pond."

"Ah! yes," said Poirot, smiling broadly.

"I hope you're not annoyed? It was very careless of me."

"But not at all, my good friend, not at all. I laid no commands upon you. You were at liberty to speak of it if you so wished. She was interested, your sister?"

"She was indeed. It created a sensation. All sorts of theories are flying about."

"Ah! And yet it is so simple. The true explanation leapt to the eye, did it not?"

"Did it?" I said dryly.

Poirot laughed.

"The wise man does not commit himself," he observed. "Is not that so? But here we are at Mr. Hammond's."

The lawyer was in his office, and we were ushered in without any delay. He rose and greeted us in his dry, precise manner.

Poirot came at once to the point.

"Monsieur, I desire from you certain information, that is, if you will be so good as to give it to me. You acted, I understand, for the late Mrs. Ferrars of King's Paddock?"

I noticed the swift gleam of surprise which showed in the lawyer's eyes, before his professional reserve came down once more like a mask over his face.

"Certainly. All her affairs passed through our hands."

"Very good. Now, before I ask you to tell me anything, I should like you to listen to the story Dr. Sheppard will relate to you. You have no objection, have you, my friend, to repeating the conversation you had with Mr. Ackroyd last Friday night?"

"Not in the least," I said, and straightway began the recital of that strange evening. Hammond listened with close attention.

"That is all," I said, when I had finished.

"Blackmail," said the lawyer thoughtfully.

"You are surprised?" asked Poirot.

The lawyer took off his pince-nez and polished them with his handkerchief.

"No," he replied, "I can hardly say that I am surprised. I have suspected something of the kind for some time."

"That brings us," said Poirot, "to the information for which I am asking. If any one can give us an idea of the actual sums paid, you are the man, monsieur."

"I see no object in withholding the information," said Hammond, after a moment or two. "During the past year, Mrs. Ferrars has sold out certain securities, and the money for them was paid into her account and not reinvested. As her income was a large one, and she lived very quietly after her husband's death, it seems certain that these sums of money were paid away for some special purpose. I once sounded her on the subject, and she said that she was obliged to support several of her husband's poor relations. I let the matter drop, of course. Until now, I have always imagined that the money was paid to some woman who had had a claim on Ashley Ferrars. I never dreamed that Mrs. Ferrars herself was involved."

"And the amount?" asked Poirot.

"In all, I should say the various sums totaled at least twenty thousand pounds."

"Twenty thousand pounds!" I exclaimed. "In one year!"

"Mrs. Ferrars was a very wealthy woman," said Poirot dryly. "And the penalty for murder is not a pleasant one."

"Is there anything else that I can tell you?" inquired Mr. Hammond.

"I thank you, no," said Poirot, rising. "All my excuses for having deranged you."

"Not at all, not at all."

"The word derange," I remarked, when we were outside again, "is applicable to mental disorder only."

"Ah!" cried Poirot, "never will my English be quite perfect. A curious language. I should then have said disarranged, *n'est-ce pas*?"

"Disturbed is the word you had in mind."

"I thank you, my friend. The word exact, you are zealous for it. *Eh bien*, what about our friend Parker now? With twenty thousand pounds in hand, would he have continued being a butler? *Je ne pense pas*. It is, of course, possible that he banked the money under another name, but I am disposed to believe he spoke the truth to us.

If he is a scoundrel, he is a scoundrel on a mean scale. He has not the big ideas. That leaves us as a possibility, Raymond, or—well—Major Blunt."

"Surely not Raymond," I objected. "Since we know that he was desperately hard up for a matter of five hundred pounds."

"That is what he says, yes."

"And as to Hector Blunt——"

"I will tell you something as to the good Major Blunt," interrupted Poirot. "It is my business to make inquiries. I make them. *Eh bien*—that legacy of which he speaks, I have discovered that the amount of it was close upon twenty thousand pounds. What do you think of that?"

I was so taken aback that I could hardly speak.

"It's impossible," I said at last. "A well-known man like Hector Blunt."

Poirot shrugged his shoulders.

"Who knows? At least he is a man with big ideas. I confess that I hardly see him as a blackmailer, but there is another possibility that you have not even considered."

"What is that?"

"The fire, my friend. Ackroyd himself may have destroyed that letter, blue envelope and all, after you left him."

"I hardly think that likely," I said slowly. "And yet—of course, it may be so. He might have changed his mind."

We had just arrived at my house, and on the spur of the moment I invited Poirot to come in and take pot luck.

I thought Caroline would be pleased with me, but it is hard to satisfy one's women folk. It appears that we were eating chops for lunch—the kitchen staff being regaled on tripe and onions. And two chops set before three people are productive of embarrassment.

But Caroline is seldom daunted for long. With magnificent mendacity, she explained to Poirot that although James laughed at her for doing so, she adhered strictly to a vegetarian diet. She descanted ecstatically on the delights of nut cutlets (which I am quite sure she has never tasted) and ate a Welsh rarebit with gusto and frequent cutting remarks as to the dangers of "flesh" foods.

Afterwards, when we were sitting in front of the fire and smoking, Caroline attacked Poirot directly.

"Not found Ralph Paton yet?" she asked.

"Where should I find him, mademoiselle?"

"I thought, perhaps, you'd found him in Cranchester," said Caroline, with intense meaning in her tone.

Poirot looked merely bewildered.

"In Cranchester? But why in Cranchester?"

I enlightened him with a touch of malice.

"One of our ample staff of private detectives happened to see you in a car on the Cranchester road yesterday," I explained.

Poirot's bewilderment vanished. He laughed heartily.

"Ah, that! A simple visit to the dentist, *c'est tout*. My tooth, it aches. I go there. My tooth, it is at once better. I think to return quickly. The dentist, he says No. Better to have it out. I argue. He insists. He has his way! That particular tooth, it will never ache again."

Caroline collapsed rather like a pricked balloon.

We fell to discussing Ralph Paton.

"A weak nature," I insisted. "But not a vicious one."

"Ah!" said Poirot. "But weakness, where does it end?"

"Exactly," said Caroline. "Take James here—weak as water, if I weren't about to look after him."

"My dear Caroline," I said irritably, "can't you talk without dragging in personalities?"

"You *are* weak, James," said Caroline, quite unmoved. "I'm eight years older than you are—oh! I don't mind M. Poirot knowing that——"

"I should never have guessed it, mademoiselle," said Poirot, with a gallant little bow.

"Eight years older. But I've always considered it my duty to look after you. With a bad bringing up, Heaven knows what mischief you might have got into by now."

"I might have married a beautiful adventuress," I murmured, gazing at the ceiling, and blowing smoke rings.

"Adventuress!" said Caroline, with a snort. "If we're talking of adventuresses——"

She left the sentence unfinished.

"Well?" I said, with some curiosity.

"Nothing. But I can think of some one not a hundred miles away."

Then she turned to Poirot suddenly.

"James sticks to it that you believe some one in the house committed the murder. All I can say is, you're wrong."

"I should not like to be wrong," said Poirot. "It is not—how do you say—my *métier*?"

"I've got the facts pretty clearly," continued Caroline, taking no notice of Poirot's remark, "from James and others. As far as I can see, of the people in the house, only two *could* have had the chance of doing it. Ralph Paton and Flora Ackroyd."

"My dear Caroline——"

"Now, James, don't interrupt me. I know what I'm talking about. Parker met her *outside* the door, didn't he? He didn't hear her uncle saying good-night to her. She could have killed him then and there."

"Caroline."

"I'm not saying she *did*, James. I'm saying she *could* have done. As a matter of fact, though Flora is like all these young girls nowadays, with no veneration for their betters and thinking they know best on every subject under the sun, I don't for a minute believe she'd kill even a chicken. But there it is. Mr. Raymond and Major Blunt have alibis. Mrs. Ackroyd's got an alibi. Even that Russell woman seems to have one—and a good job for her it is she has. Who is left? Only Ralph and Flora! And say what you will, I don't believe Ralph Paton is a murderer. A boy we've known all our lives."

Poirot was silent for a minute, watching the curling smoke rise from his cigarette. When at last he spoke, it was in a gentle far-away voice that produced a curious impression. It was totally unlike his usual manner.

"Let us take a man—a very ordinary man. A man with no idea of murder in his heart. There is in him somewhere a strain of weakness—deep down. It has so far never been called into play. Perhaps it never will be—and if so he will go to his grave honored and respected by every one. But let us suppose that something occurs. He is in difficulties—or perhaps not that even. He may stumble by accident on a secret—a secret involving life or death to some one. And his first impulse will be to speak out—to do his duty as an honest citizen. And then the strain of weakness tells. Here is a chance of money—a great amount of money. He wants money—he desires it—and it is so easy. He has to do nothing for it—just keep silence. That is the beginning. The desire for money grows. He must have more—and more! He is intoxicated by the gold mine which has opened at his feet. He becomes greedy. And in his greed he overreaches himself. One can press a man as far as one likes—but with a woman one must not press too far. For a woman has at heart a great desire to speak the truth. How many husbands who have deceived their wives go comfortably to their graves, carrying their secret with them! How many wives who have deceived their husbands wreck their lives by throwing the fact in those same husbands' teeth! They have been pressed too far. In a reckless moment (which they will afterwards regret, *bien entendu*) they fling safety to the winds and turn at bay, proclaiming the truth with great momentary satisfaction to themselves. So it was, I think, in this case. The strain was too great. And so there came your proverb, the death of the goose that laid the golden eggs. But that is not the end. Exposure faced the man of whom we are speaking. And he is not the same man he was—say, a year ago. His moral fiber is blunted. He is desperate. He is fighting a losing battle, and he is prepared to take any means that come to his hand, for exposure means ruin to him. And so—the dagger strikes!"

He was silent for a moment. It was as though he had laid a spell upon the room. I cannot try to describe the impression his words produced. There was something in the merciless analysis, and the ruthless power of vision which struck fear into both of us.

"Afterwards," he went on softly, "the danger removed, he will be himself again, normal, kindly. But if the need again arises, then once more he will strike."

Caroline roused herself at last.

"You are speaking of Ralph Paton," she said. "You may be right, you may not, but you have no business to condemn a man unheard."

The telephone bell rang sharply. I went out into the hall, and took off the receiver.

"What?" I said. "Yes. Dr. Sheppard speaking."

I listened for a minute or two, then replied briefly. Replacing the receiver, I went back into the drawing-room.

"Poirot," I said, "they have detained a man at Liverpool. His name is Charles Kent, and he is believed to be the stranger who visited Fernly that night. They want me to go to Liverpool at once and identify him."

CHAPTER XVIII

CHARLES KENT

HALF an hour later saw Poirot, myself, and Inspector Raglan in the train on the way to Liverpool. The inspector was clearly very excited.

"We may get a line on the blackmailing part of the business, if on nothing else," he declared jubilantly. "He's a rough customer, this fellow, by what I heard over the phone. Takes dope, too. We ought to find it easy to get what we want out of him. If there was the shadow of a motive, nothing's more likely than that he killed Mr. Ackroyd. But in that case, why is young Paton keeping out of the way? The whole thing's a muddle—that's what it is. By the way, M. Poirot, you were quite right about those fingerprints. They were Mr. Ackroyd's own. I had rather the same idea myself, but I dismissed it as hardly feasible."

I smiled to myself. Inspector Raglan was so very plainly saving his face.

"As regards this man," said Poirot, "he is not yet arrested, eh?"

"No, detained under suspicion."

"And what account does he give of himself?"

"Precious little," said the inspector, with a grin. "He's a wary bird, I gather. A lot of abuse, but very little more."

On arrival at Liverpool I was surprised to find that Poirot was welcomed with acclamation. Superintendent Hayes, who met us, had worked with Poirot over some case long ago, and had evidently an exaggerated opinion of his powers.

"Now we've got M. Poirot here we shan't be long," he said cheerfully. "I thought you'd retired, moosior?"

"So I had, my good Hayes, so I had. But how tedious is retirement! You cannot imagine to yourself the monotony with which day comes after day."

"Very likely. So you've come to have a look at our own particular find? Is this Dr. Sheppard? Think you'll be able to identify him, sir?"

"I'm not very sure," I said doubtfully.

"How did you get hold of him?" inquired Poirot.

"Description was circulated, as you know. In the press and privately. Not much to go on, I admit. This fellow has an American accent all right, and he doesn't deny that he was near King's Abbot that night. Just asks what the hell it is to do with us, and that he'll see us in —— before he answers any questions."

"Is it permitted that I, too, see him?" asked Poirot.

The superintendent closed one eye knowingly.

"Very glad to have you, sir. You've got permission to do anything you please. Inspector Japp of Scotland Yard was asking after you the other day. Said he'd heard you were connected unofficially with this case. Where's Captain Paton hiding, sir, can you tell me that?"

"I doubt if it would be wise at the present juncture," said Poirot primly, and I bit my lips to prevent a smile.

The little man really did it very well.

After some further parley, we were taken to interview the prisoner.

He was a young fellow, I should say not more than twenty-two or three. Tall, thin, with slightly shaking hands, and the evidences of considerable physical strength somewhat run to seed. His hair was dark, but his eyes were blue and shifty, seldom meeting a glance squarely. I had all along cherished the illusion that there was something familiar about the figure I had met that night, but if this were indeed he, I was completely mistaken. He did not remind me in the least of any one I knew.

"Now then, Kent," said the superintendent, "stand up. Here are some visitors come to see you. Recognize any of them."

Kent glared at us sullenly, but did not reply. I saw his glance waver over the three of us, and come back to rest on me.

"Well, sir," said the superintendent to me, "what do you say?"

"The height's the same," I said, "and as far as general appearance goes it might well be the man in question. Beyond that, I couldn't go."

"What the hell's the meaning of all this?" asked Kent. "What have you got against me? Come on, out with it! What am I supposed to have done?"

I nodded my head.

"It's the man," I said. "I recognize the voice."

"Recognize my voice, do you? Where do you think you heard it before?"

"On Friday evening last, outside the gates of Fernly Park. You asked me the way there."

"I did, did I?"

"Do you admit it?" asked the inspector.

"I don't admit anything. Not till I know what you've got on me."

"Have you not read the papers in the last few days?" asked Poirot, speaking for the first time.

The man's eyes narrowed.

"So that's it, is it? I saw an old gent had been croaked at Fernly. Trying to make out I did the job, are you?"

"You were there that night," said Poirot quietly.

"How do you know, mister?"

"By this." Poirot took something from his pocket and held it out.

It was the goose quill we had found in the summer-house.

At the sight of it the man's face changed. He half held out his hand.

"Snow," said Poirot thoughtfully. "No, my friend, it is empty. It lay where you dropped it in the summer-house that night."

Charles Kent looked at him uncertainly.

"You seem to know a hell of a lot about everything, you little foreign cock duck. Perhaps you remember this: the papers say that the old gent was croaked between a quarter to ten and ten o'clock?"

"That is so," agreed Poirot.

"Yes, but is it really so? That's what I'm getting at."

"This gentleman will tell you," said Poirot.

He indicated Inspector Raglan. The latter hesitated, glanced at Superintendent Hayes, then at Poirot, and finally, as though receiving sanction, he said:—

"That's right. Between a quarter to ten and ten o'clock."

"Then you've nothing to keep me here for," said Kent. "I was away from Fernly Park by twenty-five minutes past nine. You can ask at the Dog and Whistle. That's a saloon about a mile out of Fernly on the road to Cranchester. I kicked up a bit of a row there, I remember. As near as nothing to quarter to ten, it was. How about that?"

Inspector Raglan wrote down something in his notebook.

"Well?" demanded Kent.

"Inquiries will be made," said the inspector. "If you've spoken the truth, you won't have anything to complain about. What were you doing at Fernly Park anyway?"

"Went there to meet some one."

"Who?"

"That's none of your business."

"You'd better keep a civil tongue in your head, my man," the superintendent warned him.

"To hell with a civil tongue. I went there on my own business, and that's all there is to it. If I was clear away before the murder was done, that's all that concerns the cops."

"Your name, it is Charles Kent," said Poirot. "Where were you born?"

The man stared at him, then he grinned.

"I'm a full-blown Britisher all right," he said.

"Yes," said Poirot meditatively, "I think you are. I fancy you were born in Kent."

The man stared.

"Why's that? Because of my name? What's that to do with it? Is a man whose name is Kent bound to be born in that particular county?"

"Under certain circumstances, I can imagine he might be," said Poirot very deliberately. "Under certain circumstances, you comprehend."

There was so much meaning in his voice as to surprise the two police officers. As for Charles Kent, he flushed a brick red, and for a moment I thought he was going to spring at Poirot. He thought better of it, however, and turned away with a kind of laugh.

Poirot nodded as though satisfied, and made his way out through the door. He was joined presently by the two officers.

"We'll verify that statement," remarked Raglan. "I don't think he's lying, though. But he's got to come clear with a statement as to what he was doing at Fernly. It looks to me as though we'd got our blackmailer all right. On the other hand, granted his story's correct, he couldn't have had anything to do with the actual murder. He'd got ten pounds on him when he was arrested—rather a large sum. I fancy that forty pounds went to him—the numbers of the notes didn't correspond, but of course he'd have changed them first thing. Mr. Ackroyd must have given him the money, and he made off with it as fast as possible. What was that about Kent being his birthplace? What's that got to do with it?"

"Nothing whatever," said Poirot mildly. "A little idea of mine, that was all. Me, I am famous for my little ideas."

"Are you really?" said Raglan, studying him with a puzzled expression.

The superintendent went into a roar of laughter.

"Many's the time I've heard Inspector Japp say that. M. Poirot and his little ideas! Too fanciful for me, he'd say, but always something in them."

"You mock yourself at me," said Poirot, smiling; "but never mind. The old ones they laugh last sometimes, when the young, clever ones do not laugh at all."

And nodding his head at them in a sage manner, he walked out into the street.

He and I lunched together at an hotel. I know now that the whole thing lay clearly unravelled before him. He had got the last thread he needed to lead him to the truth.

But at the time I had no suspicion of the fact. I overestimated his general self-confidence, and I took it for granted that the things which puzzled me must be equally puzzling to him.

My chief puzzle was what the man Charles Kent could have been doing at Fernly. Again and again I put the question to myself and could get no satisfactory reply.

At last I ventured a tentative query to Poirot. His reply was immediate.

"*Mon ami*, I do not think; I know."

"Really?" I said incredulously.

"Yes, indeed. I suppose now that to you it would not make sense if I said that he went to Fernly that night because he was born in Kent?"

I stared at him.

"It certainly doesn't seem to make sense to me," I said dryly.

"Ah!" said Poirot pityingly. "Well, no matter. I have still my little idea."

CHAPTER XIX
FLORA ACKROYD

As I was returning from my round the following morning, I was hailed by Inspector Raglan. I pulled up, and the inspector mounted on the step.

"Good-morning, Dr. Sheppard," he said. "Well, that alibi is all right enough."

"Charles Kent's?"

"Charles Kent's. The barmaid at the Dog and Whistle, Sally Jones, she remembers him perfectly. Picked out his photograph from among five others. It was just a quarter to ten when he came into the bar, and the Dog and Whistle is well over a mile from Fernly Park. The girl mentions that he had a lot of money on him—she saw him take a handful of notes out of his pocket. Rather surprised her, it did, seeing the class of fellow he was, with a pair of boots clean dropping off him. That's where that forty pounds went right enough."

"The man still refuses to give an account of his visit to Fernly?"

"Obstinate as a mule he is. I had a chat with Hayes at Liverpool over the wire this morning."

"Hercule Poirot says he knows the reason the man went there that night," I observed.

"Does he?" cried the inspector eagerly.

"Yes," I said maliciously. "He says he went there because he was born in Kent."

I felt a distinct pleasure in passing on my own discomfiture.

Raglan stared at me for a moment or two uncomprehendingly. Then a grin overspread his weaselly countenance and he tapped his forehead significantly.

"Bit gone here," he said. "I've thought so for some time. Poor old chap, so that's why he had to give up and come down here. In the family, very likely. He's got a nephew who's quite off his crumpet."

"Poirot has?" I said, very surprised.

"Yes. Hasn't he ever mentioned him to you? Quite docile, I believe, and all that, but mad as a hatter, poor lad."

"Who told you that?"

Again a grin showed itself on Inspector Raglan's face.

"Your sister, Miss Sheppard, she told me all about it."

Really, Caroline is amazing. She never rests until she knows the last details of everybody's family secrets. Unfortunately, I have never been able to instill into her the decency of keeping them to herself.

"Jump in, inspector," I said, opening the door of the car. "We'll go up to The Larches together, and acquaint our Belgian friend with the latest news."

"Might as well, I suppose. After all, even if he is a bit balmy, it was a useful tip he gave me about those fingerprints. He's got a bee in his bonnet about the man Kent, but who knows—there may be something useful behind it."

Poirot received us with his usual smiling courtesy.

He listened to the information we had brought him, nodding his head now and then.

"Seems quite O.K., doesn't it?" said the inspector rather gloomily. "A chap can't be murdering some one in one place when he's drinking in the bar in another place a mile away."

"Are you going to release him?"

"Don't see what else we can do. We can't very well hold him for obtaining money on false pretences. Can't prove a ruddy thing."

The inspector tossed a match into the grate in a disgruntled fashion. Poirot retrieved it and put it neatly in a little receptacle designed for the purpose. His action was purely mechanical. I could see that his thoughts were on something very different.

"If I were you," he said at last, "I should not release the man Charles Kent yet."

"What do you mean?"

Raglan stared at him.

"What I say. I should not release him yet."

"You don't think he can have had anything to do with the murder, do you?"

"I think probably not—but one cannot be certain yet."

"But haven't I just told you———"

Poirot raised a hand protestingly.

"*Mais oui, mais oui.* I heard. I am not deaf—nor stupid, thank the good God! But see you, you approach the matter from the wrong—the wrong—premises, is not that the word?"

The inspector stared at him heavily.

"I don't see how you make that out. Look here, we know Mr. Ackroyd was alive at a quarter to ten. You admit that, don't you?"

Poirot looked at him for a moment, then shook his head with a quick smile.

"I admit nothing that is not—*proved*!"

"Well, we've got proof enough of that. We've got Miss Flora Ackroyd's evidence."

"That she said good-night to her uncle? But me—I do not always believe what a young lady tells me—no, not even when she is charming and beautiful."

"But hang it all, man, Parker saw her coming out of the door."

"No." Poirot's voice rang out with sudden sharpness. "That is just what he did not see. I satisfied myself of that by a little experiment the other day—you remember, doctor? Parker saw her *outside* the door, with her hand on the handle. He did not see her come out of the room."

"But—where else could she have been?"

"Perhaps on the stairs."

"The stairs?"

"That is my little idea—yes."

"But those stairs only lead to Mr. Ackroyd's bedroom."

"Precisely."

And still the inspector stared.

"You think she'd been up to her uncle's bedroom? Well, why not? Why should she lie about it?"

"Ah! that is just the question. It depends on what she was doing there, does it not?"

"You mean—the money? Hang it all, you don't suggest that it was Miss Ackroyd who took that forty pounds?"

"I suggest nothing," said Poirot. "But I will remind you of this. Life was not very easy for that mother and daughter. There were bills—there was constant trouble over small sums of money. Roger Ackroyd was a peculiar man over money matters. The girl might be at her wit's end for a comparatively small sum. Figure to yourself then what happens. She has taken the money, she descends the little staircase. When she is half-way down she hears the chink of glass from the hall. She has not a doubt of what it is—Parker coming to the study. At all costs she must not be found on the stairs—Parker will not forget it, he will think it odd. If the money is missed, Parker is sure to remember having seen her come down those stairs. She has just time to rush down to the study door—with her hand on the handle to show that she has just come out, when Parker appears in the doorway. She says the first thing that comes into her head, a repetition of Roger Ackroyd's orders earlier in the evening, and then goes upstairs to her own room."

"Yes, but later," persisted the inspector, "she must have realized the vital importance of speaking the truth? Why, the whole case hinges on it!"

"Afterwards," said Poirot dryly, "it was a little difficult for Mademoiselle Flora. She is told simply that the police are here and that there has been a robbery. Naturally she jumps to the conclusion that the theft of the money has been discovered. Her one idea is to stick to her story. When she learns that her uncle is dead she is panic-stricken. Young women do not faint nowadays, monsieur, without considerable provocation. *Eh bien!* there it is. She is bound to stick to her story, or else confess everything. And a young and pretty girl does not like to admit that she is a thief—especially before those whose esteem she is anxious to retain."

Raglan brought his fist down with a thump on the table.

"I'll not believe it," he said. "It's—it's not credible. And you—you've known this all along?"

"The possibility has been in my mind from the first," admitted Poirot. "I was always convinced that Mademoiselle Flora was hiding something from us. To satisfy myself, I made the little experiment I told you of. Dr. Sheppard accompanied me."

"A test for Parker, you said it was," I remarked bitterly.

"*Mon ami*," said Poirot apologetically, "as I told you at the time, one must say something."

The inspector rose.

"There's only one thing for it," he declared. "We must tackle the young lady right away. You'll come up to Fernly with me, M. Poirot?"

"Certainly. Dr. Sheppard will drive us up in his car."

I acquiesced willingly.

On inquiry for Miss Ackroyd, we were shown into the billiard room. Flora and Major Hector Blunt were sitting on the long window seat.

"Good-morning, Miss Ackroyd," said the inspector. "Can we have a word or two alone with you?"

Blunt got up at once and moved to the door.

"What is it?" asked Flora nervously. "Don't go, Major Blunt. He can stay, can't he?" she asked, turning to the inspector.

"That's as you like," said the inspector dryly. "There's a question or two it's my duty to put to you, miss, but I'd prefer to do so privately, and I dare say you'd prefer it also."

Flora looked keenly at him. I saw her face grow whiter. Then she turned and spoke to Blunt.

"I want you to stay—please—yes, I mean it. Whatever the inspector has to say to me, I'd rather you heard it."

Raglan shrugged his shoulders.

"Well, if you will have it so, that's all there is to it. Now, Miss Ackroyd, M. Poirot here has made a certain suggestion to me. He suggests that you weren't in the study at all last Friday night, that you never saw Mr. Ackroyd to say good-night to him, that instead of being in the study you were on the stairs leading down from your uncle's bedroom when you heard Parker coming across the hall."

Flora's gaze shifted to Poirot. He nodded back at her.

"Mademoiselle, the other day, when we sat round the table, I implored you to be frank with me. What one does not tell to Papa Poirot he finds out. It was that, was it not? See, I will make it easy for you. You took the money, did you not?"

"The money," said Blunt sharply.

There was a silence which lasted for at least a minute.

Then Flora drew herself up and spoke.

"M. Poirot is right. I took that money. I stole. I am a thief—yes, a common, vulgar little thief. Now you know! I am glad it has come out. It's been a nightmare, these last few days!" She sat down suddenly and buried her face in her hands. She spoke huskily through her fingers. "You don't know what my life has been since I came here. Wanting things, scheming for them, lying, cheating, running up bills, promising to pay—oh! I hate myself when I think of it all! That's what brought us together, Ralph and I. We were both weak! I understood him, and I was sorry—because I'm the same underneath. We're not strong enough to stand alone, either of us. We're weak, miserable, despicable things."

She looked at Blunt and suddenly stamped her foot.

"Why do you look at me like that—as though you couldn't believe? I may be a thief—but at any rate I'm real now. I'm not lying any more. I'm not pretending to be the kind of girl you like, young and innocent and simple. I don't care if you never want to see me again. I hate myself, despise myself—but you've got to believe one thing, if speaking the truth would have made things better for Ralph, I would have spoken out. But I've seen all along that it wouldn't be better for Ralph—it makes the case against him blacker than ever. I was not doing him any harm by sticking to my lie."

"Ralph," said Blunt. "I see—always Ralph."

"You don't understand," said Flora hopelessly. "You never will."

She turned to the inspector.

"I admit everything; I was at my wit's end for money. I never saw my uncle that evening after he left the dinner-table. As to the money, you can take what steps you please. Nothing could be worse than it is now!"

Suddenly she broke down again, hid her face in her hands, and rushed from the room.

"Well," said the inspector in a flat tone, "so that's that."

He seemed rather at a loss what to do next.

Blunt came forward.

"Inspector Raglan," he said quietly, "that money was given to me by Mr. Ackroyd for a special purpose. Miss Ackroyd never touched it. When she says she did, she is lying with the idea of shielding Captain Paton. The truth is as I said, and I am prepared to go into the witness box and swear to it."

He made a kind of jerky bow, then turning abruptly, he left the room.

Poirot was after him in a flash. He caught the other up in the hall.

"Monsieur—a moment, I beg of you, if you will be so good."

"Well, sir?"

Blunt was obviously impatient. He stood frowning down on Poirot.

"It is this," said Poirot rapidly: "I am not deceived by your little fantasy. No, indeed. It was truly Miss Flora who took the money. All the same it is well imagined what you say—it pleases me. It is very good what you have done there. You are a man quick to think and to act."

"I'm not in the least anxious for your opinion, thank you," said Blunt coldly.

He made once more as though to pass on, but Poirot, not at all offended, laid a detaining hand on his arm.

"Ah! but you are to listen to me. I have more to say. The other day I spoke of concealments. Very well, all along have I seen what you are concealing. Mademoiselle Flora, you love her with all your heart. From the first moment you saw her, is it not so? Oh! let us not mind saying these things—why must one in England think it necessary to mention love as though it were some disgraceful secret? You love Mademoiselle Flora. You seek to conceal that fact from all the world. That is very good—that is as it should be. But take the advice of Hercule Poirot—do not conceal it from mademoiselle herself."

Blunt had shown several signs of restlessness whilst Poirot was speaking, but the closing words seemed to rivet his attention.

"What d'you mean by that?" he said sharply.

"You think that she loves the Capitaine Ralph Paton—but I, Hercule Poirot, tell you that that is not so. Mademoiselle Flora accepted Captain Paton to please her uncle, and because she saw in the marriage a way of escape from her life here which was becoming frankly insupportable to her. She liked him, and there was much sympathy and understanding between them. But love—no! It is not Captain Paton Mademoiselle Flora loves."

"What the devil do you mean?" asked Blunt.

I saw the dark flush under his tan.

"You have been blind, monsieur. Blind! She is loyal, the little one. Ralph Paton is under a cloud, she is bound in honor to stick by him."

I felt it was time I put in a word to help on the good work.

"My sister told me the other night," I said encouragingly, "that Flora had never cared a penny piece for Ralph Paton, and never would. My sister is always right about these things."

Blunt ignored my well-meant efforts. He spoke to Poirot.

"D'you really think——" he began, and stopped.

He is one of those inarticulate men who find it hard to put things into words. Poirot knows no such disability.

"If you doubt me, ask her yourself, monsieur. But perhaps you no longer care to—the affair of the money——"

Blunt gave a sound like an angry laugh.

"Think I'd hold that against her? Roger was always a queer chap about money. She got in a mess and didn't dare tell him. Poor kid. Poor lonely kid."

Poirot looked thoughtfully at the side door.

"Mademoiselle Flora went into the garden, I think," he murmured.

"I've been every kind of a fool," said Blunt abruptly. "Rum conversation we've been having. Like one of those Danish plays. But you're a sound fellow, M. Poirot. Thank you."

He took Poirot's hand and gave it a grip which caused the other to wince in anguish. Then he strode to the side door and passed out into the garden.

"Not every kind of a fool," murmured Poirot, tenderly nursing the injured member. "Only one kind—the fool in love."

CHAPTER XX
MISS RUSSELL

INSPECTOR RAGLAN had received a bad jolt. He was not deceived by Blunt's valiant lie any more than we had been. Our way back to the village was punctuated by his complaints.

"This alters everything, this does. I don't know whether you've realized it, Monsieur Poirot?"

"I think so, yes, I think so," said Poirot. "You see, me, I have been familiar with the idea for some time."

Inspector Raglan, who had only had the idea presented to him a short half-hour ago, looked at Poirot unhappily, and went on with his discoveries.

"Those alibis now. Worthless! Absolutely worthless. Got to start again. Find out what every one was doing from nine-thirty onwards. Nine-thirty—that's the time we've got to hang on to. You were quite right about the man Kent—we don't release *him* yet awhile. Let me see now—nine-forty-five at the Dog and Whistle. He might have got there in a quarter of an hour if he ran. It's just possible that it was *his* voice Mr. Raymond heard talking to Mr. Ackroyd—asking for money which Mr. Ackroyd refused. But one thing's clear—it wasn't he who sent the telephone message. The station is half a mile in the other direction—over a mile and a half from the Dog and Whistle, and he was at the Dog and Whistle until about ten minutes past ten. Dang that telephone call! We always come up against it."

"We do indeed," agreed Poirot. "It is curious."

"It's just possible that if Captain Paton climbed into his uncle's room and found him there murdered, *he* may have sent it. Got the wind up, thought he'd be accused, and cleared out. That's possible, isn't it?"

"Why should he have telephoned?"

"May have had doubts if the old man was really dead. Thought he'd get the doctor up there as soon as possible, but didn't want to give himself away. Yes, I say now, how's that for a theory? Something in that, I should say."

The inspector swelled his chest out importantly. He was so plainly delighted with himself that any words of ours would have been quite superfluous.

We arrived back at my house at this minute, and I hurried in to my surgery patients, who had all been waiting a considerable time, leaving Poirot to walk to the police station with the inspector.

Having dismissed the last patient, I strolled into the little room at the back of the house which I call my workshop—I am rather proud of the home-made wireless set I turned out. Caroline hates my workroom. I keep my tools there, and Annie is not allowed to wreak havoc with a dustpan and brush. I was just adjusting the interior of an alarm clock which had been denounced as wholly unreliable by the household, when the door opened and Caroline put her head in.

"Oh! there you are, James," she said, with deep disapproval. "M. Poirot wants to see you."

"Well," I said, rather irritably, for her sudden entrance had startled me and I had let go of a piece of delicate mechanism, "if he wants to see me, he can come in here."

"In here?" said Caroline.

"That's what I said—in here."

Caroline gave a sniff of disapproval and retired. She returned in a moment or two, ushering in Poirot, and then retired again, shutting the door with a bang.

"Aha! my friend," said Poirot, coming forward and rubbing his hands. "You have not got rid of me so easily, you see!"

"Finished with the inspector?" I asked.

"For the moment, yes. And you, you have seen all the patients?"

"Yes."

Poirot sat down and looked at me, tilting his egg-shaped head on one side, with the air of one who savors a very delicious joke.

"You are in error," he said at last. "You have still one patient to see."

"Not you?" I exclaimed in surprise.

"Ah, not me, *bien entendu*. Me, I have the health magnificent. No, to tell you the truth, it is a little *complot* of mine. There is some one I wish to see, you understand—and at the same time it is not necessary that the whole village should intrigue itself about the matter—which is what would happen if the lady were seen to come to my house—for it is a lady. But to you she has already come as a patient before."

"Miss Russell!" I exclaimed.

"*Précisément*. I wish much to speak with her, so I send her the little note and make the appointment in your surgery. You are not annoyed with me?"

"On the contrary," I said. "That is, presuming I am allowed to be present at the interview?"

"But naturally! In your own surgery!"

"You know," I said, throwing down the pincers I was holding, "it's extraordinarily intriguing, the whole thing. Every new development that arises is like the shake you give to a kaleidoscope—the thing changes entirely in aspect. Now, why are you so anxious to see Miss Russell?"

Poirot raised his eyebrows.

"Surely it is obvious?" he murmured.

"There you go again," I grumbled. "According to you everything is obvious. But you leave me walking about in a fog."

Poirot shook his head genially at me.

"You mock yourself at me. Take the matter of Mademoiselle Flora. The inspector was surprised—but you—you were not."

"I never dreamed of her being the thief," I expostulated.

"That—perhaps no. But I was watching your face and you were not—like Inspector Raglan—startled and incredulous."

I thought for a minute or two.

"Perhaps you are right," I said at last. "All along I've felt that Flora was keeping back something—so the truth, when it came, was subconsciously expected. It upset Inspector Raglan very much indeed, poor man."

"Ah! *pour ça, oui*! The poor man must rearrange all his ideas. I profited by his state of mental chaos to induce him to grant me a little favor."

"What was that?"

Poirot took a sheet of notepaper from his pocket. Some words were written on it, and he read them aloud.

"The police have, for some days, been seeking for Captain Ralph Paton, the nephew of Mr. Ackroyd of Fernly Park, whose death occurred under such tragic circumstances last Friday. Captain Paton has been found at Liverpool, where he was on the point of embarking for America."

He folded up the piece of paper again.

"That, my friend, will be in the newspapers to-morrow morning."

I stared at him, dumbfounded.

"But—but it isn't true! He's not at Liverpool!"

Poirot beamed on me.

"You have the intelligence so quick! No, he has not been found at Liverpool. Inspector Raglan was very loath to let me send this paragraph to the press, especially as I could not take him into my confidence. But I assured him most solemnly that very interesting results would follow its appearance in print, so he gave in, after stipulating that he was, on no account, to bear the responsibility."

I stared at Poirot. He smiled back at me.

"It beats me," I said at last, "what you expect to get out of that."

"You should employ your little gray cells," said Poirot gravely.

He rose and came across to the bench.

"It is that you have really the love of the machinery," he said, after inspecting the débris of my labors.

Every man has his hobby. I immediately drew Poirot's attention to my home-made wireless. Finding him sympathetic, I showed him one or two little inventions of my own—trifling things, but useful in the house.

"Decidedly," said Poirot, "you should be an inventor by trade, not a doctor. But I hear the bell—that is your patient. Let us go into the surgery."

Once before I had been struck by the remnants of beauty in the housekeeper's face. This morning I was struck anew. Very simply dressed in black, tall, upright and independent as ever, with her big dark eyes and an unwonted flush of color in her usually pale cheeks, I realized that as a girl she must have been startlingly handsome.

"Good-morning, mademoiselle," said Poirot. "Will you be seated? Dr. Sheppard is so kind as to permit me the use of his surgery for a little conversation I am anxious to have with you."

Miss Russell sat down with her usual composure. If she felt any inward agitation, it did not display itself in any outward manifestation.

"It seems a queer way of doing things, if you'll allow me to say so," she remarked.

"Miss Russell—I have news to give you."

"Indeed!"

"Charles Kent has been arrested at Liverpool."

Not a muscle of her face moved. She merely opened her eyes a trifle wider, and asked, with a tinge of defiance:

"Well, what of it?"

But at that moment it came to me—the resemblance that had haunted me all along, something familiar in the defiance of Charles Kent's manner. The two voices, one rough and coarse, the other painfully ladylike—were strangely the same in timbre. It was of Miss Russell that I had been reminded that night outside the gates of Fernly Park.

I looked at Poirot, full of my discovery, and he gave me an imperceptible nod.

In answer to Miss Russell's question, he threw out his hands in a thoroughly French gesture.

"I thought you might be interested, that is all," he said mildly.

"Well, I'm not particularly," said Miss Russell. "Who is this Charles Kent anyway?"

"He is a man, mademoiselle, who was at Fernly on the night of the murder."

"Really?"

"Fortunately for him, he has an alibi. At a quarter to ten he was at a public-house a mile from here."

"Lucky for him," commented Miss Russell.

"But we still do not know what he was doing at Fernly—who it was he went to meet, for instance."

"I'm afraid I can't help you at all," said the housekeeper politely. "Nothing came to *my* ears. If that is all——"

She made a tentative movement as though to rise. Poirot stopped her.

"It is not quite all," he said smoothly. "This morning fresh developments have arisen. It seems now that Mr. Ackroyd was murdered, not at a quarter to ten, but *before*. Between ten minutes to nine, when Dr. Sheppard left, and a quarter to ten."

I saw the color drain from the housekeeper's face, leaving it dead white. She leaned forward, her figure swaying.

"But Miss Ackroyd said—Miss Ackroyd said——"

"Miss Ackroyd has admitted that she was lying. She was never in the study at all that evening."

"Then——?"

"Then it would seem that in this Charles Kent we have the man we are looking for. He came to Fernly, can give no account of what he was doing there——"

"I can tell you what he was doing there. He never touched a hair of old Ackroyd's head—he never went near the study. He didn't do it, I tell you."

She was leaning forward. That iron self-control was broken through at last. Terror and desperation were in her face.

"M. Poirot! M. Poirot! Oh, do believe me."

Poirot got up and came to her. He patted her reassuringly on the shoulder.

"But yes—but yes, I will believe. I had to make you speak, you know."

For an instant suspicion flared up in her.

"Is what you said true?"

"That Charles Kent is suspected of the crime? Yes, that is true. You alone can save him, by telling the reason for his being at Fernly."

"He came to see me." She spoke in a low, hurried voice. "I went out to meet him——"

"In the summer-house, yes, I know."

"How do you know?"

"Mademoiselle, it is the business of Hercule Poirot to know things. I know that you went out earlier in the evening, that you left a message in the summer-house to say what time you would be there."

"Yes, I did. I had heard from him—saying he was coming. I dared not let him come to the house. I wrote to the address he gave me and said I would meet him in the summer-house, and described it to him so that he would be able to find it. Then I was afraid he might not wait there patiently, and I ran out and left a piece of paper to say I would be there about ten minutes past nine. I didn't want the servants to see me, so I slipped out through the drawing-room window. As I came back, I met Dr. Sheppard, and I fancied that he would think it queer. I was out of breath, for I had been running. I had no idea that he was expected to dinner that night."

She paused.

"Go on," said Poirot. "You went out to meet him at ten minutes past nine. What did you say to each other?"

"It's difficult. You see——"

"Mademoiselle," said Poirot, interrupting her, "in this matter I must have the whole truth. What you tell us need never go beyond these four walls. Dr. Sheppard will be discreet, and so shall I. See, I will help you. This Charles Kent, he is your son, is he not?"

She nodded. The color had flamed into her cheeks.

"No one has ever known. It was long ago—long ago—down in Kent. I was not married...."

"So you took the name of the county as a surname for him. I understand."

"I got work. I managed to pay for his board and lodging. I never told him that I was his mother. But he turned out badly, he drank, then took to drugs. I managed to pay his passage out to Canada. I didn't hear of him for a year or two. Then, somehow or other, he found out that I was his mother. He wrote asking me for money. Finally, I heard from him back in this country again. He was coming to see me at Fernly, he said. I dared not let him come to the house. I have always been considered so—so very respectable. If any one got an inkling—it would have been all up with my post as housekeeper. So I wrote to him in the way I have just told you."

"And in the morning you came to see Dr. Sheppard?"

"Yes. I wondered if something could be done. He was not a bad boy—before he took to drugs."

"I see," said Poirot. "Now let us go on with the story. He came that night to the summer-house?"

"Yes, he was waiting for me when I got there. He was very rough and abusive. I had brought with me all the money I had, and I gave it to him. We talked a little, and then he went away."

"What time was that?"

"It must have been between twenty and twenty-five minutes past nine. It was not yet half-past when I got back to the house."

"Which way did he go?"

"Straight out the same way he came, by the path that joined the drive just inside the lodge gates."

Poirot nodded.

"And you, what did you do?"

"I went back to the house. Major Blunt was walking up and down the terrace smoking, so I made a detour to get round to the side door. It was then just on half-past nine, as I tell you."

Poirot nodded again. He made a note or two in a microscopic pocket-book.

"I think that is all," he said thoughtfully.

"Ought I——" she hesitated. "Ought I to tell all this to Inspector Raglan?"

"It may come to that. But let us not be in a hurry. Let us proceed slowly, with due order and method. Charles Kent is not yet formally charged with murder. Circumstances may arise which will render your story unnecessary."

Miss Russell rose.

"Thank you very much, M. Poirot," she said. "You have been very kind—very kind indeed. You—you do believe me, don't you? That Charles had nothing to do with this wicked murder!"

"There seems no doubt that the man who was talking to Mr. Ackroyd in the library at nine-thirty could not possibly have been your son. Be of good courage, mademoiselle. All will yet be well."

Miss Russell departed. Poirot and I were left together.

"So that's that," I said. "Every time we come back to Ralph Paton. How did you manage to spot Miss Russell as the person Charles Kent came to meet? Did you notice the resemblance?"

"I had connected her with the unknown man long before we actually came face to face with him. As soon as we found that quill. The quill suggested dope, and I remembered your account of Miss Russell's visit to you. Then I found the article on cocaine in that morning's paper. It all seemed very clear. She had heard from some one that morning—some one addicted to drugs, she read the article in the paper, and she came to you to ask a few tentative questions. She mentioned cocaine, since the article in question was on cocaine. Then, when you seemed too interested, she switched hurriedly to the subject of detective stories and untraceable poisons. I suspected a son or a brother, or some other undesirable male relation. Ah! but I must go. It is the time of the lunch."

"Stay and lunch with us," I suggested.

Poirot shook his head. A faint twinkle came into his eye.

"Not again to-day. I should not like to force Mademoiselle Caroline to adopt a vegetarian diet two days in succession."

It occurred to me that there was not much which escaped Hercule Poirot.

CHAPTER XXI
THE PARAGRAPH IN THE PAPER

CAROLINE, of course, had not failed to see Miss Russell come to the surgery door. I had anticipated this, and had ready an elaborate account of the lady's bad knee. But Caroline was not in a cross-questioning mood. Her point of view was that she knew what Miss Russell had really come for and that *I* didn't.

"Pumping you, James," said Caroline. "Pumping you in the most shameless manner, I've not a doubt. It's no good interrupting. I dare say you hadn't the least idea she was doing it even. Men *are* so simple. She knows that you are in M. Poirot's confidence, and she wants to find out things. Do you know what I think, James?"

"I couldn't begin to imagine. You think so many extraordinary things."

"It's no good being sarcastic. I think Miss Russell knows more about Mr. Ackroyd's death than she is prepared to admit."

Caroline leaned back triumphantly in her chair.

"Do you really think so?" I said absently.

"You are very dull to-day, James. No animation about you. It's that liver of yours."

Our conversation then dealt with purely personal matters.

The paragraph inspired by Poirot duly appeared in our daily paper the next morning. I was in the dark as to its purpose, but its effect on Caroline was immense.

She began by stating, most untruly, that she had said as much all along. I raised my eyebrows, but did not argue. Caroline, however, must have felt a prick of conscience, for she went on:—

"I mayn't have actually mentioned Liverpool, but I knew he'd try to get away to America. That's what Crippen did."

"Without much success," I reminded her.

"Poor boy, and so they've caught him. I consider, James, that it's your duty to see that he isn't hung."

"What do you expect me to do?"

"Why, you're a medical man, aren't you? You've known him from a boy upwards. Not mentally responsible. That's the line to take, clearly. I read only the other day that they're very happy in Broadmoor—it's quite like a high-class club."

But Caroline's words had reminded me of something.

"I never knew that Poirot had an imbecile nephew?" I said curiously.

"Didn't you? Oh, he told me all about it. Poor lad. It's a great grief to all the family. They've kept him at home so far, but it's getting to such a pitch that they're afraid he'll have to go into some kind of institution."

"I suppose you know pretty well everything there is to know about Poirot's family by this time," I said, exasperated.

"Pretty well," said Caroline complacently. "It's a great relief to people to be able to tell all their troubles to some one."

"It might be," I said, "if they were ever allowed to do so spontaneously. Whether they enjoy having confidences screwed out of them by force is another matter."

Caroline merely looked at me with the air of a Christian martyr enjoying martyrdom.

"You are so self-contained, James," she said. "You hate speaking out, or parting with any information yourself, and you think everybody else must be just like you. I should hope that I never screw confidences out of anybody. For instance, if M. Poirot comes in this afternoon, as he said he might do, I shall not dream of asking him who it was arrived at his house early this morning."

"Early this morning?" I queried.

"Very early," said Caroline. "Before the milk came. I just happened to be looking out of the window—the blind was flapping. It was a man. He came in a closed car, and he was all muffled up. I couldn't get a glimpse of his face. But I will tell you *my* idea, and you'll see that I'm right."

"What's your idea?"

Caroline dropped her voice mysteriously.

"A Home Office expert," she breathed.

"A Home Office expert," I said, amazed. "My dear Caroline!"

"Mark my words, James, you'll see that I'm right. That Russell woman was here that morning after your poisons. Roger Ackroyd might easily have been poisoned in his food that night."

I laughed out loud.

"Nonsense," I cried. "He was stabbed in the neck. You know that as well as I do."

"After death, James," said Caroline; "to make a false clew."

"My good woman," I said, "I examined the body, and I know what I'm talking about. That wound wasn't inflicted after death—it was the cause of death, and you need make no mistake about it."

Caroline merely continued to look omniscient, which so annoyed me that I went on:—

"Perhaps you will tell me, Caroline, if I have a medical degree or if I have not?"

"You have the medical degree, I dare say, James—at least, I mean I know you have. But you've no imagination whatever."

"Having endowed you with a treble portion, there was none left over for me," I said dryly.

I was amused to notice Caroline's maneuvers that afternoon when Poirot duly arrived. My sister, without asking a direct question, skirted the subject of the mysterious guest in every way imaginable. By the twinkle in Poirot's eyes, I saw that he realized her object. He remained blandly impervious, and blocked her bowling so successfully that she herself was at a loss how to proceed.

Having, I suspect, quietly enjoyed the little game, he rose to his feet and suggested a walk.

"It is that I need to reduce the figure a little," he explained. "You will come with me, doctor? And perhaps later Miss Caroline will give us some tea."

"Delighted," said Caroline. "Won't your—er—guest come in also?"

"You are too kind," said Poirot. "But no, my friend reposes himself. Soon you must make his acquaintance."

"Quite an old friend of yours, so somebody told me," said Caroline, making one last valiant effort.

"Did they?" murmured Poirot. "Well, we must start."

Our tramp took us in the direction of Fernly. I had guessed beforehand that it might do so. I was beginning to understand Poirot's methods. Every little irrelevancy had a bearing upon the whole.

"I have a commission for you, my friend," he said at last. "To-night, at my house, I desire to have a little conference. You will attend, will you not?"

"Certainly," I said.

"Good. I need also all those in the house—that is to say: Mrs. Ackroyd, Mademoiselle Flora, Major Blunt, M. Raymond. I want you to be my ambassador. This little reunion is fixed for nine o'clock. You will ask them—yes?"

"With pleasure; but why not ask them yourself?"

"Because they will then put the questions: Why? What for? They will demand what my idea is. And, as you know, my friend, I much dislike to have to explain my little ideas until the time comes."

I smiled a little.

"My friend Hastings, he of whom I told you, used to say of me that I was the human oyster. But he was unjust. Of facts, I keep nothing to myself. But to every one his own interpretation of them."

"When do you want me to do this?"

"Now, if you will. We are close to the house."

"Aren't you coming in?"

"No, me, I will promenade myself in the grounds. I will rejoin you by the lodge gates in a quarter of an hour's time."

I nodded, and set off on my task. The only member of the family at home proved to be Mrs. Ackroyd, who was sipping an early cup of tea. She received me very graciously.

"So grateful to you, doctor," she murmured, "for clearing up that little matter with M. Poirot. But life is one trouble after another. You have heard about Flora, of course?"

"What exactly?" I asked cautiously.

"This new engagement. Flora and Hector Blunt. Of course not such a good match as Ralph would have been. But after all, happiness comes first. What dear Flora needs is an older man—some one steady and reliable, and then Hector is really a very distinguished man in his way. You saw the news of Ralph's arrest in the paper this morning?"

"Yes," I said, "I did."

"Horrible." Mrs. Ackroyd closed her eyes and shuddered. "Geoffrey Raymond was in a terrible way. Rang up Liverpool. But they wouldn't tell him anything at the police station there. In fact, they said they hadn't arrested Ralph at all. Mr. Raymond insists that it's all a mistake—a—what do they call it?—*canard* of the newspaper's. I've forbidden it to be mentioned before the servants. Such a terrible disgrace. Fancy if Flora had actually been married to him."

Mrs. Ackroyd shut her eyes in anguish. I began to wonder how soon I should be able to deliver Poirot's invitation.

Before I had time to speak, Mrs. Ackroyd was off again.

"You were here yesterday, weren't you, with that dreadful Inspector Raglan? Brute of a man—he terrified Flora into saying she took that money from poor Roger's room. And the matter was so simple, really. The dear child wanted to borrow a few pounds, didn't like to disturb her uncle since he'd given strict orders against it, but knowing where he kept his notes she went there and took what she needed."

"Is that Flora's account of the matter?" I asked.

"My dear doctor, you know what girls are nowadays. So easily acted on by suggestion. You, of course, know all about hypnosis and that sort of thing. The inspector shouts at her, says the word 'steal' over and over again, until the poor child gets an inhibition—or is it a complex?—I always mix up those two words—and actually thinks herself that she has stolen the money. I saw at once how it was. But I can't be too thankful for the whole misunderstanding in one way—it seems to have brought those two together—Hector and Flora, I mean. And I assure you that I have been very much worried about Flora in the past: why, at one time I actually thought there was going to be some kind of understanding between her and young Raymond. Just think of it!" Mrs. Ackroyd's voice rose in shrill horror. "A private secretary—with practically no means of his own."

"It would have been a severe blow to you," I said. "Now, Mrs. Ackroyd, I've got a message for you from M. Hercule Poirot."

"For me?"

Mrs. Ackroyd looked quite alarmed.

I hastened to reassure her, and I explained what Poirot wanted.

"Certainly," said Mrs. Ackroyd rather doubtfully, "I suppose we must come if M. Poirot says so. But what is it all about? I like to know beforehand."

I assured the lady truthfully that I myself did not know any more than she did.

"Very well," said Mrs. Ackroyd at last, rather grudgingly, "I will tell the others, and we will be there at nine o'clock."

Thereupon I took my leave, and joined Poirot at the agreed meeting-place.

"I've been longer than a quarter of an hour, I'm afraid," I remarked. "But once that good lady starts talking it's a matter of the utmost difficulty to get a word in edgeways."

"It is of no matter," said Poirot. "Me, I have been well amused. This park is magnificent."

We set off homewards. When we arrived, to our great surprise Caroline, who had evidently been watching for us, herself opened the door.

She put her fingers to her lips. Her face was full of importance and excitement.

"Ursula Bourne," she said, "the parlormaid from Fernly. She's here! I've put her in the dining-room. She's in a terrible way, poor thing. Says she must see M. Poirot at once. I've done all I could. Taken her a cup of hot tea. It really goes to one's heart to see any one in such a state."

"In the dining-room?" asked Poirot.

"This way," I said, and flung open the door.

Ursula Bourne was sitting by the table. Her arms were spread out in front of her, and she had evidently just lifted her head from where it had been buried. Her eyes were red with weeping.

"Ursula Bourne," I murmured.

But Poirot went past me with outstretched hands.

"No," he said, "that is not quite right, I think. It is not Ursula Bourne, is it, my child—but Ursula Paton? Mrs. Ralph Paton."

CHAPTER XXII
URSULA'S STORY

FOR a moment or two the girl looked mutely at Poirot. Then, her reserve breaking down completely, she nodded her head once, and burst into an outburst of sobs.

Caroline pushed past me, and putting her arm round the girl, patted her on the shoulder.

"There, there, my dear," she said soothingly, "it will be all right. You'll see—everything will be all right."

Buried under curiosity and scandal-mongering there is a lot of kindness in Caroline. For the moment, even the interest of Poirot's revelation was lost in the sight of the girl's distress.

Presently Ursula sat up and wiped her eyes.

"This is very weak and silly of me," she said.

"No, no, my child," said Poirot kindly. "We can all realize the strain of this last week."

"It must have been a terrible ordeal," I said.

"And then to find that you knew," continued Ursula. "How did you know? Was it Ralph who told you?"

Poirot shook his head.

"You know what brought me to you to-night," went on the girl. "*This*——"

She held out a crumpled piece of newspaper, and I recognized the paragraph that Poirot had had inserted.

"It says that Ralph has been arrested. So everything is useless. I need not pretend any longer."

"Newspaper paragraphs are not always true, mademoiselle," murmured Poirot, having the grace to look ashamed of himself. "All the same, I think you will do well to make a clean breast of things. The truth is what we need now."

The girl hesitated, looking at him doubtfully.

"You do not trust me," said Poirot gently. "Yet all the same you came here to find me, did you not? Why was that?"

"Because I don't believe that Ralph did it," said the girl in a very low voice. "And I think that you are clever, and will find out the truth. And also——"

"Yes?"

"I think you are kind."

Poirot nodded his head several times.

"It is very good that—yes, it is very good. Listen, I do in verity believe that this husband of yours is innocent—but the affair marches badly. If I am to save him, I must know all there is to know—even if it should seem to make the case against him blacker than before."

"How well you understand," said Ursula.

"So you will tell me the whole story, will you not? From the beginning."

"You're not going to send *me* away, I hope," said Caroline, settling herself comfortably in an arm-chair. "What I want to know," she continued, "is why this child was masquerading as a parlormaid?"

"Masquerading?" I queried.

"That's what I said. Why did you do it, child? For a wager?"

"For a living," said Ursula dryly.

And encouraged, she began the story which I reproduce here in my own words.

Ursula Bourne, it seemed, was one of a family of seven—impoverished Irish gentlefolk. On the death of her father, most of the girls were cast out into the world to earn their own living. Ursula's eldest sister was married to Captain Folliott. It was she whom I had seen that Sunday, and the cause of her embarrassment was clear enough now. Determined to earn her living and not attracted to the idea of being a nursery governess—the one profession open to an untrained girl, Ursula preferred the job of parlormaid. She scorned to label herself a "lady parlormaid." She would be the real thing, her reference being supplied by her sister. At Fernly, despite an aloofness which, as has been seen, caused some comment, she was a success at her job—quick, competent, and thorough.

"I enjoyed the work," she explained. "And I had plenty of time to myself."

And then came her meeting with Ralph Paton, and the love affair which culminated in a secret marriage. Ralph had persuaded her into that, somewhat against her will. He had declared that his stepfather would not hear of his marrying a penniless girl. Better to be married secretly, and break the news to him at some later and more favorable minute.

And so the deed was done, and Ursula Bourne became Ursula Paton. Ralph had declared that he meant to pay off his debts, find a job, and then, when he was in a position to support her, and independent of his adopted father, they would break the news to him.

But to people like Ralph Paton, turning over a new leaf is easier in theory than in practice. He hoped that his stepfather, whilst still in ignorance of the marriage, might be persuaded to pay his debts and put him on his feet again. But the revelation of the amount of Ralph's liabilities merely enraged Roger Ackroyd, and he refused to do anything at all. Some months passed, and then Ralph was bidden once more to Fernly. Roger Ackroyd did not beat about the bush. It was the desire of his heart that Ralph should marry Flora, and he put the matter plainly before the young man.

And here it was that the innate weakness of Ralph Paton showed itself. As always, he grasped at the easy, the immediate solution. As far as I could make out, neither Flora nor Ralph made any pretence of love. It was, on both sides, a business arrangement. Roger Ackroyd dictated his wishes—they agreed to them. Flora accepted a chance of liberty, money, and an enlarged horizon, Ralph, of course, was playing a different game. But he was in a very awkward hole financially. He seized at the chance. His debts would be paid. He could start again with a clean sheet. His was not a nature to envisage the future, but I gather that he saw vaguely the engagement with Flora being broken off after a decent interval had elapsed. Both Flora and he stipulated that it should be kept a secret for the present. He was anxious to conceal it from Ursula. He felt instinctively that her nature, strong and resolute, with an inherent distaste for duplicity, was not one to welcome such a course.

Then came the crucial moment when Roger Ackroyd, always high-handed, decided to announce the engagement. He said no word of his intention to Ralph—only to Flora, and Flora, apathetic, raised no objection. On Ursula, the news fell like a bombshell. Summoned by her, Ralph came hurriedly down from town. They met in the wood, where part of their conversation was overheard by my sister. Ralph implored her to keep silent for a little while longer, Ursula was equally determined to have done with concealments. She would tell Mr. Ackroyd the truth without any further delay. Husband and wife parted acrimoniously.

Ursula, steadfast in her purpose, sought an interview with Roger Ackroyd that very afternoon, and revealed the truth to him. Their interview was a stormy one—it might have been even more stormy had not Roger Ackroyd been already obsessed with his own troubles. It was bad enough, however. Ackroyd was not the kind of man to forgive the deceit that had been practiced upon him. His rancor was mainly directed to Ralph, but Ursula came in for her share, since he regarded her as a girl who had deliberately tried to "entrap" the adopted son of a very wealthy man. Unforgivable things were said on both sides.

That same evening Ursula met Ralph by appointment in the small summer-house, stealing out from the house by the side door in order to do so. Their interview was made up of reproaches on both sides. Ralph charged Ursula with having irretrievably ruined his prospects by her ill-timed revelation. Ursula reproached Ralph with his duplicity.

They parted at last. A little over half an hour later came the discovery of Roger Ackroyd's body. Since that night Ursula had neither seen nor heard from Ralph.

As the story unfolded itself, I realized more and more what a damning series of facts it was. Alive, Ackroyd could hardly have failed to alter his will—I knew him well enough to realize that to do so would be his first thought. His death came in the nick of time for Ralph and Ursula Paton. Small wonder the girl had held her tongue, and played her part so consistently.

My meditations were interrupted. It was Poirot's voice speaking, and I knew from the gravity of his tone that he, too, was fully alive to the implications of the position.

"Mademoiselle, I must ask you one question, and you must answer it truthfully, for on it everything may hang: What time was it when you parted from Captain Ralph Paton in the summer-house? Now, take a little minute so that your answer may be very exact."

The girl gave a half laugh, bitter enough in all conscience.

"Do you think I haven't gone over that again and again in my own mind? It was just half-past nine when I went out to meet him. Major Blunt was walking up and down the terrace, so I had to go round through the bushes to avoid him. It must have been about twenty-seven minutes to ten when I reached the summer-house. Ralph was waiting for me. I was with him ten minutes—not longer, for it was just a quarter to ten when I got back to the house."

I saw now the insistence of her question the other day. If only Ackroyd could have been proved to have been killed before a quarter to ten, and not after.

I saw the reflection of that thought in Poirot's next question.

"Who left the summer-house first?"

"I did."

"Leaving Ralph Paton in the summer-house?"

"Yes—but you don't think——"

"Mademoiselle, it is of no importance what I think. What did you do when you got back to the house?"

"I went up to my room."

"And stayed there until when?"

"Until about ten o'clock."

"Is there any one who can prove that?"

"Prove? That I was in my room, you mean? Oh! no. But surely—oh! I see, they might think—they might think——"

I saw the dawning horror in her eyes.

Poirot finished the sentence for her.

"That it was *you* who entered by the window and stabbed Mr. Ackroyd as he sat in his chair? Yes, they might think just that."

"Nobody but a fool would think any such thing," said Caroline indignantly.

She patted Ursula on the shoulder.

The girl had her face hidden in her hands.

"Horrible," she was murmuring. "Horrible."

Caroline gave her a friendly shake.

"Don't worry, my dear," she said. "M. Poirot doesn't think that really. As for that husband of yours, I don't think much of him, and I tell you so candidly. Running away and leaving you to face the music."

But Ursula shook her head energetically.

"Oh, no," she cried. "It wasn't like that at all. Ralph would not run away on his own account. I see now. If he heard of his stepfather's murder, he might think himself that I had done it."

"He wouldn't think any such thing," said Caroline.

"I was so cruel to him that night—so hard and bitter. I wouldn't listen to what he was trying to say—wouldn't believe that he really cared. I just stood there telling him what I thought of him, and saying the coldest, cruelest things that came into my mind—trying my best to hurt him."

"Do him no harm," said Caroline. "Never worry about what you say to a man. They're so conceited that they never believe you mean it if it's unflattering."

Ursula went on, nervously twisting and untwisting her hands.

"When the murder was discovered and he didn't come forward, I was terribly upset. Just for a moment I wondered—but then I knew he couldn't—he couldn't.... But I wished he would come forward and say openly that he'd had nothing to do with it. I knew that he was very fond of Dr. Sheppard, and I fancied that perhaps Dr. Sheppard might know where he was hiding."

She turned to me.

"That's why I said what I did to you that day. I thought, if you knew where he was, you might pass on the message to him."

"I?" I exclaimed.

"Why should James know where he was?" demanded Caroline sharply.

"It was very unlikely, I know," admitted Ursula, "but Ralph had often spoken of Dr. Sheppard, and I knew that he would be likely to consider him as his best friend in King's Abbot."

"My dear child," I said, "I have not the least idea where Ralph Paton is at the present moment."

"That is true enough," said Poirot.

"But——" Ursula held out the newspaper cutting in a puzzled fashion.

"Ah! that," said Poirot, slightly embarrassed; "a *bagatelle*, mademoiselle. A *rien du tout*. Not for a moment do I believe that Ralph Paton has been arrested."

"But then——" began the girl slowly.

Poirot went on quickly:—

"There is one thing I should like to know—did Captain Paton wear shoes or boots that night?"

Ursula shook her head.

"I can't remember."

"A pity! But how should you? Now, madame," he smiled at her, his head on one side, his forefinger wagging eloquently, "no questions. And do not torment yourself. Be of good courage, and place your faith in Hercule Poirot."

CHAPTER XXIII
POIROT'S LITTLE REUNION

"AND now," said Caroline, rising, "that child is coming upstairs to lie down. Don't you worry, my dear. M. Poirot will do everything he can for you—be sure of that."

"I ought to go back to Fernly," said Ursula uncertainly.

But Caroline silenced her protests with a firm hand.

"Nonsense. You're in my hands for the time being. You'll stay here for the present, anyway—eh, M. Poirot?"

"It will be the best plan," agreed the little Belgian. "This evening I shall want mademoiselle—I beg her pardon, madame—to attend my little reunion. Nine o'clock at my house. It is most necessary that she should be there."

Caroline nodded, and went with Ursula out of the room. The door shut behind them. Poirot dropped down into a chair again.

"So far, so good," he said. "Things are straightening themselves out."

"They're getting to look blacker and blacker against Ralph Paton," I observed gloomily.

Poirot nodded.

"Yes, that is so. But it was to be expected, was it not?"

I looked at him, slightly puzzled by the remark. He was leaning back in the chair, his eyes half closed, the tips of his fingers just touching each other. Suddenly he sighed and shook his head.

"What is it?" I asked.

"It is that there are moments when a great longing for my friend Hastings comes over me. That is the friend of whom I spoke to you—the one who resides now in the Argentine. Always, when I have had a big case, he has been by my side. And he has helped me—yes, often he has helped me. For he had a knack, that one, of stumbling over the truth unawares—without noticing it himself, *bien entendu*. At times he has said something particularly foolish, and behold that foolish remark has revealed the truth to me! And then, too, it was his practice to keep a written record of the cases that proved interesting."

I gave a slight embarrassed cough.

"As far as that goes," I began, and then stopped.

Poirot sat upright in his chair. His eyes sparkled.

"But yes? What is it that you would say?"

"Well, as a matter of fact, I've read some of Captain Hastings's narratives, and I thought, why not try my hand at something of the same kind? Seemed a pity not to—unique opportunity—probably the only time I'll be mixed up with anything of this kind."

I felt myself getting hotter and hotter, and more and more incoherent, as I floundered through the above speech.

Poirot sprang from his chair. I had a moment's terror that he was going to embrace me French fashion, but mercifully he refrained.

"But this is magnificent—you have then written down your impressions of the case as you went along?"

I nodded.

"*Epatant!*" cried Poirot. "Let me see them—this instant."

I was not quite prepared for such a sudden demand. I racked my brains to remember certain details.

"I hope you won't mind," I stammered. "I may have been a little—er—*personal* now and then."

"Oh! I comprehend perfectly; you have referred to me as comic—as, perhaps, ridiculous now and then? It matters not at all. Hastings, he also was not always polite. Me, I have the mind above such trivialities."

Still somewhat doubtful, I rummaged in the drawers of my desk and produced an untidy pile of manuscript which I handed over to him. With an eye on possible publication in the future, I had divided the work into chapters, and the night before I had brought it up to date with an account of Miss Russell's visit. Poirot had therefore twenty chapters.

I left him with them.

I was obliged to go out to a case at some distance away, and it was past eight o'clock when I got back, to be greeted with a plate of hot dinner on a tray, and the announcement that Poirot and my sister had supped together at half-past seven, and that the former had then gone to my workshop to finish his reading of the manuscript.

"I hope, James," said my sister, "that you've been careful in what you say about me in it?"

My jaw dropped. I had not been careful at all.

"Not that it matters very much," said Caroline, reading my expression correctly. "M. Poirot will know what to think. He understands me much better than you do."

I went into the workshop. Poirot was sitting by the window. The manuscript lay neatly piled on a chair beside him. He laid his hand on it and spoke.

"*Eh bien,*" he said, "I congratulate you—on your modesty!"

"Oh!" I said, rather taken aback.

"And on your reticence," he added.

I said "Oh!" again.

"Not so did Hastings write," continued my friend. "On every page, many, many times was the word 'I.' What *he* thought—what *he* did. But you—you have kept your personality in the background; only once or twice does it obtrude—in scenes of home life, shall we say?"

I blushed a little before the twinkle in his eye.

"What do you really think of the stuff?" I asked nervously.

"You want my candid opinion?"

"Yes."

Poirot laid his jesting manner aside.

"A very meticulous and accurate account," he said kindly. "You have recorded all the facts faithfully and exactly—though you have shown yourself becomingly reticent as to your own share in them."

"And it has helped you?"

"Yes. I may say that it has helped me considerably. Come, we must go over to my house and set the stage for my little performance."

Caroline was in the hall. I think she hoped that she might be invited to accompany us. Poirot dealt with the situation tactfully.

"I should much like to have had you present, mademoiselle," he said regretfully, "but at this juncture it would not be wise. See you, all these people to-night are suspects. Amongst them, I shall find the person who killed Mr. Ackroyd."

"You really believe that?" I said incredulously.

"I see that you do not," said Poirot dryly. "Not yet do you appreciate Hercule Poirot at his true worth."

At that minute Ursula came down the staircase.

"You are ready, my child?" said Poirot. "That is good. We will go to my house together. Mademoiselle Caroline, believe me, I do everything possible to render you service. Good-evening."

We went out, leaving Caroline, rather like a dog who has been refused a walk, standing on the front door step gazing after us.

The sitting-room at The Larches had been got ready. On the table were various *sirops* and glasses. Also a plate of biscuits. Several chairs had been brought in from the other room.

Poirot ran to and fro rearranging things. Pulling out a chair here, altering the position of a lamp there, occasionally stooping to straighten one of the mats that covered the floor. He was specially fussy over the lighting. The lamps were arranged in such a way as to throw a clear light on the side of the room where the chairs were grouped, at the same time leaving the other end of the room, where I presumed Poirot himself would sit, in a dim twilight.

Ursula and I watched him. Presently a bell was heard.

"They arrive," said Poirot. "Good, all is in readiness."

The door opened and the party from Fernly filed in. Poirot went forward and greeted Mrs. Ackroyd and Flora.

"It is most good of you to come," he said. "And Major Blunt and Mr. Raymond."

The secretary was debonair as ever.

"What's the great idea?" he said, laughing. "Some scientific machine? Do we have bands round our wrists which register guilty heart-beats? There is such an invention, isn't there?"

"I have read of it, yes," admitted Poirot. "But me, I am old-fashioned. I use the old methods. I work only with the little gray cells. Now let us begin—but first I have an announcement to make to you all."

He took Ursula's hand and drew her forward.

"This lady is Mrs. Ralph Paton. She was married to Captain Paton last March."

A little shriek burst from Mrs. Ackroyd.

"Ralph! Married! Last March! Oh! but it's absurd. How could he be?"

She stared at Ursula as though she had never seen her before.

"Married to Bourne?" she said. "Really, M. Poirot, I don't believe you."

Ursula flushed and began to speak, but Flora forestalled her.

Going quickly to the other girl's side, she passed her hand through her arm.

"You must not mind our being surprised," she said. "You see, we had no idea of such a thing. You and Ralph have kept your secret very well. I am—very glad about it."

"You are very kind, Miss Ackroyd," said Ursula in a low voice, "and you have every right to be exceedingly angry. Ralph behaved very badly—especially to you."

"You needn't worry about that," said Flora, giving her arm a consoling little pat. "Ralph was in a corner and took the only way out. I should probably have done the same in his place. I do think he might have trusted me with the secret, though. I wouldn't have let him down."

Poirot rapped gently on a table and cleared his throat significantly.

"The board meeting's going to begin," said Flora. "M. Poirot hints that we mustn't talk. But just tell me one thing. Where is Ralph? You must know if any one does."

"But I don't," cried Ursula, almost in a wail. "That's just it, I don't."

"Isn't he detained at Liverpool?" asked Raymond. "It said so in the paper."

"He is not at Liverpool," said Poirot shortly.

"In fact," I remarked, "no one knows where he is."

"Excepting Hercule Poirot, eh?" said Raymond.

Poirot replied seriously to the other's banter.

"Me, I know everything. Remember that."

Geoffrey Raymond lifted his eyebrows.

"Everything?" He whistled. "Whew! that's a tall order."

"Do you mean to say you can really guess where Ralph Paton is hiding?" I asked incredulously.

"You call it guessing. I call it knowing, my friend."

"In Cranchester?" I hazarded.

"No," replied Poirot gravely, "not in Cranchester."

He said no more, but at a gesture from him the assembled party took their seats. As they did so, the door opened once more and two other people came in and sat down near the door. They were Parker and the housekeeper.

"The number is complete," said Poirot. "Every one is here."

There was a ring of satisfaction in his tone. And with the sound of it I saw a ripple of something like uneasiness pass over all those faces grouped at the other end of the room. There was a suggestion in all this as of a trap—a trap that had closed.

Poirot read from a list in an important manner.

"Mrs. Ackroyd, Miss Flora Ackroyd, Major Blunt, Mr. Geoffrey Raymond, Mrs. Ralph Paton, John Parker, Elizabeth Russell."

He laid the paper down on the table.

"What's the meaning of all this?" began Raymond.

"The list I have just read," said Poirot, "is a list of suspected persons. Every one of you present had the opportunity to kill Mr. Ackroyd——"

With a cry Mrs. Ackroyd sprang up, her throat working.

"I don't like it," she wailed. "I don't like it. I would much prefer to go home."

"You cannot go home, madame," said Poirot sternly, "until you have heard what I have to say."

He paused a moment, then cleared his throat.

"I will start at the beginning. When Miss Ackroyd asked me to investigate the case, I went up to Fernly Park with the good Dr. Sheppard. I walked with him along the terrace, where I was shown the footprints on the window-sill. From there Inspector Raglan took me along the path which leads to the drive. My eye was caught by a little summer-house, and I searched it thoroughly. I found two things—a scrap of starched cambric and an empty goose quill. The scrap of cambric immediately suggested to me a maid's apron. When Inspector Raglan showed me his list of the people in the house, I noticed at once that one of the maids—Ursula Bourne, the parlormaid—had no real alibi. According to her own story, she was in her bedroom from nine-thirty until ten. But supposing that instead she was in the summer-house? If so, she must have gone there to meet some one. Now we know from Dr. Sheppard that some one from outside *did* come to the house that night—the stranger whom he met just by the gate. At a first glance it would seem that our problem was solved, and that the stranger went to the summer-house to meet Ursula Bourne. It was fairly certain that he *did* go to the summer-house because of the goose quill. That suggested at once to my mind a taker of drugs—and one who had acquired the habit on the other side of the Atlantic where sniffing 'snow' is more common than in this country. The man whom Dr. Sheppard met had an American accent, which fitted in with that supposition.

"But I was held up by one point. *The times did not fit.* Ursula Bourne could certainly not have gone to the summer-house before nine-thirty, whereas the man must have got there by a few minutes past nine. I could, of course, assume that he waited there for half an hour. The only alternative supposition was that there had been two separate meetings in the summer-house that night. *Eh bien*, as soon as I went into that alternative I found several significant facts. I discovered that Miss Russell, the housekeeper, had visited Dr. Sheppard that morning, and had displayed a good deal of interest in cures for victims of the drug habit. Taking that in conjunction with the goose quill, I assumed that the man in question came to Fernly to meet the housekeeper, and not Ursula Bourne. Who, then, did Ursula Bourne come to the rendezvous to meet? I was not long in doubt. First I found a ring—a wedding ring—with 'From R.' and a date inside it. Then I learnt that Ralph Paton had been seen coming up the path which led to the summer-house at twenty-five minutes past nine, and I also heard of a certain conversation which had taken place in the wood near the village that very afternoon—a conversation between Ralph Paton and some unknown girl. So I had my facts succeeding each other in a neat and orderly manner. A secret marriage, an engagement announced on the day of the tragedy, the stormy interview in the wood, and the meeting arranged for the summer-house that night.

"Incidentally this proved to me one thing, that both Ralph Paton and Ursula Bourne (or Paton) had the strongest motives for wishing Mr. Ackroyd out of the way. And it also made one other point unexpectedly clear. It could not have been Ralph Paton who was with Mr. Ackroyd in the study at nine-thirty.

"So we come to another and most interesting aspect of the crime. Who was it in the room with Mr. Ackroyd at nine-thirty? Not Ralph Paton, who was in the summer-house with his wife. Not Charles Kent, who had already left. Who, then? I posed my cleverest—my most audacious question: *Was any one with him?*"

Poirot leaned forward and shot the last words triumphantly at us, drawing back afterwards with the air of one who has made a decided hit.

Raymond, however, did not seem impressed, and lodged a mild protest.

"I don't know if you're trying to make me out a liar, M. Poirot, but the matter does not rest on my evidence alone—except perhaps as to the exact words used. Remember, Major Blunt also heard Mr. Ackroyd talking to some one. He was on the terrace outside, and couldn't catch the words clearly, but he distinctly heard the voices."

Poirot nodded.

"I have not forgotten," he said quietly. "But Major Blunt was under the impression that it was *you* to whom Mr. Ackroyd was speaking."

For a moment Raymond seemed taken aback. Then he recovered himself.

"Blunt knows now that he was mistaken," he said.

"Exactly," agreed the other man.

"Yet there must have been some reason for his thinking so," mused Poirot. "Oh! no," he held up his hand in protest, "I know the reason you will give—but it is not enough. We must seek elsewhere. I will put it this way. From the beginning of the case I have been struck by one thing—the nature of those words which Mr. Raymond overheard. It has been amazing to me that no one has commented on them—has seen anything odd about them."

He paused a minute, and then quoted softly:—

"*... The calls on my purse have been so frequent of late that I fear it is impossible for me to accede to your request.* Does nothing strike you as odd about that?"

"I don't think so," said Raymond. "He has frequently dictated letters to me, using almost exactly those same words."

"Exactly," cried Poirot. "That is what I seek to arrive at. Would any man use such a phrase in *talking* to another? Impossible that that should be part of a real conversation. Now, if he had been dictating a letter——"

"You mean he was reading a letter aloud," said Raymond slowly. "Even so, he must have been reading to some one."

"But why? We have no evidence that there was any one else in the room. No other voice but Mr. Ackroyd's was heard, remember."

"Surely a man wouldn't read letters of that type aloud to himself—not unless he was—well—going balmy."

"You have all forgotten one thing," said Poirot softly: "the stranger who called at the house the preceding Wednesday."

They all stared at him.

"But yes," said Poirot, nodding encouragingly, "on Wednesday. The young man was not of himself important. But the firm he represented interested me very much."

"The Dictaphone Company," gasped Raymond. "I see it now. A dictaphone. That's what you think?"

Poirot nodded.

"Mr. Ackroyd had promised to invest in a dictaphone, you remember. Me, I had the curiosity to inquire of the company in question. Their reply is that Mr. Ackroyd *did* purchase a dictaphone from their representative. Why he concealed the matter from you, I do not know."

"He must have meant to surprise me with it," murmured Raymond. "He had quite a childish love of surprising people. Meant to keep it up his sleeve for a day or so. Probably was playing with it like a new toy. Yes, it fits in. You're quite right—no one would use quite those words in casual conversation."

"It explains, too," said Poirot, "why Major Blunt thought it was you who were in the study. Such scraps as came to him were fragments of dictation, and so his subconscious mind deduced that you were with him. His conscious mind was occupied with something quite different—the white figure he had caught a glimpse of. He fancied it was Miss Ackroyd. Really, of course, it was Ursula Bourne's white apron he saw as she was stealing down to the summer-house."

Raymond had recovered from his first surprise.

"All the same," he remarked, "this discovery of yours, brilliant though it is (I'm quite sure I should never have thought of it), leaves the essential position unchanged. Mr. Ackroyd was alive at nine-thirty, since he was speaking into the dictaphone. It seems clear that the man Charles Kent was really off the premises by then. As to Ralph Paton——?"

He hesitated, glancing at Ursula.

Her color flared up, but she answered steadily enough.

"Ralph and I parted just before a quarter to ten. He never went near the house, I am sure of that. He had no intention of doing so. The last thing on earth he wanted was to face his stepfather. He would have funked it badly."

"It isn't that I doubt your story for a moment," explained Raymond. "I've always been quite sure Captain Paton was innocent. But one has to think of a court of law—and the questions that would be asked. He is in a most unfortunate position, but if he were to come forward——"

Poirot interrupted.

"That is your advice, yes? That he should come forward?"

"Certainly. If you know where he is——"

"I perceive that you do not believe that I do know. And yet I have told you just now that I know everything. The truth of the telephone call, of the footprints on the window-sill, of the hiding-place of Ralph Paton——"

"Where is he?" said Blunt sharply.

"Not very far away," said Poirot, smiling.

"In Cranchester?" I asked.

Poirot turned towards me.

"Always you ask me that. The idea of Cranchester it is with you an *idée fixe*. No, he is not in Cranchester. He is—*there!*"

He pointed a dramatic forefinger. Every one's head turned.

Ralph Paton was standing in the doorway.

CHAPTER XXIV
RALPH PATON'S STORY

IT was a very uncomfortable minute for *me*. I hardly took in what happened next, but there were exclamations and cries of surprise! When I was sufficiently master of myself to be able to realize what was going on, Ralph Paton was standing by his wife, her hand in his, and he was smiling across the room at me.

Poirot, too, was smiling, and at the same time shaking an eloquent finger at me.

"Have I not told you at least thirty-six times that it is useless to conceal things from Hercule Poirot?" he demanded. "That in such a case he finds out?"

He turned to the others.

"One day, you remember, we held a little séance about a table—just the six of us. I accused the other five persons present of concealing something from me. Four of them gave up their secret. Dr. Sheppard did not give up his. But all along I have had my suspicions. Dr. Sheppard went to the Three Boars that night hoping to find Ralph. He did not find him there; but supposing, I said to myself, that he met him in the street on his way home? Dr. Sheppard was a friend of Captain Paton's, and he had come straight from the scene of the crime. He must know that things looked very black against him. Perhaps he knew more than the general public did——"

"I did," I said ruefully. "I suppose I might as well make a clean breast of things now. I went to see Ralph that afternoon. At first he refused to take me into his confidence, but later he told me about his marriage, and the hole he was in. As soon as the murder was discovered, I realized that once the facts were known, suspicion could not fail to attach to Ralph—or, if not to him, to the girl he loved. That night I put the facts plainly before him. The thought of having possibly to give evidence which might incriminate his wife made him resolve at all costs to—to——"

I hesitated, and Ralph filled up the gap.

"To do a bunk," he said graphically. "You see, Ursula left me to go back to the house. I thought it possible that she might have attempted to have another interview with my stepfather. He had already been very rude to her that afternoon. It occurred to me that he might have so insulted her—in such an unforgivable manner—that without knowing what she was doing——"

He stopped. Ursula released her hand from his, and stepped back.

"You thought that, Ralph! You actually thought that I might have done it?"

"Let us get back to the culpable conduct of Dr. Sheppard," said Poirot dryly. "Dr. Sheppard consented to do what he could to help him. He was successful in hiding Captain Paton from the police."

"Where?" asked Raymond. "In his own house?"

"Ah, no, indeed," said Poirot. "You should ask yourself the question that I did. If the good doctor is concealing the young man, what place would he choose? It must necessarily be somewhere near at hand. I think of Cranchester. A hotel? No. Lodgings? Even more emphatically, no. Where, then? Ah! I have it. A nursing home. A home for the mentally unfit. I test my theory. I invent a nephew with mental trouble. I consult Mademoiselle Sheppard as to suitable homes. She gives me the names of two near Cranchester to which her brother has sent patients. I make inquiries. Yes, at one of them a patient was brought there by the doctor himself early on Saturday morning. That patient, though known by another name, I had no difficulty in identifying as Captain Paton. After certain necessary formalities, I was allowed to bring him away. He arrived at my house in the early hours of yesterday morning."

I looked at him ruefully.

"Caroline's Home Office expert," I murmured. "And to think I never guessed!"

"You see now why I drew attention to the reticence of your manuscript," murmured Poirot. "It was strictly truthful as far as it went—but it did not go very far, eh, my friend?"

I was too abashed to argue.

"Dr. Sheppard has been very loyal," said Ralph. "He has stood by me through thick and thin. He did what he thought was the best. I see now, from what M. Poirot has told me, that it was not really the best. I should have come forward and faced the music. You see, in the home, we never saw a newspaper. I knew nothing of what was going on."

"Dr. Sheppard has been a model of discretion," said Poirot dryly. "But me, I discover all the little secrets. It is my business."

"Now we can have your story of what happened that night," said Raymond impatiently.

"You know it already," said Ralph. "There's very little for me to add. I left the summer-house about nine-forty-five, and tramped about the lanes, trying to make up my mind as to what to do next—what line to take. I'm bound to admit that I've not the shadow of an alibi, but I give you my solemn word that I never went to the study, that I never saw my stepfather alive—or dead. Whatever the world thinks, I'd like all of you to believe me."

"No alibi," murmured Raymond. "That's bad. I believe you, of course, but—it's a bad business."

"It makes things very simple, though," said Poirot, in a cheerful voice. "Very simple indeed."

We all stared at him.

"You see what I mean? No? Just this—to save Captain Paton the real criminal must confess."

He beamed round at us all.

"But yes—I mean what I say. See now, I did not invite Inspector Raglan to be present. That was for a reason. I did not want to tell him all that I knew—at least I did not want to tell him to-night."

He leaned forward, and suddenly his voice and his whole personality changed. He suddenly became dangerous.

"I who speak to you—I know the murderer of Mr. Ackroyd is in this room now. It is to the murderer I speak. *To-morrow the truth goes to Inspector Raglan.* You understand?"

There was a tense silence. Into the midst of it came the old Breton woman with a telegram on a salver. Poirot tore it open.

Blunt's voice rose abrupt and resonant.

"The murderer is amongst us, you say? You know—which?"

Poirot had read the message. He crumpled it up in his hand.

"I know—now."

He tapped the crumpled ball of paper.

"What is that?" said Raymond sharply.

"A wireless message—from a steamer now on her way to the United States."

There was a dead silence. Poirot rose to his feet bowing.

"Messieurs et Mesdames, this reunion of mine is at an end. Remember—*the truth goes to Inspector Raglan in the morning.*"

CHAPTER XXV
THE WHOLE TRUTH

A SLIGHT gesture from Poirot enjoined me to stay behind the rest. I obeyed, going over to the fire and thoughtfully stirring the big logs on it with the toe of my boot.

I was puzzled. For the first time I was absolutely at sea as to Poirot's meaning. For a moment I was inclined to think that the scene I had just witnessed was a gigantic piece of bombast—that he had been what he called "playing the comedy" with a view to making himself interesting and important. But, in spite of myself, I was forced to believe in an underlying reality. There had been real menace in his words—a certain indisputable sincerity. But I still believed him to be on entirely the wrong tack.

When the door shut behind the last of the party he came over to the fire.

"Well, my friend," he said quietly, "and what do you think of it all?"

"I don't know what to think," I said frankly. "What was the point? Why not go straight to Inspector Raglan with the truth instead of giving the guilty person this elaborate warning?"

Poirot sat down and drew out his case of tiny Russian cigarettes. He smoked for a minute or two in silence. Then:—

"Use your little gray cells," he said. "There is always a reason behind my actions."

I hesitated for a moment, and then I said slowly:

"The first one that occurs to me is that you yourself do not know who the guilty person is, but that you are sure that he is to be found amongst the people here to-night. Therefore your words were intended to force a confession from the unknown murderer?"

Poirot nodded approvingly.

"A clever idea, but not the truth."

"I thought, perhaps, that by making him believe you knew, you might force him out into the open—not necessarily by confession. He might try to silence you as he formerly silenced Mr. Ackroyd—before you could act to-morrow morning."

"A trap with myself as the bait! *Merci, mon ami*, but I am not sufficiently heroic for that."

"Then I fail to understand you. Surely you are running the risk of letting the murderer escape by thus putting him on his guard?"

Poirot shook his head.

"He cannot escape," he said gravely. "There is only one way out—and that way does not lead to freedom."

"You really believe that one of those people here to-night committed the murder?" I asked incredulously.

"Yes, my friend."

"Which one?"

There was a silence for some minutes. Then Poirot tossed the stump of his cigarette into the grate and began to speak in a quiet, reflective tone.

"I will take you the way that I have traveled myself. Step by step you shall accompany me, and see for yourself that all the facts point indisputably to one person. Now, to begin with, there were two facts and one little discrepancy in time which especially attracted my attention. The first fact was the telephone call. If Ralph

Paton were indeed the murderer, the telephone call became meaningless and absurd. Therefore, I said to myself, Ralph Paton is not the murderer.

"I satisfied myself that the call could not have been sent by any one in the house, yet I was convinced that it was amongst those present on the fatal evening that I had to look for my criminal. Therefore I concluded that the telephone call must have been sent by an accomplice. I was not quite pleased with that deduction, but I let it stand for the minute.

"I next examined the *motive* for the call. That was difficult. I could only get at it by judging its *result*. Which was—that the murder was discovered that night instead of—in all probability—the following morning. You agree with that?"

"Ye-es," I admitted. "Yes. As you say, Mr. Ackroyd, having given orders that he was not to be disturbed, nobody would have been likely to go to the study that night."

"*Très bien.* The affair marches, does it not? But matters were still obscure. What was the advantage of having the crime discovered that night in preference to the following morning? The only idea I could get hold of was that the murderer, knowing the crime was to be discovered at a certain time, could make sure of being present when the door was broken in—or at any rate immediately afterwards. And now we come to the second fact—the chair pulled out from the wall. Inspector Raglan dismissed that as of no importance. I, on the contrary, have always regarded it as of supreme importance.

"In your manuscript you have drawn a neat little plan of the study. If you had it with you this minute you would see that—the chair being drawn out in the position indicated by Parker—it would stand in a direct line between the door and the window."

"The window!" I said quickly.

"You, too, have my first idea. I imagined that the chair was drawn out so that something connected with the window should not be seen by any one entering through the door. But I soon abandoned that supposition, for though the chair was a grandfather with a high back, it obscured very little of the window—only the part between the sash and the ground. No, *mon ami*—but remember that just in front of the window there stood a table with books and magazines upon it. Now that table *was* completely hidden by the drawn-out chair—and immediately I had my first shadowy suspicion of the truth.

"Supposing that there had been something on that table not intended to be seen? Something placed there by the murderer? As yet I had no inkling of what that something might be. But I knew certain very interesting facts about it. For instance, it was something that the murderer had not been able to take away with him at the time that he committed the crime. At the same time it was vital that it should be removed as soon as possible after the crime had been discovered. And so—the telephone message, and the opportunity for the murderer to be on the spot when the body was discovered.

"Now four people were on the scene before the police arrived. Yourself, Parker, Major Blunt, and Mr. Raymond. Parker I eliminated at once, since at whatever time the crime was discovered, he was the one person certain to be on the spot. Also it was he who told me of the pulled-out chair. Parker, then, was cleared (of the murder, that is. I still thought it possible that he had been blackmailing Mrs. Ferrars).

Raymond and Blunt, however, remained under suspicion since, if the crime had been discovered in the early hours of the morning, it was quite possible that they might have arrived on the scene too late to prevent the object on the round table being discovered.

"Now what was that object? You heard my arguments to-night in reference to the scrap of conversation overheard? As soon as I learned that a representative of a dictaphone company had called, the idea of a dictaphone took root in my mind. You heard what I said in this room not half an hour ago? They all agreed with my theory—but one vital fact seems to have escaped them. Granted that a dictaphone was being used by Mr. Ackroyd that night—why was no dictaphone found?"

"I never thought of that," I said.

"We know that a dictaphone was supplied to Mr. Ackroyd. But no dictaphone has been found amongst his effects. So, if something was taken from that table—why should not that something be the dictaphone? But there were certain difficulties in the way. The attention of every one was, of course, focused on the murdered man. I think any one could have gone to the table unnoticed by the other people in the room. But a dictaphone has a certain bulk—it cannot be slipped casually into a pocket. There must have been a receptacle of some kind capable of holding it.

"You see where I am arriving? The figure of the murderer is taking shape. A person who was on the scene straightway, but who might not have been if the crime had been discovered the following morning. A person carrying a receptacle into which the dictaphone might be fitted——"

I interrupted.

"But why remove the dictaphone? What was the point?"

"You are like Mr. Raymond. You take it for granted that what was heard at nine-thirty was Mr. Ackroyd's voice speaking into a dictaphone. But consider this useful invention for a little minute. You dictate into it, do you not? And at some later time a secretary or a typist turns it on, and the voice speaks again."

"You mean——" I gasped.

Poirot nodded.

"Yes, I mean that. *At nine-thirty Mr. Ackroyd was already dead.* It was the dictaphone speaking—not the man."

"And the murderer switched it on. Then he must have been in the room at that minute?"

"Possibly. But we must not exclude the likelihood of some mechanical device having been applied—something after the nature of a time lock, or even of a simple alarm clock. But in that case we must add two qualifications to our imaginary portrait of the murderer. It must be some one who knew of Mr. Ackroyd's purchase of the dictaphone and also some one with the necessary mechanical knowledge.

"I had got thus far in my own mind when we came to the footprints on the window ledge. Here there were three conclusions open to me. (1) They might really have been made by Ralph Paton. He had been at Fernly that night, and might have climbed into the study and found his uncle dead there. That was one hypothesis. (2) There was the possibility that the footmarks might have been made by somebody else who happened to have the same kind of studs in his shoes. But the inmates of the house had shoes soled with crepe rubber, and I declined to believe in the coincidence of some one from outside having the same kind of shoes as Ralph Paton wore. Charles Kent, as we know from the barmaid of the Dog and Whistle, had on a pair of boots 'clean dropping off him.' (3) Those prints were made by some one deliberately trying to throw suspicion on Ralph Paton. To test this last conclusion, it was necessary to ascertain certain facts. One pair of Ralph's shoes had been obtained from the Three Boars by the police. Neither Ralph nor any one else could have worn them that evening, since they were downstairs being cleaned. According to the police theory, Ralph was wearing another pair of the same kind, and I found out that it was true that he had two pairs. Now for my theory to be proved correct it was necessary for the murderer to have worn Ralph's shoes that evening—in which case Ralph must have been wearing yet a *third* pair of footwear of some kind. I could hardly suppose that he would bring three pairs of shoes all alike—the third pair of footwear were more likely to be boots. I got your sister to make inquiries on this point—laying some stress on the color, in order—I admit it frankly—to obscure the real reason for my asking.

"You know the result of her investigations. Ralph Paton *had* had a pair of boots with him. The first question I asked him when he came to my house yesterday morning was what he was wearing on his feet on the fatal night. He replied at once that he had worn *boots*—he was still wearing them, in fact—having nothing else to put on.

"So we get a step further in our description of the murderer—a person who had the opportunity to take these shoes of Ralph Paton's from the Three Boars that day."

He paused, and then said, with a slightly raised voice:—

"There is one further point. The murderer must have been a person who had the opportunity to purloin that dagger from the silver table. You might argue that any one in the house might have done so, but I will recall to you that Miss Ackroyd was very positive that the dagger was not there when she examined the silver table."

He paused again.

"Let us recapitulate—now that all is clear. A person who was at the Three Boars earlier that day, a person who knew Ackroyd well enough to know that he had purchased a dictaphone, a person who was of a mechanical turn of mind, who had the opportunity to take the dagger from the silver table before Miss Flora arrived, who had with him a receptacle suitable for hiding the dictaphone—such as a black bag, and who had the study to himself for a few minutes after the crime was discovered while Parker was telephoning for the police. In fact—*Dr. Sheppard!*"

CHAPTER XXVI
AND NOTHING BUT THE TRUTH

THERE was a dead silence for a minute and a half.

Then I laughed.

"You're mad," I said.

"No," said Poirot placidly. "I am not mad. It was the little discrepancy in time that first drew my attention to you—right at the beginning."

"Discrepancy in time?" I queried, puzzled.

"But yes. You will remember that every one agreed—you yourself included—that it took five minutes to walk from the lodge to the house—less if you took the short cut to the terrace. But you left the house at ten minutes to nine—both by your own statement and that of Parker, and yet it was nine o'clock as you passed through the lodge gates. It was a chilly night—not an evening a man would be inclined to dawdle; why had you taken ten minutes to do a five-minutes' walk? All along I realized that we had only your statement for it that the study window was ever fastened. Ackroyd asked you if you had done so—he never looked to see. Supposing, then, that the study window was unfastened? Would there be time in that ten minutes for you to run round the outside of the house, change your shoes, climb in through the window, kill Ackroyd, and get to the gate by nine o'clock? I decided against that theory since in all probability a man as nervous as Ackroyd was that night would hear you climbing in, and then there would have been a struggle. But supposing that you killed Ackroyd *before* you left—as you were standing beside his chair? Then you go out of the front door, run round to the summer-house, take Ralph Paton's shoes out of the bag you brought up with you that night, slip them on, walk through the mud in them, and leave prints on the window ledge, you climb in, lock the study door on the inside, run back to the summer-house, change back into your own shoes, and race down to the gate. (I went through similar actions the other day, when you were with Mrs. Ackroyd—it took ten minutes exactly.) Then home—and an alibi—since you had timed the dictaphone for half-past nine."

"My dear Poirot," I said in a voice that sounded strange and forced to my own ears, "you've been brooding over this case too long. What on earth had I to gain by murdering Ackroyd?"

"Safety. It was you who blackmailed Mrs. Ferrars. Who could have had a better knowledge of what killed Mr. Ferrars than the doctor who was attending him? When you spoke to me that first day in the garden, you mentioned a legacy received about a year ago. I have been unable to discover any trace of a legacy. You had to invent some way of accounting for Mrs. Ferrars's twenty thousand pounds. It has not done you much good. You lost most of it in speculation—then you put the screw on too hard, and Mrs. Ferrars took a way out that you had not expected. If Ackroyd had learnt the truth he would have had no mercy on you—you were ruined for ever."

"And the telephone call?" I asked, trying to rally. "You have a plausible explanation of that also, I suppose?"

"I will confess to you that it was my greatest stumbling block when I found that a call had actually been put through to you from King's Abbot station. I at first believed that you had simply invented the story. It was a very clever touch, that. You must have some excuse for arriving at Fernly, finding the body, and so getting the chance to remove the dictaphone on which your alibi depended. I had a very vague notion of how it was worked when I came to see your sister that first day and inquired as to what patients you had seen on Friday morning. I had no thought of Miss Russell in my mind at that time. Her visit was a lucky coincidence, since it distracted your mind from the real object of my questions. I found what I was looking for. Among your patients that morning was the steward of an American liner. Who more suitable than he to be leaving for Liverpool by the train that evening? And afterwards he would be on the high seas, well out of the way. I noted that the *Orion* sailed on

Saturday, and having obtained the name of the steward I sent him a wireless message asking a certain question. This is his reply you saw me receive just now."

He held out the message to me. It ran as follows—

"Quite correct. Dr. Sheppard asked me to leave a note at a patient's house. I was to ring him up from the station with the reply. Reply was 'No answer.'"

** ***

"It was a clever idea," said Poirot. "The call was genuine. Your sister saw you take it. But there was only one man's word as to what was actually said—your own!"

I yawned.

"All this," I said, "is very interesting—but hardly in the sphere of practical politics."

"You think not? Remember what I said—the truth goes to Inspector Raglan in the morning. But, for the sake of your good sister, I am willing to give you the chance of another way out. There might be, for instance, an overdose of a sleeping draught. You comprehend me? But Captain Ralph Paton must be cleared—*ça va sans dire*. I should suggest that you finish that very interesting manuscript of yours—but abandoning your former reticence."

"You seem to be very prolific of suggestions," I remarked. "Are you sure you've quite finished."

"Now that you remind me of the fact, it is true that there is one thing more. It would be most unwise on your part to attempt to silence me as you silenced M. Ackroyd. That kind of business does not succeed against Hercule Poirot, you understand."

"My dear Poirot," I said, smiling a little, "whatever else I may be, I am not a fool."

I rose to my feet.

"Well, well," I said, with a slight yawn, "I must be off home. Thank you for a most interesting and instructive evening."

Poirot also rose and bowed with his accustomed politeness as I passed out of the room.

CHAPTER XXVII
APOLOGIA

FIVE a.m. I am very tired—but I have finished my task. My arm aches from writing.

A strange end to my manuscript. I meant it to be published some day as the history of one of Poirot's failures! Odd, how things pan out.

All along I've had a premonition of disaster, from the moment I saw Ralph Paton and Mrs. Ferrars with their heads together. I thought then that she was confiding in him; as it happened I was quite wrong there, but the idea persisted even after I went into the study with Ackroyd that night, until he told me the truth.

Poor old Ackroyd. I'm always glad that I gave him a chance. I urged him to read that letter before it was too late. Or let me be honest—didn't I subconsciously realize that with a pig-headed chap like him, it was my best chance of getting him *not* to read it? His nervousness that night was interesting psychologically. He knew danger was close at hand. And yet he never suspected *me*.

The dagger was an afterthought. I'd brought up a very handy little weapon of my own, but when I saw the dagger lying in the silver table, it occurred to me at once how much better it would be to use a weapon that couldn't be traced to me.

I suppose I must have meant to murder him all along. As soon as I heard of Mrs. Ferrars's death, I felt convinced that she would have told him everything before she died. When I met him and he seemed so agitated, I thought that perhaps he knew the truth, but that he couldn't bring himself to believe it, and was going to give me the chance of refuting it.

So I went home and took my precautions. If the trouble were after all only something to do with Ralph—well, no harm would have been done. The dictaphone he had given me two days before to adjust. Something had gone a little wrong with it, and I persuaded him to let me have a go at it, instead of sending it back. I did what I wanted to it, and took it up with me in my bag that evening.

I am rather pleased with myself as a writer. What could be neater, for instance, than the following:—

"The letters were brought in at twenty minutes to nine. It was just on ten minutes to nine when I left him, the letter still unread. I hesitated with my hand on the door handle, looking back and wondering if there was anything I had left undone."

All true, you see. But suppose I had put a row of stars after the first sentence! Would somebody then have wondered what exactly happened in that blank ten minutes?

When I looked round the room from the door, I was quite satisfied. Nothing had been left undone. The dictaphone was on the table by the window, timed to go off at nine-thirty (the mechanism of that little device was rather clever—based on the principle of an alarm clock), and the arm-chair was pulled out so as to hide it from the door.

I must admit that it gave me rather a shock to run into Parker just outside the door. I have faithfully recorded that fact.

Then later, when the body was discovered, and I had sent Parker to telephone for the police, what a judicious use of words: "*I did what little had to be done!*" It was quite little—just to shove the dictaphone into my bag and push back the chair against the wall in its proper place. I never dreamed that Parker would have noticed that chair. Logically, he ought to have been so agog over the body as to be blind to everything else. But I hadn't reckoned with the trained-servant complex.

I wish I could have known beforehand that Flora was going to say she'd seen her uncle alive at a quarter to ten. That puzzled me more than I can say. In fact, all through the case there have been things that puzzled me hopelessly. Every one seems to have taken a hand.

My greatest fear all through has been Caroline. I have fancied she might guess. Curious the way she spoke that day of my "strain of weakness."

Well, she will never know the truth. There is, as Poirot said, one way out....

I can trust him. He and Inspector Raglan will manage it between them. I should not like Caroline to know. She is fond of me, and then, too, she is proud.... My death will be a grief to her, but grief passes....

When I have finished writing, I shall enclose this whole manuscript in an envelope and address it to Poirot.

And then—what shall it be? Veronal? There would be a kind of poetic justice. Not that I take any responsibility for Mrs. Ferrars's death. It was the direct consequence of her own actions. I feel no pity for her.

I have no pity for myself either.

So let it be veronal.

But I wish Hercule Poirot had never retired from work and come here to grow vegetable marrows.

THE END

BIBLIOTHECA CLASSICA

Made in the USA
Coppell, TX
23 July 2024

35053617R10085